# TANKED

# Kelly Fae Wilson

Toadflax Press

Cover art by Yenthe Joline https://yenthejolineart.com/

Scene breaks and Toadflax Press logo designed by Havoc Art

Print ISBN 979-8-9994476-1-6

eBook ISBN 979-8-9994476-0-9

For Laurelin

May your spoons be plentiful and your forks be few

# CHAPTER ONE

Bullets didn't scare Tank. The mass of cameras and microphones and journalists all jostling in his face? *That* scared him.

It was the second bank robbery of the week and the third incident that night. Tank almost didn't make it there in time, what with the news vans all vying for position to follow him through the streets of Los Angeles and the reporters crowding the sidewalk in front of the bank, each trying to extract a promise for an exclusive interview after he dealt with the robbery. Even Hopper, Tank's manager, made it there before he did. Hopper leaned against an entrance column, making a point of tapping his foot and checking his watch. Shouldering through the crowd of cameras and mics, Tank avoided eye contact with his manager and headed into the bank.

Three would-be bank robbers waited for him inside. Three bullets ricocheted off his chest as soon as he stepped through the door. Tank sighed and plowed ahead.

Another shot pinged off his shoulder and hit the giant clock on the wall, cracking the face. He scrutinized the Roman numerals—those always took him a few seconds—before charging the thieves behind the teller counter.

*Four forty-five am.* His heart did a somersault. Grace might be awake already. She seemed an early riser.

He jumped the counter, and thief number one got off two more shots at Tank's abdomen. A metallic tinkling echoed through the bank as the bullets fell harmlessly to the floor.

If Grace was awake, maybe she'd have checked her messages on the BlindDate app.

The thief swung a hard left at Tank's head.

If she'd checked already, maybe she'd read the message he sent her yesterday.

Tank blocked the punch, spun the thief around, twisting his arm behind his back, and—gently—smacked his head against the counter to knock him out.

His stomach fluttered. What would Grace think of his message? Maybe he shouldn't have made it so long. It was only their third exchange, after all, and what did he know about the intricacies of communicating through a dating app? As Hopper frequently reminded him, the minutiae of social interactions had never been Tank's strength. That was part of why he needed his manager.

The other two goons jumped him from behind, slashing at him with long bowie knives. Tank frowned. Knives. Guns. Didn't they know better? You'd think the criminals in this city would have enough professionalism to watch the news. To come prepared for his impenetrable skin. His super strength. Maybe they were from out of town.

LAPD officers peered through the windows, on site to arrest the bank robbers once Tank was done with them. He had to hide his smile from them as the words of Grace's last message ran through his head. She had told him about her favorite picture book, *Seagull and Sea Dragon*. That was a good one. It had been particularly popular whenever he'd been in charge of Storytime at the library. Although he'd had to quit working at the library when he'd signed on with Hopper and took up full-time hero work, so it'd been a couple of years since he'd led a Storytime.

Tank flipped both robbers off his back. One of the bowie knives left a rip in his pants, and he sighed. It was too bad he couldn't find a uniform as durable as he was. The thieves leapt back to their feet and circled around to come at him from either side, knives raised.

Definitely from out of town.

Tank reached for the pair and clunked their heads together. Again, gently. He wasn't here to permanently damage anyone.

He had a favorite picture book too. Really, he was more of a vintage middle grade guy, but he did enjoy picture books as well. He'd agonized over telling Grace about his favorite, though. Stared at the blank screen until his eyes watered while his thoughts chased themselves, vulture-like, around his head. The book wasn't as recent or as well known. What if Grace thought he was testing her kid-lit knowledge, like some kind of ex-librarian elitist or something? Or what if she did know of the book but thought it was trivial and decided not to bother writing back to a man who loved a picture book about a tiny pixie looking for friendship?

The two failed bank robbers groaned and collapsed to the floor. Tank dragged them over to their comrade and left the three of them in a heap for the police to clean up.

Worst possibility of all, what if Grace didn't know about the book, but also didn't ask to know more about it? What if she gave the written equivalent of a disinterested "huh" and continued with her part of the conversation like he hadn't said anything at all?

A low acidic burn started in Tank's belly. In the end, he had mentioned the book but kept most of his comments focused on her book. Hadn't really talked about himself too much. Hadn't really answered her questions about him. He'd have to answer some of them soon, though, if he wanted her to keep writing to him, and he *did* want her to keep writing. Even if he wasn't ready to tell her about Tank the indestructible superhero, he could tell her more about his pre-hero life as Willard, the children's librarian. His guts gurgled at the thought, and he rubbed a hand over his belly, scoffing at himself.

*Yup, that's me. Tank, the superhero with an indestructible exterior—and killer reflux.*

The doorbell to Tank's penthouse rang through the apartment. Again. And again, before Tank could get to the door. Sometimes he thought Hopper wished he had super speed instead of strength. He pressed his thumb to the security system pad on the right side of the door. Tank didn't need the security, but he wasn't always home, and there was his cat to think about. His manager pushed through the entrance and into the open living area as soon as the door cracked open. Suit rumpled, gray hair mussed, and cheeks covered in stubble, Hopper didn't look like he'd slept at all yet.

"What took you so long getting to the bank? Fifteen minutes between calling you," Hopper tapped the earbud in his left ear, "and your arrival. If the cops hadn't already had the bank surrounded, those guys would've escaped." He leaned against the back of the couch, arms folded. "You know what the media can do with that. Any little lapse and they pounce."

Tank shifted uneasily. "Yeah, I know. Sorry. It was pretty busy last night. There was a lot of press to wade through on the way there, and before that, I had to finish up with the convenience store stick-up."

Hopper cocked an eyebrow. "You were done with that in two minutes."

Tank flushed. "With the perpetrator, yeah, but the cashier was practically a kid. He was pretty upset, I had to—"

"You had to what? Get him a blankie? Read him a story? If the kid's old enough to be working, he's old enough to take care of himself. You're not a children's librarian anymore, Tank."

Tank mumbled an apology and headed through the kitchen to the breakfast nook. The cashier had been barely sixteen, working the early shift before school. Having a gun shoved in his face had left him shaking. Tank couldn't leave him on his own like that, but he knew Hopper wouldn't accept that reasoning.

Hector "Hopper" Strickland had been the premier PR manager of celebrities and personalities before the nationwide Anti-Vigilante Act had passed, making it a requirement for anyone wishing to use superpowers for the public good to work through a licensed manager alongside law enforcement. After the law passed, Hopper made Strickland Talent Management into the premier firm for licensed hero representation. He still had celebrity clients, but Tank had become his main focus over the last couple of years. Tank's status as *the* name in hero work in Los Angeles, his full bank account, his product endorsement contracts—they were all Hopper's doing. Hopper had even arranged for the penthouse.

With its open floor plan and sleek, monochromatic decor, Hopper insisted the top floor apartment fit the public's expectations for a superhero, but Tank thought the place was like living inside the lobby of a modern art museum. One where the receptionist glared daggers if you dared to talk, and too many people wore black clothes and smug expressions.

As the one concession to his own tastes, Tank had installed a reading corner up in his loft bedroom complete with bean bag chair, extra pillows, and a tray for hot chocolate. Still, even with its stark aesthetic, the apartment beat the pants off the dingy, cockroach-infested, basement studio he'd had before Hopper took him on as a client, so who was he to argue?

"I haven't eaten breakfast yet. You hungry?" Tank set two bowls on the table and turned the chairs to take advantage of the cityscape out the floor-to-ceiling window. He scooped plain yogurt into his bowl and drizzled honey over it.

Hopper stared at the yogurt. He sighed, and his face softened. "Stomach again?"

Tank nodded. The acid that so often plagued his stomach couldn't actually damage his tissues—he was indestructible on the inside as well—but he felt the pain in his gut anyway. Being indestructible didn't mean he had no nerve endings.

He focused on his breakfast, trying to keep his eyes from glancing at the computer desk across the room. He hadn't allowed himself to check his messages after getting home from the robbery. Made himself take a shower first, started a load of laundry. If he didn't know whether or not Grace had written back yet, there was still a chance that she had. If he checked and she hadn't, that possibility was gone. Besides, it was still early, about 8 a.m. Better to be patient.

Hopper lowered himself into a chair, rubbing his forehead. "Look, I'm sorry, man. I didn't mean to come at you so harsh. I'm just trying to look out for you. You know that, right?"

"I know." Tank ate another spoonful. The yogurt cooled his esophagus and coated his stomach. His shoulders relaxed a notch. He fiddled with the dog-eared copy of *Holes* on the table and squinted against the sun on the river running through the city. "But I wasn't ... I wasn't making excuses, H, when I said it was busy last night. The warehouse fire at the dock? It wasn't random, it was arson. And the arsonist had that same creepy tattoo."

Hopper straightened. "The weird cricket thing?"

Tank nodded. Three times this month he'd apprehended someone with a tattoo of what looked like a crazed grasshopper with fangs. All three had hit some kind of industrial target but seemed more bent on destruction than stealing anything. Last night the arsonist had been raving about taking as many lives as he could.

"I was thinking I'd go talk to the detective in charge of the case today. Find out if there's a connection between the three businesses that got hit, or maybe between their owners ..." Tank trailed off and licked his spoon clean.

"No, no. I'll take care of it. You take it easy." Hopper nodded at the yogurt. "You need to be in good shape for the reception tonight."

"Wait, there's another one?" Tank asked in dismay. He'd finally gotten his copy of *Everything Sad is Untrue* and planned a quiet evening reading in the bean bag chair.

"Yeah, remember? Invite from the mayor came last week. I'm guessing she'll add something official to the evening to thank you for saving the bank this morning." Hopper looked him in the eye. "A party with the mayor is hardly the worst problem to have."

Tank ducked his head. "No, yeah, you're right. I'll be there. Thanks, H."

"Atta boy." Hopper checked his buzzing phone and rolled his eyes. "Gotta go. I wish certain pop stars were as easy to manage as you. If this one doesn't calm down soon, I may need you to help the cops arrest him. See you tonight, big guy." He clapped Tank on the shoulder and let himself out the front door.

The lock clicked behind Hopper. Tank finished his yogurt, put his bowl in the sink, and opened the door to the laundry room. A fuzzy, gray face mewed up at him.

"Yeah, I know you don't like being shut up in there, Lint, but rules are rules. Anyway, he's gone now, so you can come out." He scooped up the cat and nuzzled her nose. Hopper maintained that a cat wasn't the best choice of pet for an invulnerable superhero, but Tank figured as long as no one knew about Lint—including Hopper—she couldn't harm the persona his manager had built.

He considered the PC on the desk in the kitchen but grabbed his laptop instead and headed for the loft. The beanbag would be cozier. He settled in with a fleece blanket and opened his laptop as Lint curled up next to him.

BlindDate didn't allow pictures, which was exactly why Tank had picked the dating service. He loved his hero job. He loved helping people, and he was grateful for his success. But in the two years since he'd been doing full-time hero work, most of the women he'd met had been at some event or another of Hopper's, and they only saw him as The Tank. It had been impossible to find a date without wondering if she would have gone out with him *before* he was The Tank.

One date had been disappointed he hadn't worn his hero suit to the restaurant. Another had actually asked him to bench press her. The one time he met someone on his own, she'd hinted quite broadly she wanted an introduction to Hopper to see if he'd rep her music career.

Worst of all, the last woman he went out with said she didn't have a favorite book.

He knew this was not representative of the dating pool in general, but his career didn't put him in situations to meet someone who was in a healthy place. So, when he'd heard about BlindDate, he'd jumped right in, hadn't even talked to Hopper first. The app had matched him with Grace a few days later. She'd messaged first.

Grace still had no idea he was the superhero of Los Angeles, and the lack of pictures would help keep it that way until he decided to tell her.

He stroked Lint's ears, staring at his screen. *Don't expect anything yet.* He opened the website version of the app and clicked on Messages.

Tank sucked in a breath, heart pounding. The name Grace Kekoa beckoned at the top of his inbox.

# CHAPTER TWO

G race's fingers hovered over her keyboard. It was barely past 8 a.m. If she DM'ed Willard this early in the morning, would it make her look desperate? But she had a full day at work ahead and a doctor appointment before work on top of it.

And she didn't want to wait till tonight.

*Hi Willard! No way! I love* How the Nobble Was Finally Found! *I hardly ever find someone else who knows that book!*

It was true. As beautiful as the picture book was, it was pretty obscure. Grace still wasn't sure about the whole online dating thing, but when Willard had mentioned that book, she knew she'd keep messaging him.

*Your library sounds amazing! The kids there are lucky. I would have killed for a library like that when I was a kid ha ha. In Kahuku, the only library was shared with the high school, and it was tiny! Plus going in with all the big high school kids was a little intimidating. There was the university library in Lāʻie down Kamehameha highway, but they were super grumpy about it when actual kids tried to check out books from the kids' section. I guess they were just for "research purposes."*

She paused, looking over the full bookshelves in her bedroom. Her younger self would've killed for those too. *I actually read* The Nobble *to the keiki (that's the kids) at the charter school last week. (Vegas has a Hawaiian culture focused charter school. I go in once a week on Thursdays to help with reading.)*

*Have you ever read* The Cats of Tanglewood Forest *by Charles de Lint? There's a picture book version of the story that came out first, called* A Circle of

Cats. *That's a great one too. Although my copy got accidentally dropped in a pool a while back (maybe I shouldn't try to read and swim at the same time??) and I still need to find a new one. It's out of print now so it's not so readily available.*

She read over what she'd written so far. It needed one more question, to keep the conversation going.

*So, Los Angeles. Did you grow up there? Or is it adopted-home like me and Vegas?*

There, that was good. "And send."

"Grace," her grandmother called up the stairs. "Breakfast!"

"Coming, Tūtū." Grace stuck her head out of her bedroom to answer, then grabbed her things and headed for the door. Her computer dinged. A new message popped up from Willard.

*That was fast.* She plopped back in her desk chair, grinning.

*Hi! Wow, that would be really hard growing up without a good library. Mine was a lifesaver. L.A. is crazy ha ha. To quote Meg Ryan: 'L.A.'s a great town. It stinks! But it's a great town.' I'm a transplant. Moved here from Indiana for college and been here since. So ... fourteen, fifteen years now, I guess. How about you? What brought you to Vegas?*

Grace took a few seconds to savor the fact that he'd written back so quickly before typing out a reply.

*Similar story actually. I came out for school and my family followed a little later. After I graduated—it's been twelve years for me—we all stayed here. There's no beach in Vegas, but it's worlds cheaper than Hawai'i.* She inserted a 'shrug' emoji.

She sent the message and exhaled slowly. It was all true. There was no reason to add that she'd also come here to see a medical specialist *while* she was going to school. *Especially since the specialist never figured out what was going on.*

"Grace!" Her grandmother's voice came up the stairs again. "Come eat, bumbai you late."

"Almost pau!"

She turned back to the screen. *Indiana, huh? I've never been there; do you ever miss it? Do you still have family there?*

Willard's answer came thirty seconds later. *Not really. I have my work here, that keeps me busy. Sometimes too busy. I actually have a work party thing I have to go to tonight. I'd rather read this new book I just got though.*

She tapped her fingers on the desk, frowning. That was vague. And he didn't answer her question about family. *I hear you. I have a work trip I'm leaving for later today, but it's a* work work *trip, not a* fun work *trip, you know? Although a work party at a library with book lovers certainly beats a normal office party, yeah?;)*

Three little dots appeared on the thread showing he was writing. They vanished, then reappeared, and Grace wondered what he was having a hard time saying until his message arrived.

*Too bad Vegas is such a drive, it'd be way more fun if you could come.*

Her heart sped up. Was he suggesting they meet?

Footsteps pounded up the stairs. "Ho, sis. Tūtū going flip. Why you take so long? Move your 'ōkole."

Grace ignored her brother's question. "James Pono Kekoa, did you sleep here again last night? What's the point of having your own place if you're here all the time?"

"'Cause I don't get one Tūtū breakfast at my place." He handed her a plate of steaming eggs, toast, and fried SPAM and leaned over her shoulder to check the screen. "Better not let Tūtū know you writing one haole guy." He winked.

"You—" Too late, Grace slammed her laptop shut. BlindDate didn't allow pictures, but there was demographic info on each person's profile. Willard was listed as Caucasian. She smacked James affectionately on the arm.

"You like this one?" he asked.

"I think I do. No tell, yeah?" *At least not yet.*

"Shoots, but you gonna owe me." James sauntered out of her room.

She rolled her eyes. "Don't I always." Her stomach jumped as she reread Willard's last message, and she set her breakfast aside. Meeting up sounded ... intriguing. But it would need more planning.

*I'd love to come if I could. Maybe the next time we could work it out if I knew more in advance.* Her grandmother yelled up the stairs again, and Grace checked the time. She really would be late if she didn't leave now. She dashed off another few lines. *I have to run, I have a doctor appointment before I can finish getting ready for the work trip, but I'm so glad we got to 'chat.'*

*A doctor appointment? Everything ok?*

Grace smacked her palm against her forehead. She hadn't meant to include that part. *Yeah, routine stuff is all. No worries.* She snorted. Routine for *her.*

*Ok, that's good. I'm glad we got to 'talk' too. This was fun, let's do it again soon.*

"Yes," Grace smiled and hugged her arms around her chest. "Let's."

Still smiling, Grace pushed through the double doors and hurried to the reception desk.

"Hey, Charlotte. Sorry I'm running behind."

The woman at the desk nodded. "No worries. She'll be right with you. You look happy this morning, though. What's that about?"

Grace smirked. "Oh, nothing."

"Uh-huh." Charlotte turned back to her screen. "We'll get it out of you sooner or later. Normal room." She pointed down the hall.

"Thanks." Grace moved through the empty waiting room and into her usual exam room. A hospital gown laid on the table. She sighed, trying to hold on to her good humor, before pulling her shirt over her head to change.

*Usual. Normal.* Useless words. If Grace had her way, they'd be erased from the English language entirely because there was no such thing as "normal." Especially for her.

She paused in front of the mirror over the sink before tying the gown, examining a vicious purple splotch that covered the right side of her ribs. Another bruise spread from her left trap down her shoulder blade. The bruising had started when she was a child. She bruised much more easily than other kids, but the contusions appeared even when she hadn't hurt herself. No bumps or scrapes required. They came and went on different places on her body, and of varying severity, but they never left for good. At first, the doctors had thought she was simply anemic and that she'd grow out of it with time and iron supplements.

She didn't.

As a teen, they tried to attribute it to hormones—even though no one else her age bruised every time they got emotional—and told her she'd grow out of it as she became an adult.

She hadn't.

And the older she got, the longer the bruises took to fade.

Now, in her mid-thirties, all she really knew about her mystery condition was that stress and heartache made it worse.

With her natural optimism, she'd signed up for BlindDate, reasoning that if heartache made it worse, maybe having someone to love would help. The No Pictures Allowed rule removed the stress of worrying she might have a bruise on her face when a guy asked for more pictures. Sure, eventually she'd have to meet someone—*Maybe Willard. Hopefully Willard*—in person, and maybe she'd have bruises that day that her clothes or makeup didn't cover. But if that someone had come to know and like her without knowing what she looked like, if he already liked her for her, then the bruises wouldn't matter so much. She'd be able to tell him about it as just another part of her.

A quick knock came at the door and Dr. Oracion entered. "Hey there. Running on Hawaiian time?" She chuckled.

"Yes, sorry. But ..." Grace stretched the word out, grinning.

Dr. Oracion grinned back. "Oh my gosh, he messaged you again?"

"Yes!" Grace laughed at herself. Here she was, a grown woman who owned her own business, but Willard made her squeal like a schoolgirl with her first crush.

"Show me!" The doctor rushed to her side, as giddy as she was, and not for the first time, Grace blessed the stars that had brought them together when they were both still in grad school, Grace in sustainability and the doctor in med school. "Dr. O," as Grace teasingly called her back in school, had stuck by her in the search for both diagnosis and cure, something Grace knew she wouldn't have found in a doctor who wasn't also her friend. They dissected Willard's messages for a minute, laughing together.

*Almost 'normal,'* Grace thought. But normal wasn't why she was sitting on an exam table. She sighed, tucked away her phone and showed Dr. O the latest bruise.

"How's it feel?" The doctor probed it gently.

Grace winced. "Tender. And oddly, kind of ... hot? Almost like a sunburn."

"Interesting." Dr. Oracion made a note on her chart before retrieving a tube from a drawer. "Try the cream for the week, see if it helps at all."

Grace lifted her hair out of the way for the doctor to rub in the mixture of arnica, vitamin K, aloe vera and comfrey. Sometimes it helped. Sometimes it didn't.

"Any news on the other idea?" Grace ventured.

Dr. Oracion washed her hands and pulled up a rolling stool. "We're still looking. It seems highly unlikely that with all the different powers manifesting in people these days, there wouldn't be *anyone* with some kind of healing ability other than jumpers."

Grace nodded. Jumpers were teleporters and it was a well-documented fact they had a healing factor that kicked in when they jumped. Since their atoms reconstituted every time they teleported, they reconstituted whole, any injury sustained before the jump, healed. But Jumpers also tended to choose crime over heroism. Something about being able to teleport made it too easy to go that route. Since the ability to jump wasn't a common one, and there were no jumpers registered as working heroes, they were hard to find. The one time Dr. O had found one, she got mugged for her trouble.

"Yeah, it's just finding them." Grace tapped a finger against the paper sheets. "Not everyone with an extra ability makes it known to the world."

"You should know," the doctor said wryly.

Grace snorted. She didn't condone the path of most jumpers, but she understood not wanting to work within the Anti-Vigilante Act. "It's ridiculous. All the regulations and the red tape and—"

Dr. Oracion held up a hand to stop her. "Stress, my friend. Stress."

Grace exhaled heavily but let the subject drop. "Right."

"Like I was saying," the doctor continued. "We're still looking. I have a couple new rumors I want to trace. Your job, in the meantime, is to avoid extra stress. Try not to climb onto too many social soapboxes, ok?"

Grace shook her head. "No promises."

# CHAPTER THREE

The valet's eyes widened as Tank climbed out of his Mustang Dark Horse in front of the mayor's Tudor-style mansion. Ford had given him the car as part of a sponsorship, and Hopper had insisted it helped build his image, but Tank found the engine ... loud.

He gave the valet an apologetic smile as he handed over the keys. "Hopefully you don't get a noise citation parking this thing."

"Huh?" The teen's eyebrows crinkled. "Oh, the car! Yeah, it's epic, man, but would you mind, maybe ...?" He pulled out his phone and mimed taking a selfie. "The guys'll never believe I parked The Tank's car."

Tank flushed. "Sure, no problem." He posed with the valet, then turned toward the house.

The Getty House was in fine form. Lights planted throughout the landscaping gave the mayoral residence a gentle glow—bright enough to be inviting, but soft enough to avoid glare. Sconces lined the path leading around the side of the house to the spacious grounds behind, and Tank strolled that way, familiar enough with the place after so many of these functions to feel comfortable.

His uniform was not so comfortable.

He couldn't deny that the olive greens and solid white star matched his namesake, and the cargo pockets on the pants were large enough to hide a book, but whatever his suit was made out of was stiff across his chest and through the armpits. Maybe he could talk to Hopper about getting it adjusted. He had no idea who made the things—when Tank was first learning about his powers, he used sweats for training, and they'd be shredded by the end of every session.

Hopper had connections that Tank, on his own, just ... didn't. Aside from the legality issues, it was one more reason his manager was good for him.

The gate to the gardens stood open, security personnel on either side, and Tank nodded to them as he passed. They didn't ask for I.D.

Party sounds drifted toward him. At the end of the path, the yard opened onto swaths of lawn and dignitaries.

At the corner of the house, a young boy in a child's version of a fancy suit leaned against the bricks. "Tank," he whisper-shouted.

Tank knelt to talk to the mayor's son. "Hey, Gerard. What are you doing hiding in the bushes?"

"Saving you." Gerard glanced over his shoulder at the partygoers like they were all secretly villains. "You really want to hang out with *them?* All they talk about is numbers and the news."

Tank studied the garden, rubbing his chin. "I don't know, last time I had a pretty interesting conversation with the flamingo statue in the fountain."

Gerard rolled his eyes. "Gimme a break. Do I look like a seven-year-old?"

"You are a seven-year-old."

"Only until April, then I'm eight. Come in the house with me, I have the new issue of Miles Morales. It's sick!"

"Shut up!" Tank grinned. "The one with the new costume? I don't even have that one yet."

"Come on, let's go." Gerard pulled on Tank's hands, hopping up and down.

Tank got to his feet. Comics with a seven-year-old sounded way better than a garden party with the city's finest. "I wish I could, bud, but I have to go talk to the *grown-ups.*" He rolled his eyes.

"Why?" Gerard whined. "You're not a grown-up."

Tank laughed. "That's one of the nicest things anyone's ever said to me. Tell you what—" He pulled a Wolverine issue out of one of his cargo pockets "—You go inside and read Miles and Logan for me, ok? No reason we both have to suffer."

Gerard snatched the comic, eyes gleaming. "Sweet. My mom won't let me read this one."

"Wait, really?"

Gerard ignored the question and stowed Wolverine safely inside his suit jacket. With one more glance between the party and Tank, he laid a hand over his heart. "Ye who are about to die, we salute you."

"I don't think that's quite how that quote goes."

Gerard turned on his heel and ran for the French doors leading into the house.

"Your mom lets you watch Gladiator, but not read Wolverine?" Tank called after him.

Gerard waved before disappearing through the doors. Tank faced the party and sighed. If he was going to metaphorically die, he might as well get it over with.

Hopper met him halfway to the crowd on the lawn and handed him a drink. "Good, you're here." He shot a look back at the house. "Were you talking to Gerard again?"

Tank nodded. "He wanted to talk comics."

Hopper frowned. "I told you, when you put on that suit, you put on the persona too. It's not Book Club time. If you really want, we can talk to the mayor about having you help with a ribbon cutting at a new school or library or something. People like that. But you gotta leave Willard at home."

Tank ducked his head. "Yeah, sorry."

"Come on, big guy." Hopper clapped him on the shoulder. "The CEO of First Federal wants to shake your hand."

Thirty-seven minutes, two lemonades, three canapes and fourteen hand-shakes later, Tank managed to find a quiet corner by the fountain. He scrolled through the message thread with Grace from that morning, a genuine smile replacing the forced-public-proximity one he'd been wearing.

When he read Grace's line about a librarian party being more interesting than a normal office party, the smile faltered. He hadn't thought about it when he'd said he had a work thing that night. As soon as she'd written back, he'd realized his mistake. She thought he was talking about the library. Where he no longer worked. He wasn't ready to tell her about The Tank yet, so he'd improvised the line about his co-workers not wanting to talk about books. It wasn't strictly untrue. The mayor had never told him anything about her favorite read.

He *had* thought about it when he said the party would be more fun with Grace there. Almost hadn't sent it. But amazingly, she'd seemed interested in the idea of meeting.

"Excuse me?" someone asked.

Tank fumbled his phone, nearly dropping it in the fountain, caught it again and shoved it back in his pocket. Hopefully Hopper hadn't seen that. A Polynesian woman stood in front of him. Black hair skimmed her hips and the light from the party glittered on her bronze skin. She wore a white and yellow flower behind her right ear and, for a fraction of a second, all Tank could think was Grace had somehow made it to the party after all.

*Don't be an idiot,* he berated himself. *There are thousands of Polynesian people in L.A. Even the mayor is Tahitian on one side. You have the idea of meeting Grace on the brain, that's all.*

"Elodie Seeker, Fashion Seeker Designs." She held out her hand. "I believe I have you to thank for saving my employees. I own the warehouse that burned last night."

"Oh, yes. Um ..." Tank could practically hear Hopper saying "*No umming.*" He cleared his throat and shook her proffered hand. "I'm sorry we couldn't save more of the building, Ms. Seeker."

"Please don't be. Clothes can be replaced. Walls can be rebuilt. My people are the important thing."

"How are they doing?"

"Some mild smoke inhalation, but thanks to you, everyone will be fine. I did want to ask you about something though, if you don't mind."

"Sure." Tank stole a glance at the main knot of party goers. Hopper was watching them, a funny look on his face, and Tank straightened his shoulders. The mayor tapped Hopper on the shoulder and the two of them started across the lawn.

"Was there anything unusual about the man you caught?" Elodie asked. "Anything identifying like a tattoo perhaps?"

Tank hesitated. As far as he knew, the fact that several different perpetrators shared the same tattoo wasn't public knowledge. "Why do you ask?"

Elodie glanced over her shoulder and stepped closer. "Did it happen to be an insect with fangs?"

"I'm sorry, Ms. Seeker. I can't disclose facts about an open investigation. I mean, I know it was your warehouse," he amended. "But it's probably best if you speak to the detective in charge."

She shook her head, and her voice grew more urgent. "I know that wasn't the first person with one of those tattoos you've stopped."

Tank narrowed his eyes. "How do you know that?"

"I have information for you." Elodie ignored his question. "And I need your help. Two days ago—"

"Tank," Hopper interrupted, reaching them, Mayor Dupont with him. The mayor kissed Elodie on the cheek.

"Elodie, I'm so glad you could make it. I see you've met our resident hero. This is Tank's manager, Hector Strickland."

He turned a smile on Elodie and held out a hand. "Everyone calls me Hopper."

"Elodie Seeker." She shook his hand, stress no longer evident in her voice.

"Tank, I don't suppose you've seen Gerard?" the mayor asked. "He was supposed to stay out here during the party, but ..." She raised one hand in a helpless gesture. "When does he ever listen?"

"Oh." Tank cleared his throat and tried not to glance at the house. *At least one of us gets to read something tonight.* "I'm sure he'll turn up."

"Kids," Hopper said. "Anyway, sorry to interrupt, but they need you at the podium for the toast, big guy." He pointed toward a small platform surrounded by guests and cameras.

Elodie moved toward the crowd along with them. "Tank, it was good to meet you. I hope we can talk more later." She handed him a business card before breaking off to find a spot in the audience.

"Yeah. You too." Not knowing what else to do with it, he tucked the card into his phone case.

Hopper watched Elodie walk away then elbowed Tank in the ribs. "Nice, big guy. And you got a phone number. You gonna call her later?"

"What? No. I don't think that's what she meant." *Besides, I'd rather talk to Grace.*

Hopper clucked his tongue. "Eh, we'll see. But we gotta do this toast first anyway."

Tank's steps slowed as they approached the podium. He hated this part. If the mayor was simply making a toast, why did there have to be a podium? Why were there reporters? He got into the hero business to help people, not to be the center of attention.

"Hey, hey." Hopper urged him forward. "It's alright, you don't have to talk. Just stand next to the mayor and look imposing. I'll be at the back if you need a face to focus on."

"Sure, imposing." Tank swallowed and took his place next to Mayor Dupont on a platform that afforded a clear view of the back of the mansion.

He didn't feel imposing. But he was wearing the uniform. Like Hopper said, he had to wear the persona too. *Come on, you're bulletproof, and you've got super strength. You can handle imposing.* He tried to arrange his expression into something Hopper would approve of, but one of the reporters near the front cocked her head, a quizzical look on her face, and he sighed at himself. *Or not.*

The microphone squeaked as the mayor began speaking. "Thank you for joining us tonight, everyone. I am delighted to host this gathering in honor of The Tank."

The press personnel and party goers applauded. Tank's cheeks heated, but he raised a hand in acknowledgement. "Crime rates have plummeted since he began working alongside LAPD, and last night, he once again proved his worth, saving both lives and the First Federal Bank."

Tank's mind wandered away from the speech. Maybe there'd be another message from Grace tomorrow. Either way, at least the party was almost over. He stared longingly at the gate, thinking about leaving.

"Please join me in a toast to—"

The back wall of the house exploded.

Glass burst outward, and flames roared from the broken windows. Tank yanked the mayor down in a crouch. Someone screamed. Half the crowd dropped to the ground, and the other half scattered.

The mayor's head of security rushed over, shouting into a walkie talkie. "Was anyone in the house?"

Horror froze Tank in place for a heartbeat.

Gerard.

Gerard was in the house. Curled up somewhere with the comic he'd given him.

His muscles unlocked, and Tank bolted across the lawn. Hopper called after him, but he ignored it. What remained of the French doors blazed lightning hot. Tank barreled through them.

He took half a second to orient himself in the house. The parlor. He was in the parlor overlooking the gardens. That meant Gerard's room was to the right and up the stairs.

"Gerard!" He took the stairs three at a time. The house shivered and groaned. A chunk of the ceiling crashed down, smashing into his shoulders. He heaved it over the burning railing with a grunt. The flames caught his sleeve, and bitter fumes filled his nostrils as the fabric melted. He smacked the flames out as he ran faster. He felt the heat, but it couldn't damage him.

Gerard didn't have that advantage.

He yelled the boy's name again. Smoke, thick and black, clogged the upstairs hallway. Tank plunged through the haze, blinking against the sting, to the fourth door on the left. Furniture lay overturned through the room, displaced by the initial explosion. Pages fluttered in a gust of hot air, and Tank caught a glimpse of an X-Men cover before it burst into flames next to a wardrobe leaning against the far wall. He shoved the wardrobe aside.

"No. No, no, no, no."

Gerard lay crumpled beneath. Blood welled from the side of his head and scorch marks covered his side.

Sirens sounded in the distance.

Tank scooped the boy up, trying to move his neck as little as possible. The house rocked on its foundations and the inferno roared anew outside the bedroom door. There was no going back that way.

"Sorry, buddy." Tank talked to the unconscious child as he kicked out the window frame. "No way out but down."

He cradled the boy close to his chest and launched out the window to the ground below.

# CHAPTER FOUR

S moke clung to Tank's skin, acrid and out of place with the antiseptic smell of the hospital. Tank pressed his bulk into a corner, out of the way of the wall of doctors and nurses around Gerard's bed, sending out a vague prayer of gratitude that the hospital was only three minutes from the mayor's house.

Still, what if that was three minutes too long?

Raised voices and running steps came from the corridor, and Mayor Dupont burst into her son's room, blouse untucked and face blotchy from crying. Tank eased himself out of the room to give her space and sank into a plastic chair in the waiting area near a wall mounted TV playing the local news on mute.

*This is my fault.* The mayor had asked her son to stay at the party. She'd asked Tank where Gerard was. *And I didn't say anything. Willard, you big dumb oaf.*

The elevator at the end of the hallway dinged, and Hopper strode out, arguing with someone on the phone. He hung up and slumped into the chair next to Tank. "How is he?"

"Not sure yet. They're still working. What about the fire?" Tank asked. "What do we know so far?"

"Nothing yet. They're still putting it out."

"It could have been a gas leak ..." His voice sounded tired in his own ears.

"Could've been," Hopper agreed. "Except."

"Except, that was a very visible event with VIPs from all over the city. But then, I don't know, H. The hospital is three minutes away. The fire station, one minute. Those distances are on purpose, in case of emergencies like tonight. Anyone who wanted to plan something would've done their homework and known that. And they couldn't have been targeting the mayor directly, because they'd have known she and everybody else were going to be outside all evening and the house was going to be empty."

"Almost empty." Hopper grunted.

"Almost empty," Tank agreed heavily. "Still, what would anyone hope to get out of blowing up the house with help so close?"

"Don't forget, you're included in that help. Seems pretty stupid to plan something with you around. But, you said yourself, the event was visible," Hopper pointed out. "Maybe they wanted to be noticed."

Tank frowned. "Noticed? Has anyone claimed responsibility?"

"Not that I've heard yet. I'll ask when I talk to the Point."

Tank glanced down the hall to Gerard's room. "I want to be there when you talk to her this time, H." As his manager, Hopper acted as the liaison between Tank and law enforcement agencies, including first responders like fire and medical teams. The Point of Contact Officer, or Point was a position created by the AVA as part of the liaison relationship. There was nothing in the Anti-Vigilante Act that disallowed Tank from talking to the Point or other officials, but Hopper preferred taking care of the details himself.

"No, don't worry about it, I can fill you in on what she says." He went to a vending machine in the corner before Tank could protest further.

The TV flickered with static. A nurse fiddled with the remote, and the picture and volume returned together.

"... this is Jen Abara at KTLA with breaking news. We've been given a ..." she faltered. eyes flicking off camera. "... a video to play ..."

Tank narrowed his eyes and moved closer to the TV. The news anchor was sweating. She glanced to her left again. "Hopper, come look at this."

Jen Abara kept talking. "... from someone who has a message for Los Angeles's resident hero."

A cold burn cut through Tank's guts. "Someone's in that studio who shouldn't be."

Hopper whipped out his phone. "Calling Point now."

The screen flipped to a nighttime beach scene, black waves crashing on the shore. A group of people waited out of the camera's light. Pixels covered all of their faces.

"People of Los Angeles, the cleansing begins with you." Their voices were modified, run through some kind of software so that each voice sounded the same timbre and pitch, but layered one over the other, like a choral version of fun house mirrors. "The beast is coming; your destruction is nigh. Human beings are a plague upon this earth. We are Abaddon and we will fight plague with plague."

Tank squinted at the video. Each of the people on the beach had at least part of a tattoo showing somewhere on their body. The same tattoo he'd found on the arsonist.

"Hopper," he said.

Hopper folded his arms tightly over his chest. "I see them."

"To the one called The Tank," the voices continued. "We tried to tell this people to turn from their pollutions, but each time we struck to point out their filth, you prevented our message from reaching them. Know that we will no longer tolerate your interference. Consider the Mayor's house our last warning. Step aside or be swept aside."

"I guess it wasn't a gas leak," Hopper muttered.

"People of Los Angeles, the cleansing begins with you." A man at the front of the group lifted a hand and the ground shifted. It agitated, undulating.

The nurse came up behind Tank and Hopper, mouth open. "Is the sand moving?"

Small clumps shot into the air, buzzing viciously. The buzz thrummed louder, and the clumps coalesced into a wave that hovered around the speakers.

"That's not sand," Hopper whispered.

The man on the beach raised his arm, and the hovering wave followed. Individual wings and serrated legs stuck out from the mass. The camera light glinted off exoskeletons.

"No," Tank said, trying not to gag. "They're insects, like the tattoos."

The man thrust his hand toward the camera, and the wave attacked, smashing into the lens like bullets.

Tank fidgeted with his phone in the back of the patrol car on the way to KTLA's broadcast building. After the video had cut out, the Point had texted Hopper saying the police had the exits covered, but they wanted Tank there. Whoever had forced the broadcast hadn't tried to leave the building yet.

Tank glanced at his screen again. No messages.

"Stop checking." Hopper snatched the phone away and shoved it back in Tank's cargo pocket. "Dupont said she'd call as soon as Gerard woke up. You need to focus."

"Yeah, sorry," Tank said. The mayor practically had to shove him out the door to get him to leave before Gerard woke up, but in the end, he'd gone. That was his job. Tank closed his eyes, trying to clear his head.

All his other jobs he'd known more or less what to expect. Usually, it was average humans committing predictable crimes. Not that he'd never dealt with creative or intelligent foes, and he had faced a few criminals with powers—jumpers could be tricky—but mostly he'd been able to barrel his way into a situation and incapacitate the culprits without much harm to them, simply because there wasn't anything they could throw at him to hurt him. Recently, a number of them had surrendered as soon as he arrived. He handed them over to the police, and no one got hurt.

The people in the Abaddon video didn't seem the type to surrender.

Hopper seemed to be thinking along the same lines. "Listen, these guys aren't playing. No softball tonight, ok? Remember, you're The Tank."

"Right." Tank nodded but his reflux boiled at the thought that he might have to truly hurt someone tonight.

The officer driving pulled up alongside other squad cars on Sunset Blvd, their lights strobing red and blue on the white columns of Sunset Bronson

Studios. A line of palm trees ran down the street, parallel to the columns, and a wrought-iron fence separated the sidewalk from the studio's entrance courtyard. Inside the courtyard, the KTLA radio tower soared over the street.

It was covered in bugs.

They swarmed over the giant number five suspended halfway up, a mass of squirming insect bodies. Something crunched under Tank's boot—the creatures choked the sidewalk. He shivered. The Goosebumps books had never been his favorite, but especially not the ones with creepy bugs.

Tank followed Hopper to where a detective stood glaring at the bugs crawling over the tower.

"Locusts," he said with a shudder. "Nasty."

"Locusts?" Tank inspected the creepy crawlies on the sidewalk closer. "I guess that makes sense with the tattoo, but where'd they all come from?"

Hopper kicked the insects away. "Who knows? What's the status?"

"Whoever's in the studio is refusing to come out but hasn't communicated any demands either." The detective nodded at Tank. "I think maybe they're waiting for you."

"Alright, get in there." Hopper removed two earpieces from a small box and handed one to Tank. "I'll be right here."

"Sounds good, H." Tank fit the earpiece into his left ear and started for the entrance.

Inside the building, more locusts thronged the stairwell, jumping from floor to wall to railing. Tank followed the trail of insects upstairs, nerves jumping in his belly.

In the hallway at the top of the stairs, Tank eased open the first of two doors leading to the sound stage. The news anchor, Jen, sat frozen behind her desk, staring to her left where a man paced, silhouetted against the weather report greenscreen and carrying a small duffle bag over his shoulder. Despite his pacing, the man kept a handgun trained on Jen.

There were no locusts in the room.

Tank was on the wrong side of the room from the gunman. He couldn't run straight at the guy from the angle he was at, or he'd have time to shoot the hostage. Throwing something was out too; the gunman might shoot on impact. Tank crept through the dark spaces of the studio to hide behind a bank of cameras. If he could get to a better position, he could launch himself between the gun and the anchorwoman. She'd be safe and he could take down the gunman.

The man came to a stop in front of the news desk, gun still aimed at the anchor's face, and to Tank's surprise spoke with a received British accent. "Shall we get acquainted while we wait for The Tank? I'm NineSix."

She stared at him.

"A bit out of the ordinary, I know. Do you know where it comes from?" He went on without waiting for an answer. "Revelations chapter nine, verse six. *And in those days shall men seek death and shall not find it.*"

Tank snuck from the cameras to a stack of boxes, rolling through his feet to keep quiet. He paused when NineSix explained his name. *What's that supposed to mean?*

"And your name?" NineSix asked.

The anchor barely opened her mouth. "Jen Abara."

"Ah, what a lovely blouse, Jen Abara."

She didn't answer.

"Designer, is it? New as well. We can't very well go on television in second-hand, off-the-rack clothing, now can we? Did you know," NineSix went on, "so much clothing ends up in landfills every year—heaven forbid you be seen in public wearing last season's outfit—that you could fill the entire Sydney harbor with them?"

Jen swallowed and shook her head.

"Another fun fact. Locusts eat cotton crops." The man swirled a hand in the air and a cloud of insects gathered to it. Tank did a double take. Where had the bugs come from?

"Shall we find out if they eat cotton *after* it's made into fabric as well, while we wait for our little friend?" He threw the gob of insects at her. Jen screamed and covered her head, but NineSix called them back like a yo-yo before they reached her. He laughed and swung the duffle bag off his shoulder onto the desk, letting the mini swarm drop onto the floor. "Or perhaps he's not coming?" NineSix zipped open the bag. Studio lights glinted off metal.

"H," Tank breathed just loud enough for the earpiece to pick up. "He's got a bomb."

Hopper swore and Tank heard other voices in the background calling for the bomb squad.

"In which case—if you'll excuse the horrible pun—I might as well *blow* this joint." NineSix turned his back to Tank's hiding spot and flipped open a panel on the side of the metal cylinder to reveal a digital countdown. Gun or not, Tank couldn't wait any longer. He judged the distance between him and NineSix. He could make that jump, knock the man out and be done with it. No maiming or killing needed. He coiled.

His phone trilled in his pocket.

It rang through the quiet studio like an air raid siren. Tank scrambled to shut it off—*Stupid, stupid, stupid!* He'd left notifications on earlier in case the mayor called.

NineSix whipped his head around, a vicious grin spreading on his face when he saw Tank. He jabbed a button on the cylinder, then whirled in a circle. The locusts zoomed back to him, circling him like a tornado, and he sped through the second door.

Tank cursed himself, head flipping between the door and the bomb on the desk. Numbers ticked down on the display.

*30, 29, 28 ...*

*No time to go after NineSix.*

Jen whimpered, eyes wide.

"Go, run!" Tank waved his arms at the door and she bolted. He snatched up the cylinder, throwing the shoulder strap over his chest, and ran back to the hall.

*17, 16, 15 ...*

He kicked out the nearest window, crawled through and began to climb. The building's smooth sides offered no purchase, and he punched hand holds into the wall on the way up. At the top, he scrambled over the edge of the roof, yanking the bomb off his shoulder.

*6, 5, 4 ...*

A quick glance at the sky to check for passing planes, and he ran, launching himself in the air. At the apex of the jump, he hurled the device straight up. A deafening boom shattered the sky.

A tsunami of air tumbled him across the roof and buffeted the street. Palm trees bent and swayed. Car alarms wailed. Tank jumped to his feet and sprinted to the edge of the roof. NineSix had to still be close by—he'd only had thirty seconds—but all Tank saw was the LAPD officers sheltering from the force of the blast.

He ran to each side of the building, but there was no NineSix. Tank growled and pounded a fist on the ledge.

The roof access door flew open, and Hopper stormed out. "What the hell was that? Please tell me that wasn't your phone going off." He tapped his earpiece.

Tank pulled the offending phone out of his pocket and held it out to Hopper like a kid caught with contraband at school. "I'm sorry, H." His voice came out hoarse. "I forgot to turn off notifications. The mayor ..."

"You forgot to silence your phone?! What kind of rookie mistake is that? That guy got away because you *forgot?*" Hopper snatched the phone and swiped open the screen. "And who the hell is Grace?"

Tank snapped his head up. "It was from Grace?"

Hopper glared at the notification, face reddening. "BlindDate? You got on a dating app?"

Tank didn't answer. Hopper shut his eyes and inhaled deeply, pinching the bridge of his nose.

"Sorry," Tank managed.

Down on the street, the police had regained their feet. News vans assembled at the perimeter. Sirens blared and voices clamored.

Hopper blew out a breath and handed the phone back. "I've gotta go do damage control." His face was still red, but his voice had gentled. "You get yourself back to your apartment without being waylaid by the press, or attracting extra attention, understand? I'll come by in the morning and we'll talk about this."

"Yes, H." Tank sat against the roof ledge, out of sight of anyone on the street. He'd have to wait a while for the crowds to die down enough for him to leave unseen. The BlindDate notification still glowed on his screen. He swiped it open, even as he wondered if he should ignore it as penance. The message was short.

*Hi, Willard! Just thought I'd see how your work thing is going. If it's super boring, we can chat here instead. I could use a laugh after my day ha ha.*

*Boring? I wish.* He couldn't tell Grace his "work party" had featured two explosions, a burning house, an injured kid and a psychopath covered in bugs. To say nothing of his mistakes. Even if he'd been ready to tell her about his real job, that was not the introduction he'd choose. His head was swimming with too many things to be able to answer like a normal person, but it was late enough it wouldn't look weird if he didn't answer the message until tomorrow. He peeked over the side of the roof. Hopper was still talking to the mass of reporters in the front of the studios.

He texted the mayor. *Any news?*

The answer came quickly. *No, he's still out.*

He bounced a heel up and down, his mistakes drilling into his stomach, until a crack appeared in the cement. He rolled his eyes at himself but stilled his leg.

He'd messed up so many times that night. Sure, he pulled Gerard out of the fire, but would the kid have been in the fire if he hadn't given him the X-Men issue? And he'd kept the bomb from detonating in the building, but would NineSix actually have armed it if his phone hadn't gone off?

He had to make it right. But what could he do? He was just the muscle. Hopper kept track of the information, the business contacts. Earlier when Tank had said he wanted to talk to the Point, Hopper had said no. And now he'd told Tank to go home and wait. Because he'd only mess things up more.

But Gerard was unconscious in the hospital, and who knew how long the fire department's investigation would take, even if he could convince Hopper to let him be there. Whoever these locust-loving crazies were, Tank had to stop them. And for that, he needed more information.

He pushed himself to a crouch, snuck through the access door, hurried down the stairs, and out the back door.

But he wasn't going home to sit and wait.

He was going to call Elodie Seeker.

# CHAPTER FIVE

T ank kept to the less populated streets. Technically, his penthouse wasn't in walking distance from the news studio, but that wasn't a problem for him. Strictly speaking, he didn't have super speed, but his strength and durability allowed him to run much faster and longer than the average human.

Running like that attracted attention though. And Hopper said to not be noticed.

He nodded to a couple passing on the sidewalk, like nothing was amiss. *Yup, nothing to see here. Just your average superhero trying to not screw things up.* He extricated Elodie's business card from his phone case and punched in her number.

"Elodie Seeker." Her alto slid like silk over the line.

"Ms. Seeker? This is Tank."

"Tank?" The alto slid up a notch with urgency. "Oh my gosh, the house exploded and then I didn't see you after that. What happened? Are you okay?"

He halted in the middle of the sidewalk. Nobody ever bothered to ask him if he was okay. He was The Tank. "Yeah, I'm alright. Um ... walking home cause my car's still at the mayor's." He faltered. *You're rambling. Get to the point.* "Listen, Ms. Seeker, I was wondering if we could talk? Earlier, it sounded like you had more to tell me."

A clinking noise, like silverware on plates came over the line and a voice in the background said something Tank didn't catch.

"Sorry," he said. "It sounds like you're busy. I can call back later."

"No, no." Elodie stopped him. "I'm just picking up dinner. I only left the mayor's a few minutes ago. The cops wanted statements from everybody at the party, and the fire department wanted to make sure we were all okay before we left, so it took a little while. Have you eaten?"

"Oh, I guess not."

"Okay, I'll grab something for you too and swing by and pick you up. I can give you a lift to your place and we can talk there. Text me where to find you."

Tank shared his location with her, and they hung up. He'd expected that to be harder. But Hopper had been working with him on being less awkward around people. Maybe it was taking?

Except she was bringing food. Take-out meant things like garlic and onions and spices past his heat tolerance. And eating take-out with someone he didn't really know meant awkward explanations about how he couldn't just up and *eat* food, like a normal person, because reflux made its own rules.

He snorted. He might be bullet proof, but Tank often wondered if all anyone would have to do to finish him off was shove a bowlful of raw onions down his throat.

His phone buzzed with a text from Hopper. *Finished with press. Any word from Dupont?*

*No. Gerard still out.*

*Ok. LAPD has an APB out for the guy from the studio. Meet me tomorrow, I should have info from the fire dept. We'll fix it, big guy.*

*Sure, H.*

"Wouldn't have to fix it if I hadn't broken it," Tank muttered. He opened Grace's message again.

*Hi, Willard! Just thought I'd see how your work thing is going. If it's super boring we can chat here instead. I could use a laugh after my day ha ha.*

When he wrote back tomorrow, he'd ask what happened to make her need a laugh. Better yet, think of a way to make her laugh.

Headlights pulled up at the curb, and Elodie Seeker beckoned him to the car.

"I wasn't sure how you felt about spicy things, so I got your curry mild," she said as he slid into the passenger seat. "I hope that's ok." A gentle, spiced smell wafted from Thai House take-out bags on the floor at Tank's feet, and his stomach growled, despite himself.

"Mild's perfect, thanks." *Maybe it'll work. I can pick out extra onions.* He wasn't sure what else to say, so he gave directions to his apartment.

In the penthouse, Lint sauntered into the living room, complaining loudly.

"You have a cat?"

Tank blanched. He hadn't shut her in the laundry room before he left, not expecting company that evening. He was about to scoop her up and put her in the loft when Elodie reached down and scratched behind Lint's ears, crooning.

"Her name's Lint." He shuffled his feet. Hopper always said a cat didn't fit the persona of The Tank, but Elodie looked pleased.

"Hey, Lint." She gave the cat a bit more love. The living room lamp silhouetted her figure, highlighting the curve of her hips, and Tank suddenly remembered Hopper's comments about calling her later.

"Okay if we eat in here?" he asked. The couches and coffee table would keep more professional distance between them than the dining table.

"Sure." Elodie set the bags on the coffee table and handed him a Styrofoam container and a pair of chopsticks. "What happened at the mayor's? Where did you go?"

Tank looked up from his curry. Of course. She wouldn't know about Gerard. "I went to the hospital with the ambulance. The mayor's son was in the house."

She stopped chewing. "Mareva's boy was inside?"

"Gerard, yes." He didn't elaborate on why Gerard had been in the house.

"Is he ok? Do they have a suspect?"

Tank noted she didn't mention the possibility of the explosion being an accident. "He's not awake yet but he's stable. I'm guessing since you were busy with the cops and the fire department you didn't see the news."

She shook her head, and Tank filled her in on the broadcast hijacking and Bronson Studios. Again, he didn't elaborate, only telling her the man had escaped. He wasn't ready to rehash his screw-ups out loud. Elodie rose and paced in front of the window while he talked. Watching her, Hopper's comments came back once again. He ignored them. Yes, Elodie was beautiful. So what?

Los Angeles was full of beautiful people. How many of them had read *How the Nobble Was Finally Found*?

"I wanted to tell you at the party." She ran a hand through her hair. The flower from earlier was gone. "I'm sorry, if I'd thought they were going to try something tonight, I would've tried harder. I have the warehouse here in L.A., obviously, but my company's headquarters are in Las Vegas. Two days ago, we caught someone trying to break in. He had rags and gasoline." She stopped pacing. "And a tattoo of some kind of grasshopper with monster teeth."

Tank sucked in a breath. "They're not just hitting L.A."

"No. When my security team apprehended him, we called Slingshot in to consult."

"Slingshot." Tank thought through the list of other heroes he knew about. He'd met very few of them personally. The Anti-Vigilante Law forbade heroes working as a team. "He works the Vegas area? Has some kind of matter manipulation, right?"

She nodded. "Matter manipulation and a highly intuitive grasp of physics. He can't move large objects—things up to the size of a fist work best, and the rounder the better. But the actual material doesn't matter as long as it's dense enough. So he couldn't fling a couch at someone with his mind, and something like a rubber spatula is the wrong density and shape—"

Tank was momentarily distracted by the idea of trying to stop criminals with a quiver full of spatulas. *There's gotta be a picture book idea in there somewhere.*

"—but I've seen him do impressive things with a handful of ball bearings. It's not as general purpose as super strength," she motioned to Tank, and his cheeks heated, "but Slingshot gets pretty creative with it. And he does a lot of community service outside of straight up hero work." She gave a half smile. "Vegas loves her superhero."

Tank wondered who Slingshot's agent was that they allowed him time for community service. Hopper had suggested a library ribbon cutting or something similar as a concession to Tank's interests, but that wasn't the same as being directly involved.

Elodie went on. "Slingshot saw the tattoo on our arsonist and told us he'd already been investigating a group of ecoterrorists with locust tattoos that calls itself Abaddon. Their aim is to kill as many people as possible in the name of protecting the planet. Their name is based on some kind of beast in the book of Revelations."

"I think their video tonight mentioned a beast," Tank offered. "Had Slingshot found out anything else?"

"Not much, he wanted to do some more research. He did say he thinks their base is near Las Vegas, even though they've been hitting targets here and not there. My business being the exception."

*Grace is in Vegas.* The urge to message her right then and make sure she was safe slammed into him. But he didn't have a good way to explain a message like that without revealing he was The Tank. He consoled himself with the fact that she'd sounded fine in her last message.

Elodie continued. "Slingshot sent me here to talk to you—he'd found out about the attacks in L.A. and how you stopped them—while he kept working on uncovering more of their plan."

Tank frowned. "Slingshot sent you to talk to me? Why didn't the Las Vegas police contact LAPD? Or the FBI? If Abaddon is working in more than one state, I think it would go to the FBI, wouldn't it?" He was fairly sure that was how it worked, but Hopper handled all that stuff. "Either way, they should be sharing info with somebody."

"The police in Vegas can't share any information," Elodie said slowly. "Because they don't have any information."

"They weren't able to get anything out of the guy you caught?"

"No. Because I never turned him over to the police. Slingshot's investigation of Abaddon, and his assistance to me weren't exactly through the normal channels." She looked at him meaningfully.

Tank's mouth dropped open. "Wait, you mean his manager didn't know? Slingshot was doing all this ... on his *own*?"

Elodie nodded and set down her chopsticks. "And he sent me here to ask you to come to Vegas to help. He thinks Abaddon is big. And if we want to stop them, we'll need a team."

"Come to—I can't—" Tank swallowed. "I can't work without Hopper. And I'm not allowed to work with another hero, that's one of the biggest stipulations in the Anti-Vigilante Act."

"Anti-Vigilante Act." She snorted. "All that does is prevent people like you from doing the good you set out to do when you chose this line of work. Come to Vegas and help us."

"I can't," he repeated. "It's illegal."

"And burning down businesses and killing people *is* legal?" she asked, nostrils flaring.

"No! But—" Tank groaned. He didn't get into hero work to turn away people who needed help. Elodie's business had already been targeted twice, and if Abaddon made good on the threats in their video, *everybody* was going to need help. But legally, his hands were tied. "I'm really sorry, but it's not up to me. Slingshot should know that."

"He does know that, but he's prepared to do what needs to be done. Isn't that what The Tank does? Charge ahead and do what needs to be done?" She put her hands on her hips, a challenge on her face.

Tank shrank away from her. Exhaustion—mental and emotional if not strictly physical—settled on his shoulders. The night replayed in his mind: Gerard in his burning room, NineSix disappearing, the bomb lighting up Sunset Boulevard like the noon sun. "That *is* what The Tank is supposed to do, but I don't ..."

The challenge faded from her expression. "You don't what?"

"I don't know that I can be what you need to stop Abaddon. I don't know that I can be that kind of charge-ahead hero that Hopper says I have to be." He winced, worrying that sounded as lame to her as it did to him. "Sorry. You want to finish eating?"

She sat next to him on the couch. "No, tell me what you mean."

Tank blew out a breath. He'd rather open up this way to Grace, but Grace still thought he was a librarian. He couldn't talk to her about Tank stuff yet. "It's just, when we picked the name, The Tank, I thought of it as something impenetrable."

"Like your skin?"

"Yes, but also like a shield, or a bulwark. Something that protects those behind it. I want to protect people; I want to help them. I believe that's what these gifts are for. But I worry Hopper sees The Tank more like something that runs over and smashes anything in its path."

Elodie studied him a moment, tapping a finger against her chin. "You need a new suit."

He blinked. "What?"

"A new suit. Let me make you one. Whenever I don't know what to do in a situation, I design myself a new outfit and my path becomes clear. Besides," she fingered his burnt sleeve, "this one's toast, and I could make you one that lasts longer. Come on." She stood and tugged on his arm until he got to his feet. She looked him over, retrieved a tape from her purse and set about taking measurements.

Tank craned his neck, watching her circle him. "But my path isn't up to me."

She stopped and held his gaze. "Your path is always up to you."

Tank held his breath. Elodie's eyes were earnest, with no trace of her earlier agitation. He found he was glad. In that moment, the thought of her being upset with him made his stomach cramp.

She looked away and shrugged. "And if you don't want to think about your path just yet, then let me make the suit as a thank you for saving my employees. You can come pick it up at my place tomorrow night."

"That fast?" Tank didn't know much about sewing but twenty-four hours didn't sound like enough time to design and make a hero suit.

She smirked. "That fast. I'll text you my address. And bring something of yours that's a favorite."

"What do you mean?"

"A favorite," she reiterated. "You know, like a favorite movie, or song, a book. Something like that."

Tank's brow crinkled. "You want me to bring my favorite book?"

"Yes, a book would be great. You do read, right?"

He stifled a laugh. "Yeah, I read. I'll bring my favorite."

"Good. It helps me know if I need to make any last-minute changes." She gathered her things and gave Lint a farewell scritch under the chin. At the door she turned back. "But Tank? In the meantime, think about that path."

# CHAPTER SIX

Grace shoved her laptop across the desk and ran her hands through her hair. She stared out her window, searching for inspiration in the glass and cement of the cityscape.

*Maybe I need a break.* She pushed her chair out from the desk just as the phone buzzed. Hopefully that was James. She wanted to fill him in on her last appointment with Dr. Oracion, but he hadn't texted her back.

She checked the screen. *Not James.* A grin spread across her face. It was from Willard.

*Morning! Sorry I didn't get back to you sooner. The work party got a bit livelier than expected.*

Grace started with a wide-eyed emoji. *Hey, no worries. Livelier in a good way, I hope?*

*Not exactly. We had some party crashers and security had to step in.*

She raised an eyebrow. *Wow. Librarians in L.A. must really know how to party if you've got gate crashers. Are you ok?*

Willard didn't answer right away, and she wondered if her last line had landed wrong.

*Yeah, I'm ok. It got taken care of. How about you? You mentioned needing a laugh. What's up?*

Grace scooped her water bottle off a stack of papers and refilled it at the sink to give herself time to think of an appropriate answer. It was still too early to talk about doctor appointments.

*Just work. I have a project to finish on this work trip and I'm still trying to figure it out is all. But thanks for asking : )*

*Ah, I'm sorry. You work in sustainability, right?*

She resettled in her chair, casting a rueful glance at the paper towers of abandoned rough drafts on her desk. *I do. I do a lot of work on ways to make various processes zero or near zero emissions. There's always a better way to do a thing, right?*

He came back with a big smiley face and a thumbs up. *Absolutely! That's awesome work. And you're clever, I'm sure you'll figure out whatever problem you're working on. You got this.*

Grace beamed and held the phone to her chest before answering. *Thanks for the confidence.*

*In the meantime, I have a little news that might make you smile.*

*What's that?*

Willard sent a gif of a drum roll. *I found a copy of* A Circle of Cats.

Grace gasped. "No way!" *Oh my gosh! Really?*

*Really. It's a used copy since, like you said, it's out of print.*

*Used copies are better,* she typed, grinning. *They already have love in them.*

*Exactly! Where should I mail it?*

She sat up straight, thinking. The mail got delivered mid-morning. If he sent it to the house, Tūtū would find it first and then there would be questions. Grace wasn't quite ready for questions yet. She loved her grandma, loved all her family, but sometimes it seemed that since they couldn't protect her from the near constant bruising, they'd protect her from everything else.

*Send it to the charter school, then I can read it to the kids right away. Thank you, Willard!* She added the school's address in Summerlin West and hit send. She paced the length of her desk twice, debating, then sent one more message. Two red hearts.

Willard responded immediately with two red hearts of his own. *I'm so glad it made you happy.*

Grace did a little happy dance before reclaiming her chair, Willard's thoughtfulness and confidence in her giving her a creative boost. She grabbed a new piece of scratch paper.

Flow set in and the world faded away, the pencil lines on the paper Grace's only focus. An hour later, she surfaced, pleased with her work so far. The phone buzzed again.

She frowned at it, not quite ready to fully emerge from her creative cocoon and communicate with the outside world. Unless it was Willard again.

She'd been trying to keep a rein on her feelings. They'd only messaged a handful of times, and they'd never met in real life. But every time they "talked," she thought her cheeks would crack from smiling.

She grabbed the phone, but it wasn't Willard. It was from Dr. Oracion.

*Call me. I think I found one.*

# CHAPTER SEVEN

A familiar building rose ahead of Tank. He walked slowly through the park, eyes on the library where he'd worked before signing with Strickland Talent. A mom herded three kids that looked under five years old into the library. Tank checked his watch and realized with a pang it was Storytime.

He smiled ruefully. Maybe they'd read *Seagull and Sea Dragon* again today. Although, it was the second week of the month, when they always did a Storytime featuring holidays from that month. Out of habit, he started structuring the hour in his head. Maybe something for St. Patrick's Day, since it was March. But March also featured National Barbie Day, and there were plenty of Barbie picture books and early chapter books. The March before quitting the library, he'd read *Froggy Bakes a Cake* for National Pound Cake Day, and the kids had decorated paper chef hats.

He shook his head. *Not why you're here.*

When Hopper had texted to meet here, of all places, Tank's reflux kicked into high gear. There was a lecture coming for sure.

To fortify himself, he'd dropped into his favorite used bookstore on the way here. He'd found a couple comic issues, but when *A Circle of Cats* showed up on the shelf like the Holy Grail, he couldn't believe his luck. Those two red hearts from Grace had buoyed him all the way here.

But now, standing in front of a place that should've reminded him of joy, his stomach burned.

"There you are." Hopper strode up, sipping at a to-go coffee cup. "Where's your car? I didn't see it in the parking lot."

Tank turned away from the library to focus on his manager. "I took an Uber."

Hopper quirked an eyebrow. "Why?"

"Well, I haven't picked up my car from the mayor's yet." He thought that'd be obvious. It was too late last night to worry about it, and he hadn't had a chance to get over there yet this morning.

Hopper shrugged like he still didn't get it. "Why didn't you have the valet service deliver it to your building?"

Tank shifted. "I guess I didn't want to bug anyone. I can go get it later."

Hopper waved the comment away. "You're a superhero serving this city 24/7. Bug people. Ask for what you want."

Tank nodded but didn't say anything.

"Anyway." Hopper strolled through the grass toward the library and Tank followed. "I asked you to meet me here because I want to talk to you."

Tank shut his eyes. *Here it comes.*

"I still haven't heard anything from the mayor about Gerard, have you?"

"No." Tank's voice was small. He knew where Hopper was going.

"I'm not gonna say that it's your fault that kid is in the hospital. It's not your fault. Those guys from the video last night—it's their fault. You saved Gerard. But, Tank, buddy ..." Hopper faced him, shaking his head.

Tank nodded miserably. "He wouldn't have been in the house if I hadn't given him a new comic."

"Exactly." Hopper jabbed a finger at the library. "You have to leave this behind. You came to me wanting to help people, to use your gifts to protect those weaker than you. Yes?"

Tank's voice barely registered a whisper this time. "Yes."

"Ok, then let me help you do that. You can't have a foot in two worlds. You can't be two people. You gotta be The Tank. Read on your own time if you want, in the loft in your apartment or whatever. Maybe we can even have you face for a literacy advocacy non-profit, that's good press. But when you walk out that front door, when you put that uniform on, you aren't Willard Meeks anymore. You are The Tank. Let others read to people, or sing lullabies—do the

soft stuff. That's their job. You gotta handle the tough stuff. That's your job.
And you gotta *be* tough enough that nothing gets through you. Get it?"

Tank shoved his hands in his pockets. "Yeah, I get it."

"Good." Hopper started walking again. "One more thing."

Tank held his breath. *More?*

"This woman, Grace. I don't think that's a good idea. She's probably after
her fifteen minutes of fame, dating The Tank."

"No, there are no pictures allowed on the app," Tank hastened to explain.
"She doesn't even know I'm in hero work—she lives in Las Vegas, not here in
L.A. She calls me Willard." He said the last words softly, appreciating the fact,
even if the name Willard wasn't the whole truth of himself anymore.

Hopper looked at him and grunted. "I get how that's appealing, but you
gotta keep your head in the game. She's a distraction, as we saw last night. I
want you to drop the dating service. I'm your manager, and I hope by now,
your friend. If you're looking for a relationship let me help you. We'll find you
someone who aligns with your career goals better."

Tank's brow wrinkled in confusion. Drop BlindDate? Drop Grace? Usually
he saw how Hopper's directions would help him become who he needed to be
to help people the most effectively, but cutting off contact with Grace did *not*
make sense. "What do you mean?"

Hopper patted his shoulder. "Don't worry about it too much right now, big
guy. We can discuss it more later. I want to talk about what we're going to do
about these locust tattoo people too."

"Right." Uneasy, Tank let the topic of Grace drop. He'd have to come up with
some good arguments between now and "later" to convince Hopper he should
keep talking to Grace. "I did find out something interesting last night."

Hopper shot him a look. "Last night? You were supposed to go straight
home."

"And I did. Basically. But I called Elodie—"

"Elodie?"

"Yeah. Or, Ms. Seeker, that is. You met her at the mayor's last night. She gave
me her card, said she wanted to talk. She makes clothes. I mean, she's a fashion

mogul ... or something." He fumbled through his explanation. "She picked me up—I didn't have the car, right?—and we brought dinner back to my place."

"Yes, I remember who Elodie Seeker is. And you had dinner last night at your place?" Hopper grinned. "Now there's a good choice. Plenty of visibility for you both."

Tank gaped at him, face burning at Hopper's suggestion. "No, she had information for me about Abaddon. She didn't get to finish explaining at the party, so I called her to find out what she knew. It wasn't a date."

Hopper smirked. "But it could be. What kind of information did she have?"

"She knows where their headquarters are."

Hopper ground to a halt. "She what?"

"Or, at least, she knows that they're based out of Las Vegas. We don't know the exact location." Tank filled him in on the arson attempt on Elodie's Vegas facilities and what her security team had learned. "They called in the Vegas hero, Slingshot, to help."

"Slingshot, huh?" Hopper paced a circle, rubbing his jaw. "Ok. I can reach out to his manager and see if we can compare notes."

"About that." Tank shuffled his feet, unsure if he should tell Hopper that Slingshot had been working on his own.

"Feet," Hopper said. Tank stilled. "About what?"

"Nothing." It wasn't his place to discuss whatever Slingshot was doing. And if Hopper was going to call Slingshot's manager, he'd find out for himself.

Tank's phone dinged. A text alert, not the BlindDate alert. Just as well. If he got another message from Grace right now, he'd get it from Hopper for sure.

"Who's that?" Hopper asked.

Fire raced up Tank's esophagus as he read the message. "It's the mayor. Gerard's awake."

The hospital's main lobby echoed with footsteps and P.A. announcements. Tank hurried through the assortment of couches and fake plants to a bank of elevators.

Hopper tapped his arm. "Hey, I'm gonna duck out for a few minutes and see if I can get ahold of Slingshot's rep. That way you can have a few minutes with the kid."

"Thanks, H.". Tank pushed the call button and tapped his foot impatiently while Hopper found a seat in a quiet corner. When he stepped out of the elevators on Gerard's floor, a nurse was bustling down the hall, shaking her head.

"Hi, excuse me?" Tank caught her attention. "I'm here to see Gerard Dupont. Is it okay to go in?"

"Yes, His Highness is receiving visitors," she said, rolling her eyes. "You're The Tank, right? Tell him to take his pain meds, maybe he'll listen to you more than me." She threw her hands up and took a post at the nurse's station.

Tank chuckled to himself. Gerard making his opinions known was a good sign.

"Tank!" The boy's face lit up when Tank stuck his head in the door.

"Hey, bud." He glanced around the room. No one else was there. "Where's your mom?"

"She went downstairs to get me some ice cream. I woke up two hours ago, so she finally thinks it's safe to leave my side or something, I guess."

"Ah, ice cream seems in order. How are you feeling?" Tank pulled a plastic chair next to the bed and had to hide his smile as Gerard launched into an animated description of the hospital staff's shortcomings. "They keep trying to get me to take pain killers, but they'll make me sleepy. I need to be sharp, alert." He snapped his fingers. "And they don't even have any comics!"

"Ludicrous conditions," Tank agreed, stifling his laughter.

"And Mom refuses to bring me any from home. She says I'm grounded from comics." He made a face. "Like it's Miles Morales's fault someone blew up our house."

Tank's amusement fizzled out. "Ah, yeah." He cleared his throat, tried to lighten his tone. "Hey, maybe take it easy on the nurses, despite the lack of comics, ok? They're just trying to help you."

Gerard slouched against his pillows, knocking one to the floor. "Wolverine wouldn't need to take pain killers."

Tank retrieved the pillow and tucked it behind the boy. "Well," he said softly. "We can't all be Wolverine. Although maybe ..." He reached for his backpack with the comics he'd bought that morning but then stopped. Gerard wouldn't have been in the explosion if he'd told the mayor he'd given him a new issue. And Hopper's voice echoed in his head. *You have to leave this behind.*

"Maybe what?" Gerard asked.

Tank shook his head. "Nothing."

Gerard squinted at him. "You're siding with my mom, aren't you? Come on, hand it over." He held out a hand, every inch the prince the nurse had called him. Despite Hopper's bleak instructions, Tank choked back another laugh.

"Hand over what?" he asked, feigning innocence.

Gerard rolled his eyes. "I'm not a grown up, remember? That means I'm not stupid."

"Ouch!" Tank clutched at his heart. "What does that say about me?"

"Don't be silly." Gerard dismissed his objection. "I already told you, you don't count as a grown up."

Tank couldn't hold in his laughter this time. "Thank goodness for that. You'll tell me if I ever start acting like one, right?"

The boy shrugged. "Duh."

A soft rush of air sounded as the door opened. Hopper strode in carrying a gift shop bouquet of carnations. "Hey, how's the patient? I brought you something."

Gerard wrinkled his nose at the flowers and turned a pointed look on Tank. "See? I don't think you're in any danger."

"Any danger of what?" Hopper demanded.

"Of acting like a—"

"Nothing, nothing," Tank covered. The last thing he needed was another lecture.

Hopper grunted. "Fine. I need to talk to you a minute." He pulled Tank to the far corner of the room. "I managed to get a hold of Slingshot's manager, Mateo Delagarza."

"What did he say?"

Hopper's face turned grim. "He said he hasn't seen Slingshot since Tuesday. He can't find him."

"What? But Elodie saw him Monday morning."

"Yeah," Hopper said. "So it sounds like she was the last one to see him. His rep went to his apartment looking for him." He paused and glanced meaningfully at Gerard. The boy was watching them, face intent.

Tank turned toward the wall to keep the conversation private. "And?"

"The apartment was torn apart. And crawling with locusts."

"They're thinking Abaddon kidnapped him?"

"Could be, could be." Hopper stared out the hospital window. "But apparently Delagarza didn't know Slingshot went on that call to Elodie's. He took that job on his own."

"Oh ... wow." Tank shoved his hands in his pocket, avoiding Hopper's gaze. "Did Delagarza say why he thought Slingshot would do that?"

Hopper retrieved a bag of corn nuts from his coat pocket and tossed a handful in his mouth. "No. And I'm thinking maybe there were locusts in Slingshot's apartment because Abaddon kidnapped him, *or* maybe there were locusts in Slingshot's apartment because he's joined up with Abaddon."

Tank gave a low whistle. Rogue heroes weren't unheard of, but they were uncommon. The AVA stipulated severe repercussions for any hero who went off the rails. Turning villain equaled a death sentence. "But why would he be investigating them if he were part of them?"

Hopper shrugged. "Maybe he was looking into them and decided he liked what he saw. Or maybe he lied to Elodie when he said he'd been looking into them."

"Hello? It's very rude to keep other people out of the conversation," Gerard said, tapping his fingers on the bed railing.

"Almost done, kiddo. Here, watch cat videos for a minute." Hopper tossed Gerard his phone and turned back to Tank. The boy shot Hopper's back a disgusted look but tapped at the screen.

"How do we handle this?" Tank kept his voice low. "If Slingshot is MIA, how are we supposed to swap info or make any kind of strategy?"

"That's the interesting part. There's a bit of a loophole, let's say, in AVA regulations for circumstances like this."

"What kind of loophole?"

"Basically, since Slingshot is missing, Las Vegas doesn't technically have a hero working the area. And if the missing hero's manager agrees, which Delagarza already did, another hero can come in, temporarily of course, until the first is found. We can go to Vegas, and you can stop Abaddon at their heart."

Go to Vegas. Tank swallowed. This would be the biggest thing he'd undertaken in his career, but it would mean keeping millions of people safe. More, if Abaddon truly meant their threat about "cleansing" the whole world.

*And*, he couldn't keep the thought from coming, *Grace is in Las Vegas.* He'd be keeping Grace safe. Maybe he could deliver the book in person. See her face. If Hopper met her too, his manager would come around. After all, Hopper wanted what was best for him.

"But it's still on a technicality," Hopper qualified, crunching more corn nuts. "We go in quiet. Local law enforcement will know we're there and will be working with us, and it sounds like we'll want to talk to Elodie's team, but we don't advertise our presence. I'll book our flights. We should be able to leave in the morning."

"Elodie's team?" Tank supposed he'd be going to Vegas like she'd asked him to, but he still couldn't give her the team she'd wanted. Slingshot was missing and the AVA wasn't.

"Her security team," Hopper clarified.

"Oh, right. Of course." *Dumb, Tank, dumb.* "Because they have that terrorist in custody."

"Yeah, him. Whatever info there is to be had so far, Elodie's team has it. But even after we get that info, I'm thinking we should work with them as much as we can." He elbowed Tank in the ribs.

The door shushed open again, and Mayor Dupont swept in carrying a thick milkshake. She looked like she hadn't slept all night, but she smiled when she saw them. "Tank, I'm so glad you came. He asked for you as soon as he came to."

They joined the mayor by the bed while she set about fussing over Gerard and arranging his shake on a tray.

"So tomorrow, big guy," Hopper repeated.

"Tomorrow will be good." Tank nodded. His apartment building had complimentary pet sitting, so Lint would be covered. "Gives me time to get the new suit from Elodie tonight."

"What new suit?" Hopper tossed his empty corn nuts bag in the trash. "We didn't talk about any new designs."

*Shoot.* He'd forgotten to tell his manager about that part. "She volunteered last night. To design a new uniform, I mean, with better functionality. For me."

"Elodie's making you a new suit? And so fast." Mayor Dupont looked up from her ministrations. "You're lucky. Her waiting list is miles long."

"Is it now?" Hopper crossed his arms with an I-told-you-so expression. "And you're picking it up where?"

Tank blushed from his cheeks to the back of his neck. "Her house."

"Excellent. Wear your leather jacket and that short-sleeved blue T-shirt. They emphasize all of this." He gestured at Tank's physique.

"Hopper, that's not why I'm going."

Mayor Dupont grinned. "Oh, is there a new development in the life of Los Angeles's favorite superhero?"

"No, there's not—"

"Elodie's a fantastic woman, Tank," she continued. "I give my full approval." Her phone buzzed and she excused herself to the hallway.

Hopper pulled Tank aside once more. "Listen, I think Vegas could be a great opportunity for you, big guy. But you have to be on board with what we talked about earlier. Abaddon aren't petty thugs robbing a convenience store. They're organized, they have resources, and they have a mission. You can't leave the kid gloves on." He shot a look at Gerard. "You gotta *be* The Tank. Leave Willard at home."

Gerard threw up his hands. "Are you two done with the blah-blah-blahing? And Tank, my eyes are going to dry up in my skull from X-Men withdrawal. Did you bring me another issue or what?"

"Hey." Hopper pulled his attention back. "You get it?"

Tank fingered his backpack strap, staring at the bandage on Gerard's arm, the bruising on his forehead. How many other kids would Abaddon put in the hospital, or worse, in the ground, because he couldn't bury his old self like Hopper kept telling him to?

He hardened his jaw. None. "I get it, H." He turned back to Gerard and let his very real regret show on his face. "Sorry, bud. I'm afraid I didn't."

# CHAPTER EIGHT

The moon rose over L.A. as Tank pulled his Tesla up to the gate at Elodie's driveway. A woman with Seeker Security embroidered on her uniform leaned out of the guardhouse window.

"Clubs are downtown, pal."

"Oh, no, I—" Hopper's admonition to *be* The Tank played in his mind and he lifted his chin. "The Tank. Here to see Ms. Seeker."

The woman's face cleared and her tone became more friendly. "Oh, yes. She said you were coming. Sorry, we get a lot of guys pulling in claiming to be '*lost.*' And I'm from her Vegas office, so I didn't recognize you right off. Slingshot fan, myself."

"Ah, yes. Elodie said Vegas loves her superhero."

"—loves her superhero." She finished the sentence with him with a grin, and Tank hoped for the sake of the people of Las Vegas that Hopper's suspicions were wrong. "Go on up." She pushed a button, and the gate slid open. Tank gave a little wave and drove ahead.

Jacaranda trees lined the driveway, lights glowing between each. Purple blossoms dripped down to touch the top of the car as he parked next to the house.

He climbed out of the car, tugging his shirt smooth. After a lengthy wardrobe consultation with Lint, he'd gone with Hopper's suggestion of the blue tee and black leather jacket.

"Not because I'm trying to impress anyone," he'd told the cat. "Just because you got fur all over my other choices." Lint hadn't looked convinced.

Classical columns and tall windows framed the front of the house, but woven wood blinds tempered the formality. Tank rang the doorbell and stepped a pace back from the door.

Light flooded over him as the door swung open. Elodie greeted him in leggings and an oversize shirt. *Comfortable for working in,* he thought. The shirt looked soft. He gave himself a mental shake. What a dumb thought. What did it matter if Elodie's shirt was soft?

"Hey, come on in. Shoes off, if you don't mind." She pointed to a shoe rack by the door.

"Oh, right. Sure." He slipped off his low boots and padded after her. The entryway opened into sitting rooms on either side of it. Splashes of green from an indoor palm, and a potted umbrella tree accented a cream, gold and black color scheme. He paused at a plant he didn't recognize. Jewel green needles covered the branches, reminiscent of evergreens, but gentler than any he was familiar with.

"What kind of plant is this?" he asked.

"Hmm?" Elodie turned back.

"I mean," he fumbled. "If you don't mind me asking." *Dumb question, Tank. You're here for a costume, not a horticulture lesson.*

She smiled. "Not at all. It's a Norfolk Island Pine. Are you into botany?"

Tank bit his lip. He knew what Hopper would say. *Houseplants are not tough.*

"No, not specifically. I just know a few basics from—" He cut himself off before he could bring up helping kids research for school projects at the library. That was something he missed. Collecting miscellaneous bits of knowledge while helping others learn. But Hopper's scowl flashed through his mind. *Leave Willard at home.*

He couldn't talk to Elodie about Willard stuff.

"Just from around, I guess," he finished lamely. "But you? You're into botany?"

She ran a finger over the plant's needles. "I find having living things around helps me be creative." She nodded to a wide staircase at the far end of the entry.

Cream steps and a polished wooden banister curved up to the second floor. "Shall we?"

Upstairs, the second floor spread open as one large room. Floor to ceiling windows along the front and back walls ensured plenty of natural light during the day. Now, in the evening, they proffered a fantastic view of the galaxy that was L.A.'s night lights.

"Welcome to my workshop." Elodie proceeded to a standing-height worktable that ran along most of the far wall. A pair of folding screens with koi swimming on the panels converted a corner into a dressing room. A corps of dress dummies presided over fabric, sewing machines, sergers, dress racks, measuring tapes, scissors and all the organized chaos indicative of someone who routinely lost themselves in their work.

"It's incredible." Tank craned his neck to take in the room as a whole. It gave off the same pleasantly cluttered feeling as a used bookstore or the library stacks. All Elodie's workshop needed was a reading nook.

"Thanks." She folded herself into an armchair in front of the bank of windows overlooking the driveway. "So, did you remember to bring your favorite book?"

Tank sat gingerly in the chair next to her and pulled a battered paperback from his inside jacket pocket. He'd had it sewn in specially so he could carry small volumes with him, having never acclimatized to e-readers.

"I did." He ran a hand over the cover, spiderwebbed with wear lines. His heart pounded with sudden nerves. This wasn't merely 'a good book' to him. It had been his escape all through junior high and high school. The number of times he'd read the book didn't quite match the number of times his uncle had called him a big oaf, or a dumb ox. But it was close.

The paper was soft and kind on his skin as he thumbed through the pages. "What does ..." he started. "How does knowing a favorite book help with finishing the suit?"

Elodie watched him, elbow on armrest, chin in hand. "Fair question. The functionality of a garment is crucial. In your line of work, even more so. But if a garment is solely functional, we can't really call it fashion. Fashion is an expression. It finds the inner you and presents it to the outside world. I can't make that suit uniquely yours until I know what makes you uniquely you. What fuels The Tank, you could say."

Tank coughed. What fueled him? What fueled him was the whole problem. He couldn't present his inner self to the world—his inner self was what Hopper kept telling him to bury.

"I ask clients to bring a favorite of something to help me see them better," Elodie continued. "I'm glad you brought a book, though. I find a person's taste in books shows a side of themselves they may aspire to but haven't found yet. I can help them bring it forward, help them realize it."

Tank's mouth formed a little 'O.' He hadn't heard such a beautiful view on books in a long time. "Wow. I didn't know fashion design was so psychological."

Elodie smiled and held out her hand. "May I?"

He offered her the book with both hands. On the cover a great, black horse stood proudly on a rock at the edge of the sea.

Elodie examined it with interest. "*The Black Stallion?*"

"By Walter Farley, yes." Tank's voice was quiet.

"Tell me why it's your favorite."

He floundered. If he had imagined having this conversation with someone, it would've been with Grace, not Elodie.

"Please know that anything my clients tell me stays with me," she said gently. "No leaks."

Tank nodded, sucked in a breath and began. "I was mostly raised by my uncle. He was ... not kind. And in school, I had all this size already—" he pointed to his chest "—but not the extra strength. And my skin wasn't impenetrable yet. But it had this," he paused, remembering. "Numbness. It made me clumsy. It's hard to perform delicate, fine motor motions when you almost can't feel your fingers. And you know high school kids. They can be, well, the way they can be. So, they'd do things to me, hurt me, from behind, because I couldn't feel it. Half the time it was the other guys from football, the ones that were supposed to be my teammates." Acid crawled up his esophagus, a physical reminder of the pain in the memory. "I wouldn't know they had cut me again until a teacher would ask me why my shirt was bloody."

Elodie stared at him, horrified. "They *cut* you?"

Tank lifted his shirt and turned so she could see the network of scars crisscrossing his back.

"Oh, Tank," she whispered. "I'm so sorry. Your teachers did nothing?"

He tugged his shirt back into place and faced her. "They didn't believe me that I couldn't feel it. They thought I must have been cutting myself, for attention. And my uncle told the admin that I was a clumsy oaf and always falling into things." His face twisted. "They'd seen me having trouble with the other kids. But school officials and teachers are busy. Hundreds of students to keep track of, plenty of paperwork to get buried in. It was easier to let it go than try to deal with a complicated problem.

"But this book." He tapped the volume. "When Alec gets stranded on the island The Black becomes his friend, his protector. The Black was this strong, powerful being standing between Alec and the pain of the world—the fact that his father was dead, that he was lost in a harsh environment—and later when they started racing and none of the adults wanted to take this kid seriously, The Black made them see Alec's true worth. I—" He faltered again, cleared his throat against the lava searing his insides. "I wished so bad that I had someone like The Black to do that for me. So later, when the numbness faded and the strength kicked in, when no one could cut me anymore, I decided I would be The Black for others who needed it."

Elodie stared at the book, not speaking. When she finally lifted her head, it was to wipe away a tear. She handed him the book and held his gaze. "Thank you for sharing that with me."

"Thanks for listening." To his own surprise, he didn't break eye contact. Neither did Elodie. The burn in his throat receded. A different warmth kindled in his chest, and he was glad to be sharing this moment with her.

"I have to confess, you are not what I expected," she said, her voice soft. "When Slingshot sent me out here, and I looked up The Tank online ... Well,

I've had more than enough experience dealing with so-called alpha males to have recognized one in your public hero persona. But that's not who you are, is it?"

He swallowed. *As Hopper frequently reminds me.*

Elodie pushed out of her chair. "I'm going to make one final adjustment to the suit and then you can try it on."

She disappeared behind the folding screens for two minutes before reemerging and beckoning him over. "Ok, it's on the hanger. Come out and show me when you have it on."

Tank left the book and his jacket on the chair. "How did you make changes so fast?"

"It's what I do. Quick, quick. I want to see it on you." She pushed him toward the changing area, laughing.

Tank flinched. Except for Hopper, people didn't touch him. He didn't know if they were secretly afraid of him, or if it was just that there weren't very many people he knew well enough for that, but people didn't touch him. Just like they didn't ask if he was ok.

But Elodie had asked last night. And now, here she was, her hands on his back, despite his scars, teasingly pushing him forward. Familiar, close. Like friends. He relaxed and allowed her to shoo him behind the screens where her creation waited.

The pants and form-fitting top weren't done in camo like the old ones. Elodie had kept the suit green, but opted for a more energized shade, reminiscent of the Norfolk Island Pine downstairs. The solid star still decorated the chest, but it shone a glossy black, exactly how he'd always imagined The Black's coat to look in the sun. Lines of the same iridescent darkness ran from the wrists, around the sleeves, and converged at the star.

The suit went on twice as fast as the old design, and when Tank examined himself in the mirror, he saw how the ribbons of black curved to accent his musculature. The pants still sported cargo-style pockets, but even superheroes needed someplace to put their car keys.

"How's it coming?"

Tank stepped out from behind the screen and spread his arms. "Ta da."

Elodie's eyes lit up like the sun. She clapped her hands and rushed to his side. "Oh, it looks so good!" She smoothed her hands over the star, and across the shoulders, nodding to herself. "The neckline's not too tight?"

"Nope, it's way better than the old one." Tank took in her beaming face. "You really love doing this, don't you?"

She laughed and walked a slow circle around him. "I really do. Now, your old suit was not nearly as bulletproof as you are."

"True. Hopper had to get them replaced pretty regularly; they'd get all full of holes or ripped up. We could've added Kevlar to the design to make them last longer, but it seemed like a waste since I don't need it."

"Hmm, yes. And it's way too bulky. It'd impede your movements."

"Exactly."

She planted her feet in front of him. "I've been working on a new kind of fabric for a while, and this is the inaugural use of it. The suit should be much more durable than your old one and move with your body better." She knelt, slid a finger into the waistband and gave it a tug.

*Just checking the fit,* Tank thought. But goosebumps raised on his skin, and the new closeness between them ratcheted a notch higher until she hummed in satisfaction and got to her feet.

*Just checking the fit,* he repeated. "Elodie, this is amazing. Thank you so much."

"You are so welcome." She beamed again, gold threads swirling through the deep brown of her eyes.

A text alert rang from Tank's jacket, and they both jumped. He crossed to the chair and checked the message.

"Flight info from Hopper."

"Flight info?" Elodie busied herself straightening supplies at the worktable.

"Flight info—oh my gosh, I forgot to tell you." He smacked a palm on his forehead. "You know how you asked me to come to Vegas? And I said I couldn't? It turns out there's some loophole, clause thing that Hopper found, so we can."

She turned from the table, fabric scraps trailing from her hands. "You're coming to Vegas?"

"Tomorrow morning, in fact. Hopper wants to work with your security team, question the guy that tried to start the fire, that kind of thing." He didn't mention Hopper's ulterior motive of pushing he and Elodie together. Working with Elodie's people made sense. *But H is nothing if not a multitasker.*

"Great." She tossed the scraps into a small bin of other shredded fabric, face alight. "You can have whatever access you need to him. I would love it if we worked together on this."

"Perfect." He rolled his shoulders, and bent through his knees, feeling how the new suit stayed right with his body. "I think we'll make a great team."

She nodded in satisfaction, watching him move. "Definitely. How did you work it out?"

"Hopper got a hold of Slingshot's manager. No one's seen Slingshot since you talked to him Monday morning, and his apartment was ransacked." Tank slowed his movements as he relayed what Hopper had told him. It wasn't the best reason for being able to go. "They're considering him a missing person."

Elodie paled and leaned against the table. "Slingshot's missing?"

Tank hurried to her side. *Way to go, dummy, throwing that out there like that.*

"Are you ok? You look like you're about to faint." He searched the worktable for a water bottle or anything to help her.

"Yes, sorry. I'm fine." She straightened. "A little surprised is all. Like I said, Vegas loves her hero." She ran her hands over his shoulders again, inspecting the suit. "You're sure it's comfortable? Nothing you want to change?"

Tank searched her face, but she seemed recovered. "Nothing. It's great."

"Ok, go ahead and change out of it."

After he'd donned his street clothes once more, Elodie produced what looked like a shaving kit.

"Pop this latch here and align the suit like this." She lay the left cuff over a secret compartment in the shaving kit and the suit folded in on itself into an impossibly condensed size, fitting neatly in the compartment.

He held it with awe. "How did you—never mind. I will just accept that you are a genius."

"I'll take genius. Also, if it goes through an X-ray machine, like in an airport, all they'll see is the shaving kit, no suit. I know you're on a special dispensation to work outside L.A., but in case you ever need it."

"Impressive." He couldn't think what he'd ever be doing that he needed to hide his super suit, but Elodie was, nevertheless, a genius, and he told her so again as she walked him to his car.

She leaned down to the open driver's side window as he started the engine. "This was fun, Tank," she said, eyes soft. "I'm glad we got to talk."

"Me too. See you in Vegas?"

"I'll be a day behind you, there's something I have to take care of here before I can leave, but then, yes. I'll tell Leona, my head of security, to look for you and Mr. Strickland to visit sometime tomorrow." She straightened and patted the car door. "Till then, be careful. You're fun to design for, I'd hate for anything to happen to you." Her eyes laughed at the joke of anything hurting him.

He joked back. "Hey, I'll be wearing an Elodie original. What could happen?"

He smiled to himself the entire drive home.

# CHAPTER NINE

A forest of tents spread across the sidewalk. Grace's heart clenched as she and Dr. Oracion walked through them to the shelter, offering small smiles to whichever of the tents' residents seemed receptive to the gesture. She wished she could give them more.

"I see that look," Dr. Oracion said.

"I know. But I can't help thinking about that folktale where the guy is granted a wish, and he wishes that whenever he reaches into his pocket, he pulls out the exact amount of money he needs." Her eyes ranged over the tents. "If we had that wish we could help so many people."

The doctor pulled open the door to the Madeleine Alliance for the Unhoused. "Yes, but we don't have that wish, so we can't. At least not today. But if we can find this Alice person, we can help her *and* you."

"You're right," Grace conceded. "Thanks for flying out to help me with this."

"I wouldn't miss it." The doctor strode ahead of Grace down a corridor, sneakers squeaking on the painted cement floor. Even in jeans and a T-shirt, she carried tools of her trade with her in a backpack. If they did manage to find Alice and, if she turned out to have some kind of healing factor like the rumors said, and *if* she consented to help them, they'd need the backpack.

Grace blew a stray hair out of her face. That was a lot of ifs.

Dr. Oracion knocked at an office labeled Rene Silva.

*She's so young,* Grace thought when Rene answered the door. The doctor had said Rene directed the shelter's addiction recovery services and was consulting with a private non-profit on a tiny homes project for unhoused people. She'd also been unhoused herself for over ten years.

But she didn't look over twenty-five.

The inside of her upper arm prickled, and Grace tried to banish the image of a fifteen-year-old on the streets. Another bruise right now wouldn't help anyone.

Rene waved them inside a small office. "You must be Grace Kekoa. The doctor here told me a little bit about your situation. Please, have a seat." She scooped files off a couple of chairs and deposited them on the floor next to a golden retriever wearing a therapy dog vest.

"So, Alice." Instead of taking the third chair, Rene sat on the floor next to the dog and stroked its ears.

"Alice," Dr. Oracion said. "Tell us a little more about her."

"She's been in and out of this area for a while. I think she might have family outside of town that try to get her to stay with them, but ... It's not an unusual story." She shrugged. The dog nestled its head on her knee for more pets, and she continued, "Anyways, I noticed in the last year or two how good Alice's constitution is. Seemed like if a flu or something went through the community, she never got it, or if she cut herself or got scraped up, she healed really fast. I didn't think about it too much until a couple weeks ago. Alice keeps a little dog with her, Henry. Some kind of terrier mix, I think. And this cyclist accidentally clipped the dog in the park, right? Henry ran out in front of him, barking, and the cyclist couldn't turn in time, and Henry's leg got broken."

Grace winced. "Poor thing."

"Yeah, the guy felt really bad. He offered to take Henry to the vet, but Alice grabbed the dog and ran. But here's the thing." Rene leaned forward. "Two days after that Alice stopped in here with Henry, and he was fine. Trotting around like nothing had happened."

Grace exchanged a look with the doctor. "Did Alice mention anything about it?"

"No." Rene leaned back against the wall. "And, who knows? Maybe the dog is the one with an ability instead of Alice. But last week when a couple of the nurses who volunteer here and know Dr. Oracion mentioned what she was looking for, and what you—" she pointed at Grace "—were offering for it, I figured it couldn't hurt to let you know. If you can help Alice, get her off the streets like that, I want her to have that shot."

"Thank you, Rene," Dr. Oracion said. "I hope we can help her too."

Rene gently shifted her dog's head and pushed to her feet. "I asked her to come in today to talk to you. She's in the cafeteria. I have to warn you though, she's jumpy. Doesn't trust people."

"She ran from the cyclist." Grace followed Rene and the doctor out of the office back toward the lobby.

"Exactly. She tends to think people are government operatives out to get her, things like that."

"We'll go slowly," Grace promised. Paranoia and other mental health issues weren't uncommon in the unhoused population, but if Alice really did have a healing ability, maybe she wasn't wrong to be overly cautious. Dr. Oracion's team couldn't be the only ones searching for people who hadn't made their powers public.

The cafeteria was empty, other than a few volunteers cleaning and an older woman sitting at one of the tables. Alice clutched Henry in her arms, rocking back and forth.

"Maybe I should start," Rene suggested. She eased into a seat across the table from Alice while Grace and Dr. Oracion waited a step back. "Alice, these are the women I told you about. This is Dr. Oracion, and this is her patient, Grace Kekoa. They'd like to help you. Is it alright if they talk to you for a minute?"

Alice scratched Henry under the chin, not looking at them, and gave a swift nod.

Grace sat next to Rene. "Hi, Alice. Your dog's really cute." Alice's gaze raked over Grace, and she wondered what the older woman must think of her. If she came across as presumptuous, thinking she could swoop in and fix someone's life—and her own health in the process—or if Alice was truly interested in the exchange she was going to propose.

"His name's Henry," Alice finally said.

"Cool, Henry's a good name. I have a dog too, back home in Vegas. Her name's Teapot."

Alice quirked an eyebrow. "Teapot?"

"She's a teacup poodle mix, but when we adopted her and brought her home, my dad thought we said tea*pot* instead of tea*cup*. It stuck."

Alice smiled a little.

"Rene said Henry got hurt a couple weeks ago. Is he okay now?"

Alice mashed her lips together and turned her face away, running a hand over the dog's left foreleg.

"It's alright," Rene said. "You can tell them."

Alice fixed Grace with a stare like a challenge. "I fixed it."

Grace's heart lurched—it was real, this was real—but she kept her face calm. "That's amazing. How did you do it?"

Alice shook her head like a stubborn toddler and buried her face in Henry's neck.

Grace exchanged a look with Dr. O. "Alice, can I give Henry a present?"

The woman raised her head just enough to see over the dog's fur. "What is it?"

Grace positioned both hands over the table between her and Alice, palms pressed together. "What's Henry's favorite color?"

"Yellow."

Light glowed from between Grace's hands, like a hidden flashlight. She pulled her hands apart slowly, fingers splayed, and a Henry-sized, yellow dog sweater materialized in the air between her palms. She snapped her fingers, the sweater detached from her hands and slid to the table.

Alice reached for it with trembling fingers, eyes on Grace.

"I can do some unusual things too," said Grace. "I'd love to hear how you helped Henry."

Alice swallowed. "I bled on him. There was a cut on his leg from the bike. I sliced my hand and bled on the cut and the bone knit. My blood is different."

Grace nodded. That was exactly how Dr. Oracion had theorized a healing factor could be shared with someone.

"Since you healed Henry, has his leg hurt him again at all?" the doctor pressed.

"I don't think so."

Grace made a mental note of the information. Obviously, a transfusion between humans would use a greater quantity of blood than Alice would have dripped into Henry's wound, so they'd have to work out the ratios of what Grace would need, but if the effects were permanent—

Her breath quickened at the idea. The pain, the stress. The uncertainty of not knowing how this affliction would affect her on any given day, the bigger worry of not knowing how this was going to alter her life long term. All of that—gone.

"Alice," Grace began. She had to tread carefully through the next part. "I'm so glad you were able to help Henry. How would you feel about helping me?"

Alice screwed up her face. "You want me to bleed on you? You aren't even injured."

"No, I don't exactly want you to bleed on me. But Dr. Oracion and I would like to bring you to Las Vegas with us."

Alice blanched and Grace hurried to add, "Henry too, of course. Henry will absolutely be with you. We'd like to set you up with a home in Vegas. We'll provide whatever medical care you need, a stable job. We can help you have a healthy life and get on your own feet again. And while we're doing all that, I'd be so grateful if you let Dr. Oracion take some blood samples."

Alice clutched her dog closer.

"And if it looks like your beautiful gift will work on me, consent to give me some transfusions. I've been sick for a long time, and I'd like to heal, just like Henry."

Alice sucked in a breath and held it, her face turning red.

"It's ok, Alice." Rene reached across the table. "No one's making you do anything."

"No, no, of course not," Grace put in. "This is completely voluntary."

Alice let her breath out with a shriek and jumped out of her chair. She ran, dog in her arms, for a door across the cafeteria. Dr. Oracion swore.

Grace leapt to her feet. "Alice, wait, please!" She chased her through the door to a back alley with a loading dock.

Halfway down the street, Alice was still shrieking. "My blood!"

"Grace," Dr. Oracion called behind her.

But this was the closest they'd come. She had to try. Grace sprinted down the alley, around the building and through the forest of tents, hurdling over someone's backpack as Alice pulled away.

A knot of people to her right shifted, and she careened into a man's elbow. The air whooshed out of her lungs, and she went down. Her midsection throbbed—stress wasn't the only thing that produced the bruises. Sucking oxygen back in, she struggled to her feet.

Dr. Oracion caught up to her and wrapped an arm around her for support. "What hit you? Where?"

Grace coughed. "Elbow, stomach."

The doctor turned back toward the shelter. "Come on, let's take a look."

Grace stayed rooted to the pavement, eyes trained on where Alice had disappeared. "We could have helped us both."

"We could always have people hunt her down." Dr. Oracion's tone was wry, and Grace huffed a grudging laugh. She'd never allow someone's super abilities to be used against their will and her friend knew it.

"How did such an old woman run so fast?" Grace hobbled along the sidewalk, still leaning on the doctor.

"Maybe she has super speed too? Or maybe you aren't as fast as you think you are."

"Um, ouch."

Dr. Oracion grimaced. "The truth hurts, my friend."

Grace rubbed her diaphragm. "Tell me about it."

# CHAPTER TEN

The air was drier in Las Vegas. Only an hour-long flight separated the two cities, but Tank felt the difference as soon as he stepped outside Harry Reid International Airport.

Hopper picked up the rental car, and Tank eased himself into the passenger seat. The tires squealed as his manager turned out of the parking lot. Tank smiled wryly. Maybe they should have driven to Vegas. The way Hopper drove, it might have been faster.

"Ok, order of operations," Hopper said. "We meet up with Delagarza at Slingshot's apartment and take a look for ourselves, then check into the hotel. I heard from Leona Amherst, Ms. Seeker's head of security, this morning."

"Right, Elodie said she'd put her in touch."

"We're meeting Leona's team at 2 p.m. at Fashion Seeker Designs headquarters." He adjusted the A/C on the dashboard.

"Sounds good, H. Do you want me suited up before we get to Slingshot's apartment?" Elodie's "shaving kit" was nestled safely in his backpack, right next to *A Circle of Cats*. Tank hadn't let the bag out of his sight the entire flight.

"Better not. I want to see it before we show it to anybody. But I do want to hear how last night went." Hopper grinned, throwing a quick glance at Tank.

Tank squirmed. "It went fine." Better than fine. He'd arrived at the house of a business contact but left the house of a friend. And the gold and deep brown of Elodie's eyes had featured in his dreams last night. *Not that that's important,* he told himself. *It was simply my brain processing the day. Because of rehashing high school stuff.* Either way, Hopper had bigger ideas than friendship where Elodie and he were concerned, and Tank didn't want to encourage him. "The suit fits really nicely. I think you'll like it."

"Uh-huh. Ok." His manager cocked an eyebrow, like he knew Tank wasn't filling him in, but he let it drop.

Grateful for the reprieve, Tank turned to the window. He'd never been to Las Vegas before. The overwrought opulence of the Strip flashed by as Hopper maneuvered through traffic. Billboards advertised shows and casinos and something called the Las Vegas Health Challenge. Once off the interstate, they navigated through stucco and cactus neighborhoods. Tank couldn't help but wonder if one of the houses they passed belonged to Grace.

Hopper pulled into a block of apartments with a mural splashed the length of one side. Solar panels angled on the roof and several parking spots were reserved for electric vehicles.

Tank pointed out the features to Hopper. "That's cool." He wished his building at home would do things like install solar panels. It wasn't as if Los Angeles lacked sun.

Hopper grunted and climbed an outdoor staircase. Three floors up, he rang a doorbell. Tank adjusted his backpack on his shoulder. He hardly noticed the weight of the pack, but Elodie's suit inside the bag pressed on his thoughts. Again, he thought of the depths of her eyes, and how she'd squeezed his hand after he'd explained his past. He shifted guiltily. For the first time, he regretted the fact that BlindDate didn't allow pictures. Perhaps if he had a picture of Grace, he'd stop thinking about Elodie.

The door opened and Hopper held out his hand. "Hector Strickland, Strickland Talent Management. Thanks for meeting us here, Mr. Delagarza."

Slingshot's manager nodded and shook Hopper's hand. "Thanks for coming. I'm hoping you can help us find Slingshot." He smiled but his eyes tightened as he looked Tank over. "This must be your client."

"Yes, this is Tank. Tank, Mateo Delagarza."

"I'm sorry Slingshot's missing, Mr. Delagarza. You must be worried."

Delagarza didn't respond and didn't shake Tank's proffered hand. Tank flushed and shoved his hands in his pockets.

"The insects have been removed, as you can see. They responded to fumigation like any other bug." Delagarza stepped aside, letting them into the front room. A galley kitchen done in white and blue tile extended off the living room, and a hallway sprouted off to the left. "But I haven't righted any of the furniture."

Hopper whistled. "Looks like your boy put up quite a fight."

The apartment was trashed. The kitchen table lay on its side, glass top fissured with cracks. One of the chairs was splintered near the front door and the other had been tossed into the hallway. A body-sized hole had been crushed into the wet bar to the right of the entry. Across the room, a desk was snapped in half, all the drawers yanked out and broken.

"Or made it look like he did," Hopper added under his breath and wandered into the kitchen to look around.

Delagarza stared out the window, arms folded and lips mashed together. Tank wondered if all managers used the same expression when they were stressed. Maybe they practiced it in manager school. Still, Mateo Delagarza had good reason to worry. Embarrassed by Hopper's assumption, Tank stepped closer to Slingshot's manager.

"We'll find him, Mr. Delagarza," he said softly. "Don't worry."

Delagarza swallowed and waved at the apartment. "Look through whatever you need." He stomped outside to lean against the balcony railing.

Tank picked his way past the shattered chair in the hall to Slingshot's bedroom. Other than the bed, closet, and a nightstand pushed over on its side, the space was bare. No photos or personal effects. No leashes or food bowls or litter box.

He found nothing under the bed, but when he turned his head, he caught a different view of the nightstand; the drawers had been ransacked like the desk in the living room and were strewn on the floor. But above, a thick manilla envelope dangled by a piece of tape from the frame where the bottom drawer should go.

"Hello." Tank eased the rest of the tape free. "How did whoever trashed the apartment miss you?" He dumped the contents of the envelope on the bed and sifted through them. A copy of the Abaddon manifesto, newspaper clippings detailing fires, break-ins, traffic accidents involving oil-tankers, and a sketch of a stylized locust with a mouth full of needle-like teeth made up most of the pile. The rest looked like diagrams of chemical formulas.

The most recent clipping was about the first two run-ins he'd had with Abaddon in L.A., before he knew there *was* an Abaddon. The others were from cities around the country, and Tank sucked in a breath. Abaddon was active in more places than Elodie had thought. He shoveled everything back into the envelope and hurried to find Hopper.

"H, I found Slingshot's research. It looks like they're already moving on other cities, testing the water, even if they haven't claimed responsibility for it yet."

"What?" Hopper hissed. "Are you sure?"

Tank shrugged. "You can go through the articles if you want."

Hopper clapped Tank on the arm. "Let's get out of here and get checked into the hotel."

"Shouldn't we show this to Mr. Delagarza, too? Keep him in the loop?"

Hopper glanced to where Delagarza brooded on the balcony. "Nah, look at him. He's clearly broken up. He doesn't need one more thing on his mind." He strode out the door, leaving Tank to follow.

The other manager gave them a curt nod as they passed. Tank hesitated at the top of the stairs, wishing he could say something to comfort the man. But Delagarza returned to staring at nothing, and Hopper leaned on the horn in the parking lot. Tank gave up and jogged down the stairs. Finding Slingshot and stopping Abaddon were the best things he could do to help Mateo Delagarza.

At the hotel, Hopper stuck his head into Tank's room to say he had an errand to run. "But I'll be back in time to go meet with Seeker Security."

"Ok, thanks, H." Tank gave a half-wave.

Per usual, Hopper had booked rooms far more luxurious than Tank felt he needed. The bottles of vitamin water, labeled Las Vegas Health Challenge, were ok, but the chilled champagne was over the top, and he made a mental note to have the hotel staff take it back.

*Alcohol and reflux do not mix.*

A Gideon's Bible sat on the bedside table. Both Abaddon and NineSix took their names from the Book of Revelations, maybe the same book could grant some insight into the terrorists. Tank scanned through the pages, stopping when he caught the word locusts in chapter nine.

"Locusts ... smoke ..." he murmured to himself. "Hurt men not the earth—ok, fits with the eco-terrorism thing. Seek death and not find it—that's NineSix's verse ... The angel of the bottomless pit, Abaddon ... and a key to the pit." He tucked the Bible in the nightstand drawer. Regardless of what people said about Vegas, Tank doubted they'd find a literal bottomless pit in the city. But maybe the terrorists had taken that as inspiration for their headquarters.

*A nightclub front with 'pit' in the name? Or maybe 'angels'?* It was a place to start anyway. He'd bring it up when he and Hopper met with Elodie's team later.

The meeting wasn't for a while, so he unpacked his carry-on and backpack, wavering between the dresser drawer and the bathroom for the secret shaving kit. Ultimately, he decided on the nightstand, where it was close at hand, but didn't look too out of place. The next thing he pulled out of his bag was *A Circle of Cats.*

He stilled. Traced his fingers down the cover. Grace had been interested in meeting. Today was even Thursday, the day she volunteered at the school. He had the address for the school, and two hours to kill before meeting with Elodie's team. Hopper wouldn't be happy about it if he found out.

But wasn't Hopper always telling him to go after what he wanted?

He plugged the address into his phone and ordered an Uber, indulging in a brief daydream of Grace being so happy to meet him that they read the book to the kids together. Two hours wasn't a long time, and it was a twenty-five-minute drive each way, but then, the first time they met shouldn't be too long anyway, especially since it was a surprise.

The daydream soured.

What if Grace didn't want a surprise? What if she got angry that he'd shown up unannounced? Or she took one look at him and said, "No oafs, thank you very much."

His breath grew shallow, and he hugged the book to his chest.

BlindDate didn't allow photos—that was the whole point, to give people a chance to be attracted to who a person was, rather than what they looked like. Meeting in person added another layer of complexity. He'd met plenty of women at Hopper's parties who found The Tank attractive, but he doubted any of them would give Willard Meeks the time of day. Grace had given him more than that so far. He wasn't sure what he'd do if she took it all back.

If only dating were as harmless as bullets.

He flipped open the shaving kit. Elodie's black-and-green creation unfolded, gleaming up at him.

Beautiful. It was beautiful. When he'd worn it at Elodie's, he'd felt almost beautiful too.

He stripped down and changed into the suit for extra confidence. Hopper didn't want it out in public before he approved it, but he could wear street clothes over it.

Calm flowed through him as soon as he had the uniform on. He took a deep breath, stashed the shaving kit case in a cargo pocket, and scooped up the picture book.

"Looks like you're my wingman, Mr. de Lint."

Behind the school, red rock cliffs grew from the distant desert like stone giants. A Hawaiian flag flew on the front sidewalk. Tank placed a hand on his stomach, wishing the churning would stop. A green cuff poked out from his shirtsleeve. He smiled, heartbeat slowing, and headed through the entrance.

In the foyer, a front office watched over a set of double doors that Tank assumed led to the rest of the school. The doors looked like the kind in hospitals that needed a nurse to press a button to buzz guests through. He approached the desk where a receptionist was simultaneously on the phone and the computer.

"The air duct people are coming today. Yeah, ok. Bye." She hung up the phone but didn't look up from her computer as she gave Tank a rote greeting. "Aloha, and welcome to Ninth Island Charter School. Do you have an appointment with someone today?"

"Hi." Tank cleared his throat. "No, actually, I'm looking for Grace Kekoa? I was told she volunteers here on Thursdays?"

The receptionist quit typing to stare at him but didn't answer.

He mentally kicked himself. Why was everything he said coming out as a question? If Hopper heard it, he'd tell him, yet again, to *be The Tank.*

*But I'm here as Willard. I can't be The Tank right now. That's not who Grace knows.*

"My name is Willard Meeks; she's not expecting me. I just have something for her. We've been messaging ... that is ..." He stumbled under the woman's scrutiny.

"Sorry, Ms. Kekoa is not here this week," she said, not sounding very sorry. "She's out of town. I can take whatever you want to leave for her."

"Oh, no." Tank took a step back, clutching the book. "That's alright. I'll hold on to it till I see her." He retreated another step with a small parting wave. "Thanks."

Outside, he stashed the book in his backpack, face in flames.

*Stupid! She's not even here.* All that worry and she was out of town. He remembered now, she'd mentioned a work trip.

Cheeks still hot, he checked the time. 12:40. Maybe he'd walk a while before calling another Uber. As useful as they were, the drivers generally wanted to make conversation, which was not what Tank wanted right now. And he had plenty of time to get back to the hotel before Hopper did. Yes, a walk by himself to calm down.

A residential neighborhood curved out from the school's cul-de-sac, low houses imitating the desert floor. The clear blue of swimming pools peeked through backyard fences, waiting for use, even in March. Tank tipped his head back, drank in the deeper blue of the sky, picturing the color spreading through his belly, cooling the pain. His breathing slowed, deepened.

Someone bashed into his side. "Dude, watch it!" A man wearing a Desert Air Duct Services jumpsuit and carrying a duffle bag glared at Tank, rubbing his shoulder.

"Sorry." Tank held up his hands in apology.

The man shoved past, grumbling about brick walls in the middle of the sidewalk.

Tank winced. Brick wall. Great. "Sorry again."

The repairman shot a fist into the air with his middle finger pointing at the sky. Tank rolled his eyes but then paused. A locust tattoo spread across the back of the man's hand.

For half a second, he wondered if he should call Hopper before going after the guy. But then he'd have to tell Hopper where he was, and Hopper would ask why. If he apprehended the guy on his own, and took him straight to Elodie's team, they could lock him up with the other Abaddon member, and maybe Hopper would be happy enough about having two people in custody that he'd forget to ask Tank where he'd found the guy.

*Sure, that'll work*, he thought doubtfully. But he had let NineSix escape in L.A. He couldn't let another terrorist just walk away.

"Hey, Buddy," he called. "Let me make it up to you." It'd be best if he could apprehend him without making a scene; they were supposed to keep a low profile here in Vegas.

The repairman adjusted the duffle bag on his shoulder and walked faster.

"Wait up, I want to ask you about that tattoo." Tank jogged after him and the man took off running.

Tank caught him in half a block, back on the school's cul-de-sac. His shirt ripped as he tackled the man to the ground, rolling to take most of the impact himself—he didn't want to smash the guy's face into the concrete, he still had to take him to Elodie's place in an Uber. He dragged him back to his feet, one arm wrapped around his neck.

"I'm guessing you're not really an air duct repairman."

The man struggled. Or tried to. Tank tightened his arm, and he gave up. Using his free hand, Tank yanked on the duffle bag until it ripped. Plastic bags of white powder tumbled to the ground.

"What is this, cocaine? What were you planning to do with it?"

His captive didn't answer. Tank shook the bag again and a work order for air duct cleaning at Ninth Island Charter School fluttered to the ground.

"The school?" Tank's insides flared hot, for once not from his stomach. Maybe smashing this guy's face into the sidewalk wasn't such a bad idea after all.

It was only after the crack of his forehead on concrete that Tank realized he'd never be able to take the guy in an Uber with his face messed up.

He sighed. Looked like he'd have to call Hopper after all.

# CHAPTER ELEVEN

H opper's face was murder as he pulled up to the curb. Tank wondered again if all managers practiced that expression. Maybe they had lip-mashing-glare contests at conferences.

Plastic sheeting covered the back seat; Hopper must have picked it up on the way. Tank laid the unconscious Abaddon operative on the bench seat, ripped off a corner of the plastic, wrapped the bags of powder in it and tossed them in the trunk. He sucked in a breath and closed his eyes for half a moment. Then climbed in the passenger seat.

The car sped down the street before Tank had the door closed.

"Do I want to know why you were halfway across town?" Hopper kept his eyes glued straight ahead.

Tank folded his hands in his lap. "Probably not."

"Are you gonna try to tell me it had nothing to do with this Grace woman?"

"No." Tank's voice came out a whisper. He hated this feeling. Like he was back in the principal's office in high school, trying to explain how he had managed to knock into yet another piece of breakable school property, or why the back of his shirt was bloody again.

"And?" Hopper asked. "What happened? Did you see her?"

Tank faced away to watch the houses fly by. Hopper was driving way too fast for a residential neighborhood. "She wasn't there. I forgot she was on a work trip."

His manager grunted. "Well, at least you happened to intercept that guy." He hooked a thumb toward the back seat. "We'll take him to Ms. Seeker's team. We've gotta go straight there now anyway."

The knot in Tank's chest eased a bit.

Hopper sighed, his face smoothing out. "You've always been so easy to manage, Tank. You listen, you follow instructions, you're well behaved, unlike certain other clients I could mention. Don't ..." He lifted a hand in a helpless gesture and let it fall back to the steering wheel. "Don't let this crush mess up your career, ok? I don't want to see you get hurt."

"Yeah, ok, H." Tank gave the easy answer, trying not to think too far ahead. He hadn't even met Grace in person yet, but he wasn't willing to give up on the connection they'd built.

Out the window, the houses shifted to an industrial area. They stopped at a large warehouse on the north side of the city, with bare desert behind it. The Fashion Seeker Designs logo swirled across the front of the building. The font slanted at an elegant angle, suggesting quality and expense, but the colors seemed to smile, the way Elodie had when she'd seen him wearing her design.

"Bring him." Hopper shoved out of the car and stomped to the front doors while Tank slid the man from the back seat and slung him over one shoulder. The guy was still unconscious. Maybe Tank had smashed his face on the ground too hard.

No. Whether the powder was cocaine or something else, the guy's intent had been to hurt kids. There had been just the right amount of face smashing. Hopefully he'd have an awesome headache when he woke up.

The lobby was done in cream, gold, and green, with black accents, similar to Elodie's house in L.A. Arches and tall windows gave the room an open, airy feeling. Tank maneuvered his captive around to a cradle hold, worried about blood dripping on the spotless carpet.

Hopper checked in with the woman at the desk and ushered Tank down a wide corridor and up an elevator. A white woman in a tight, silver braid and charcoal-gray uniform greeted them on the third floor. Red patches weathered her cheeks, like she'd spent a good deal of time working outside. Seeker Security was emblazoned on her left sleeve.

"Leona Amherst, head of Seeker Security." She shook both their hands, Tank adjusting his burden to reach. "This is Marlena Silva." She pointed to another Seeker Security-clad woman standing behind her, younger than Leona, with golden skin and dark hair.

"I see you brought us another one," Leona said. "Let's put him down here."

Leona led them down the hall and through a set of double doors to what looked like a medical office reception area. She opened a door down another hall to an exam room. Paper sheets crinkled as Tank laid the man down on the bed.

"You have your own doctor's office here?" he asked.

Leona didn't answer but another woman joined them and began examining the patient. She wore a lab coat and scrubs, but Seeker Security was still printed above the coat pocket. Going off the many families he'd helped in his library days, Tank guessed her to be Filipina American. The library had allowed him to interact with kids and parents of so many different backgrounds. It was one of the many things he missed.

"Sofia," Leona said addressed the woman in the lab coat. "You got him?"

She nodded. "I'll get him cleaned up."

"Thanks." She led Tank and Hopper back to the first hallway. "We can talk in the conference room."

Floor-to-ceiling windows ran the length of the corridor, giving a view of the production floor two stories below. Tank slowed to watch. Employees whipped out garments on sergers, or cut pieces at tables, or pushed racks of clothing across the floor. All of the employees were women. Different skin tones and hair colors, different ages, but all in dark gray uniforms with Seeker Security on their sleeves.

"The security team and the garment production team are the same?" Tank asked Leona.

She chuckled and kept walking. "This is a different sort of place. I'll let Ms. Seeker explain."

Tank watched the production floor a moment longer, disappointed. There was a story behind this team of Elodie's, and he wanted to hear it. Still, Elodie should be back in Vegas in a day or two. "Yeah, I can ask her the next time I see her."

"The next time is now."

"Elodie?" Tank turned.

She stood behind him in a white, sleeveless turtleneck, slacks, and red heels, with a white and yellow flower tucked behind her right ear. Tank's palms turned sweaty.

"I thought you weren't back for another day or two?" he asked.

She laughed. "Oh, I see how it is. You get a free suit off me and then we're done?"

"No, no." Tank backtracked. "I just thought—I mean, you said you had something to finish in L.A."

"I'm kidding, Tank, relax." She strode into the conference room to the head of the table.

Hopper nudged Tank in the ribs. "Look at you, all nervous and sweaty." Tank braced for another lecture, but Hopper only laughed. "I told you she was a good choice for you. You like her."

"What?" Tank hissed. Whether he approved or not, Hopper knew Tank was interested in Grace.

"Coming, gentlemen?" Elodie called. Leona and Marlena already waited at the table.

"Yeah, yeah." Tank gave a nervous laugh and went to take a seat a few chairs down from the end, but Hopper held out the one immediately to Elodie's right.

"You take this one, big guy. You're the one with the information." Hopper slipped him the envelope from Slingshot's apartment under the table.

"Oh, right." Tank emptied the contents onto the table for everyone to see "We found—"

Hopper kicked him under the table.

Tank sighed. *Right. Speak more assertively.* "I found this in Slingshot's apartment. It looks like research into Abaddon." He sifted through the articles.

"Including incidents other than in Los Angeles that Slingshot appears to have suspected Abaddon was responsible for. I'm guessing this research is why they kidnapped him. He got too close. Someone in Abaddon found out, and they nabbed him before he could tell the police."

"That's one theory," Hopper said. "We should look at others as well."

Elodie raised an eyebrow. "What other theories?"

Hopper shrugged. "Just one really. Slingshot's in with Abaddon."

Elodie and Leona both stared at him, stony faced. Leona spoke first. "Excuse you?"

Hopper continued unfazed. "He was working on this research without his manager or any kind of law enforcement backup, and the smash-up at his apartment looked a little too perfect." He spread his hands. "I'm just saying. We should consider all possibilities."

Elodie raised her chin. "Not that one. Trust me, our most recent consultation with Slingshot was not the first. He'd never turn rogue; he loves his city too much."

"But then why do all this on the sly?" Hopper pressed. "Why collect all this information about crimes in places outside his own territory? He knew he couldn't do anything out of his own jurisdiction."

Elodie laced her fingers together. "Slingshot disagrees with the idea of exceptional people staying strictly regional. He feels what affects one affects all and that heroes should be working together. After all," she said wryly, "criminals don't bother to confine themselves to city borders."

Tank fidgeted in his seat, remembering her impassioned plea at his apartment. He'd always played by the rules, assumed the rules were written by people with the public's best interests at heart, but when Elodie spoke about it, it gave him pause.

She continued, "Slingshot routinely kept an eye on things out of state, looking for patterns, anything like that. He started following—or," she cleared her throat. "I imagine he started following the incidents in L.A. and followed threads back here to Vegas and found Abaddon's base."

"Sounds like you know him pretty well." Hopper raised an eyebrow.

Elodie sat straighter. "I designed his suit. I like to know a bit about my clients before creating a piece." She smiled at Tank.

"Strictly professional, then," Hopper said under his breath. He kicked Tank under the table again. Tank ignored it.

"Before we go further," Elodie said. "I want to clarify how this is going to work so we're all on the same page. Hopper, you worked out a special dispensation under the AVA to have Tank here in Vegas. Which means Slingshot's manager agreed to you being here, LVMPD knows you're here, and you report to them, but you and Tank have to keep your presence quiet, correct?"

Hopper nodded. "Correct. No media interviews or anything. And part of our job in being here is to find Slingshot, whatever his reason for disappearing."

Elodie's eyebrow quirked but she didn't respond to Hopper's implication. If they found Slingshot and he had gone rogue, Tank would be obligated to hand him over to the authorities. Tank fiddled with a corner of the Abaddon manifesto, hoping that scenario never materialized. Elodie was adamant Slingshot was innocent in that regard, and he hated the thought of her being disappointed.

"As for us," Elodie said. "We now have two members of Abaddon in custody. Las Vegas police don't know about either one of them. And I want it to stay that way. I understand you have to work through them." She looked at Tank. "But I don't want the police knowing that you're also working with us."

Tank's brow furrowed. "Why not?"

"I'm sorry, Tank." Her voice softened and she laid her hand over his. "I have reasons. For now, I need you to trust me."

Tank held her gaze, the gold threads in her eyes shimmering. Last night, he had trusted her with his past. He could trust her with the present until she was ready to tell him her reasons. He nodded.

"Thank you." She leaned back in her chair.

Tank threw a sideways glance at Hopper. His lips were mashed together like he wanted to argue, but his eyes were glued to where Elodie's hand had rested on Tank's. Tank almost chuckled at the internal argument raging in his manager's head.

"Hopper?" he prompted.

Hopper cleared his throat and waved a hand. "I'm good with that for now."

"Excellent," Elodie said. "So, we know Abaddon is here in Las Vegas. We pinpoint where they're operating from and then ..." She turned her gaze on Tank.

He swallowed. She was waiting for him to say something, but his thoughts felt tangled in the gold in her eyes. The petals of the flower behind her ear played against the bronze of her skin. He wondered what color Grace's eyes were. What her skin would look like next to soft petals.

Hopper kicked him for the third time.

"Right," he fumbled. "We find their base, then I go in and clean up."

Elodie tilted her head. "Are you ok?"

"Yeah, sure." He straightened and flattened his hands on the table, trying to look confident. Or at least attentive. "So, we need to pinpoint where their base is. I, uh, had sort of an idea." Tank cleared his throat. Presenting his own ideas wasn't typically how he and Hopper operated. Usually, they talked together beforehand about whatever Tank would say for a meeting or conference. "I was reading in Revelations, since that's where they got their name. In one of the verses it talks about Abaddon being the angel of the bottomless pit, so I just thought—"

Hopper was watching him, chin in hand. Tank couldn't tell if he was pleased or irritated that he'd put forward an idea himself.

"I thought maybe we look for front businesses with anything like that in the name, or in the concept?"

Hopper jumped in. "Good thought, big guy. Let's all research that." Leona and Marlena started brainstorming businesses, and Hopper leaned close to Tank. "Way to take the initiative. Good job."

Tank exhaled in relief and grinned.

"That might be a starting place, but that's going to be a whole lot of businesses to sort through, so I'll point out that we already have two people in this facility who know where Abaddon's headquarters are," Leona said. "We could *ask* them."

"We're not torturing anyone, Le." Elodie's voice was firm.

She shrugged. "Applying a little pressure would be the fastest way to get what we needed."

"No." Elodie elongated the word. Tank glanced between the two women. This was obviously not the first time they'd had this conversation.

Leona sighed. "Fine. But, you know, tell me if you change your mind. I can be quick." She said it like a joke, but the glint in her eye left Tank in no doubt as to her sincerity. Where had Elodie found these women on her "security team"?

"I agree torture is off the table," he said. "But Leona's also right that my idea would take too long." Next to him, Hopper frowned at him backtracking so fast on his idea, but Tank pressed on. "If one of them were to escape," he said, putting air quotes around the word. "We could follow him till he reported back to wherever or whomever he reports back to." He winced inside. That sounded dumb out loud. *That's what I get for improvising.*

"We thought about doing that," Leona said. "But I'm sure he'd assume he was being followed. I would if it were me."

"True. But what about the guy we brought in—"

Hopper kicked his ankle again, and Tank held in an exasperated sigh. It was a good thing he couldn't bruise.

"The guy *I* brought in today. He doesn't even know he's been here, so maybe he wouldn't think he was being followed?"

Leona pursed her lips. "Maybe. If it were me, and I woke up on the sidewalk after being knocked out, I'd still assume I had a tail, but it might still be worth a shot."

"I'll ask Sofia if he's still unconscious." Elodie shot off a text.

"Marlena and I can change into street clothes, drop him back where Tank found him, and follow him when he wakes up. Tank's is the only face he's seen, so that'll help." She checked her watch. "We'll have to wait a little while before leaving him there. Kids'll be walking home from school in not too long. We don't want someone to find him unconscious on the sidewalk and call an ambulance."

"That's fine, Le."

"With any luck, when he comes to, he'll head back to his creepy crawlies. Two good ideas today, big guy." Hopper patted Tank on the shoulder.

Tank's shoulders relaxed. "Thanks, H."

"I think we should keep one of the bags of powder he had on him though," Hopper continued. "See if we can figure out what it is."

"I agree." Elodie tapped one of the chemical formula diagrams in Slingshot's pile of research. "Maybe it matches one of these."

Elodie's phone buzzed. "Sofia says he's still out." Leona pushed her chair back and tapped Marlena on her shoulder. "We better head out. I need phone numbers from you two so I can keep everyone informed." She indicated Tank and Hopper, and they added themselves to Leona's contacts.

"Excellent." Elodie rose from the table. "Tank, Hopper, while we wait to hear, do you want to come get something to eat? I haven't had time to eat since last night."

At the idea of eating, the usual, internal wrestling match between Tank's taste buds and his digestive system set in. He was bullet proof, fireproof—everything proof. Why was *food* so hard? He turned to his manager to stall.

"Hopper, you hungry?"

Hopper was staring at his phone, a frown etched into his forehead. "Actually, it looks like I need to go take care of something. One of these days I'm gonna drop all my other clients and only do you, big guy." His face cleared as he looked between Tank and Elodie. "But you two should go eat, that's a great idea."

Tank blushed at Hopper's clunky attempts to push them together. Hopefully Elodie hadn't noticed. *Although I don't know how she could miss it.* "That's ok, I can get something at the hotel."

"No, no." Hopper ushered him closer to Elodie. "Go, eat. Enjoy the city while you have a minute. We've got a little time before we hear back from Ms. Amherst." He leaned in close and laid a hand on Tank's elbow. "Just, no side trips, right?"

Tank grimaced. "Yeah, right, H."

"That's my boy." Hopper hurried out of the conference room, leaving Tank alone with Elodie.

"So, did you have something in mind?" he asked. "Food-wise, I mean."

She rubbed her hands together and strode toward the door. "I am dying for a malasada."

Tank tried to keep the surprise from showing on his face when Elodie parked in front of a dingy two-story building in a shabby shopping center. Everything he'd seen about Elodie so far—her house in L.A., her business, her manners, even her movements—exuded class and elegance. The hole-in-the-wall diner next to a payday loan place didn't match. Not that the "normal people" vibe bothered him; his life before Strickland Talent Management hadn't exactly been five stars. But it did surprise him.

"What exactly is a malasada?" Tank stretched as he got out of her car. Between flying in, the Uber, Hopper's car, and the conference room, he'd spent way too much time sitting down today. Hopefully he could get out for a run later, or maybe Hopper could arrange some time in a junk yard somewhere, find some cars to flip.

Her eyes widened. "You've never had a malasada?"

He shook his head.

"My poor, deprived friend." She pantomimed wiping away a tear. "Your life is about to change." She made a ta-da motion at the restaurant sign. Silhouettes of the Hawaiian Islands and a bright-green sea turtle made up the logo over the door.

"Hawaiian food?" Tank immediately thought of Grace. Had she eaten here before? A daydream swept through his head, clear as a scene in a book. He'd walk into the restaurant. Grace would be sitting at a table—of course he'd know it was her, fellow book nerds always spotted each other. He'd walk up, confident and comfortable and ...

And what? Introduce the stunning fashion designer he was having dinner with? The daydream evaporated.

*Tank, you're so dumb.* Aside from the fact that Grace was still out of town, it was ridiculous to think she'd eaten here simply because it was a Hawaiian restaurant. *Don't make stupid assumptions.*

"Yes," Elodie said, holding the door for him. He yanked his attention back to their conversation. "Although, technically malasadas are Portuguese. So much of modern cuisine in Hawai'i comes from people of other cultures that immigrated to the islands. It's not Hawaiian food, but it is Hawai'i food, if that makes sense." She shrugged. "Basically, by now it all counts as local."

"Sounds great." Tank maneuvered his bulk through the door, hoping local food didn't run heavy on onions.

"El, howzit, girl?" An aproned man behind the counter smiled as Elodie approached.

"Hey, Uncle. What kine malasadas get?" Elodie's speech patterns slipped seamlessly from high fashion mogul to Hawaiian Pidgin. She chatted, seeming perfectly comfortable with both her own elegant appearance and the more casual surroundings and conversation. Tank marveled at the ease with which she melded the two aspects of herself.

*If only it were that easy.*

"Mahalo, Uncle!" Elodie gathered up a couple of to-go bags and Tank held the door for her on the way out.

"Are we not eating here?"

"Nope, your boss is right. We've got a little time. You should see some sights before things get busy."

Tank paused, taken aback by the word "boss." True, a manager and a client were more like business partners than anything else, and either of them could exit the business relationship when they wanted, but technically, *he* employed Strickland Talent Management.

"Hopper's not my ... boss."

Elodie gave him a look and the words died on his lips. They slid into the car, and she laid a hand on his arm.

"Tank, you're intelligent and you're kind. Don't get me wrong, Strickland gets great results." She held her breath for a moment. "But I think you'd be happier if those results were on your own terms."

Tank stared at her, mouth open. He didn't have a response to that. He tried and failed to smile and cast about for something else to talk about while Elodie backed out of the parking lot.

"What kind of flower is that?" The petals behind her ear smelled sweet, similar to honeysuckle.

"It's a plumeria, my favorite." She touched a petal, not commenting on the change of topic. "They smell like home."

"Do lots of people wear them? Back home, I mean?"

She nodded. "If someone is wearing theirs over their right ear it means they're available. Over their left ear means they're taken. I missed them after moving here. Fortunately, Vegas is a decent place to grow them. They don't do quite as well as back home, but they do grow."

Red cliffs grew on the horizon. They were near the same area as Grace's school. Tank snuck a look at the BlindDate app, just in case. No new messages. Elodie headed south and west again, leaving city and suburbs behind for rocky desert. She stopped in a parking lot flanked by red and yellow hills. The scent of warm, dry dirt washed over Tank as he got out of the car.

"There's a picnic spot here I like." Elodie scooped up the to-go bags from the back seat.

Scrappy trees spread their branches next to a picnic pavilion. Behind it, a boardwalk trail snaked over a splash of vivid growth, a moment of green amid the red rocks. The tree leaves shushed against each other in the breeze, murmuring a desert song. Tank tipped his face up to the sky and breathed deep. Between the movement of the trees and the steadiness of stone, the violence and urgency of Abaddon seemed far away.

"And that, right there, is why I love this spot." Elodie opened the takeout containers and handed Tank a fork. "It makes me stop and breathe too."

"It's beautiful," he murmured. "Too bad I don't have a book with me. That spot under the trees looks perfect for reading."

"What an enchanting idea. I know *The Black Stallion* is your favorite, but I take it you are a regular reader?"

He chuckled. "You could say that, yes."

"Good. More people should be. Here, I got you a sampler plate so you can try several things." She sat at the table and pointed out various dishes. "We've got kalua pork, some laulau, some poke. SPAM musubi too, because it's obligatory if you've never eaten food from Hawai'i. Aaaand, malasadas for dessert." She held up a bakery bag with a flourish.

Tank took a deep whiff of the smorgasbord. "Smells amazing." He hoped he wasn't going to pay too dearly for eating it.

"So," Elodie said after a few minutes of concentrated chewing. "Why don't you have a book with you?"

"I do. I mean, not with me right now, but I brought a couple on the trip. But I left one at the hotel, and the other in Hopper's car. He doesn't like me to bring them to meetings. Which makes sense, that would be weird, right? I'm supposed to be paying attention. I mean, I *am* paying attention, it's just—" He cut himself off. *Nice one, genius. Stop talking.*

She waved it away. "I get it. I've been in plenty of meetings where I wished I had a book instead. But, speaking of Mr. Strickland again, I want to talk to you about something."

Tank swallowed and set his fork down, guessing where she was going.

"It seems like he perhaps has some ideas about you and me being an 'us.'"

"I'm so sorry, Elodie," Tank stammered, cheeks burning. "He gets these ideas in his head sometimes—"

"No, no, don't apologize. It's not your fault, and it's not that you aren't very attractive," she spoke over him.

He blinked. Did she just call him attractive?

"And kind and smart—"

"Well, you too. I mean, you're clever and creative—"

"And you have such a gentle presence—"

"I'd have to be blind not to notice how beautiful you are—"

"But I'm already interested in someone," Elodie finished.

Tank exhaled like he'd been punched in the gut. In relief. Of course, in relief, because he was waiting for Grace's next message. Yes, that was it. "Yeah, yeah. Me too, actually."

Elodie's face relaxed. "Ok, good. We're on the same page then." Her phone rang before Tank could formulate an answer. She frowned at the screen. "Sorry, I'll be right back." She took the call by the car, her back to him.

Tank exhaled and ran a hand through his hair. Sure, they were on the same page. He just needed to figure out what book they were reading.

*No, I don't,* he told himself. *Because I am waiting for a message from Grace. Grace, who loves the same books, and reading to kids. And who calls me Willard.* To prove it, he yanked his phone out and checked the app again. Miraculously, a notification popped up while he stared at the screen. A quick glance told him Elodie was leaning against the car, still facing away. He opened the message, holding his breath.

*Willard! I just got a message from the office at the school. I'm so sorry I missed you! I am back in town now (got in this afternoon). What brings you to Vegas? How long will you be in town? I'd love to meet up.*

Warmth filled his chest. Grace wanted to meet. No, she'd 'love' to meet.

Elodie returned to the table. "Sorry about that."

Tank grinned, feeling like he was glowing. "No problem." He stuffed the phone back in his pocket. He'd answer Grace as soon as he got back to the hotel. "Do I get to try these famous malasadas now?"

Elodie did a little dance in her seat. "Yes, malasada time!" She handed him what looked like a doughnut with no hole. Crystals of sugar stuck to Tank's fingers and sweetness tickled his nose. He took a bite.

"Wow." He ate another. "Oh my gosh. Where have these been all my life?"

Elodie laughed. "Right?"

Tank tried a bite of a chocolate filled one. "Mmm, yeah. Life changing. I will forever measure my life now as Before Malasadas and After Malasadas."

"Definitely. In fact, we should document this most momentous of occasions." She grabbed her phone, still laughing, and hurried to his side of the table to snap a selfie of the two of them. Tank tried to smile, to look relaxed, but Elodie's arm was pushed against his, and the fragrance from the plumeria was derailing his thoughts. As soon as she texted him the photo her phone rang again.

She grimaced in apology and Tank laughed. "The glamorous life of a designer, right?"

"Yeah." She snorted. "A phone glued to my ear, what an accessory. I imagine it's *almost* as glamorous as being a superhero."

"Oh, yes. I never feel more glam than when I'm scrubbing the smell of smoke out of my clothes," he teased back.

"Here's to champagne and dramatic poses." She raised her malasada in a toast and took another bite before answering the phone. Tank set about cleaning up the picnic while she listened but paused when the jokes drained out of her face.

"On our way." She leapt to her feet and ran for the car. "We have to go."

"Was that Leona?" Tank dumped the picnic trash in a garbage can and still made it to the car before her. "Did they follow the guy?"

"They did." Tires squealed on the way out of the parking lot. "But he didn't go back to Abaddon."

"Where'd he go?"

"Your hotel. And now it's on fire."

# CHAPTER TWELVE

E lodie paired her phone with the car's Bluetooth, Leona still on the line.

"What do you mean my hotel is on fire?" Tank braced as Elodie sped around a curve.

"I mean, it's on fire. Can't you hear that?" A roaring was trying to swallow Leona's voice. "We followed him to the lobby, but it was so crowded we lost him. He must have set off some kind of bomb. The fire spread too fast for him to have simply started it in a broom closet."

"Why was the lobby so crowded?" Tank asked. "Is there some kind of event this weekend?"

"No," Leona said. "Apparently someone called all the local media outlets and spilled the beans about Slingshot being missing. Whoever it was also told them there was a press conference about it in the lobby of *your* hotel."

Tank groaned and looked at Elodie. "Abaddon." He kicked himself. His good idea hadn't turned out to be so good. "They must have followed us."

"Or they have someone working in that hotel," Elodie said. "Leona, what's your status?"

"We're still looking for the bastard." Another roar whooshed through the speakers.

"Wait, Le, are you still in the hotel? The hotel that is on fire? You're not calling from outside?" Elodie's voice rose, and she leaned forward like she could retrieve her team through her phone.

"Of course we're still in the hotel, target is not yet acquired. He's gotta still be up here. The fire crews have it contained to the top floors; it hasn't spread down—"

"And are you *in* the top floors?" Elodie's voice slid another notch higher. "Get out, Le. He's probably already gone."

"Yes, ma'am." Leona disconnected.

Elodie sped up, the directions on her phone indicating they'd be there in five minutes. A column of smoke billowed ahead, visible even from the freeway, a smear of orange and black amidst the glint of evening sun on high-rises.

Tank's phone buzzed. "Hopper, are you ok? Where are you?"

"Fine, I'm fine." Despite his reassurances his voice sounded ragged. Sirens shrieked in the background. "But Leona texted she'd followed our guy to our hotel, and then I didn't hear anything else. I was almost there and the top exploded. What's going on?" Tank filled him in as Elodie raced through the streets.

Two blocks out from the hotel, cops were turning traffic back. Elodie jerked into a parking spot, and they dashed through an alley and between buildings, emerging opposite the hotel into a horde of evacuated hotel guests and on-lookers. Sirens and shouting and car horns filled the space between bodies. A sidewalk table-display for the Las Vegas Health Challenge had been knocked over and abandoned. The crowd huddled together behind plastic police bar-riers, watching the fire, and Tank grabbed Elodie's hand to keep from getting separated. A familiar gray head bobbed through the crowd.

"Hopper!" Tank threaded his way through the press to where Hopper spoke with a fire crew official and a woman in a business suit.

Hopper spun. "You made it. Listen, this is the fire chief and the hotel man-ager. You've got to go in."

"Go in?" Tank threw a glance at the chief and the manager, wondering how much they knew. "I thought we were supposed to keep a low profile? Or did they not get everyone out yet?"

"No, there are still three people unaccounted for. The fire crew has a base set up on the twenty-seventh floor, a floor below the fire—"

A bank of windows exploded, raining glass on the street below. Tank grabbed Elodie and Hopper, shielding them. The fire chief took off, yelling about getting the spectators moved farther back.

Tank pulled Hopper, Elodie, and the hotel manager behind a fire truck. "Ok, so I go in and find those three, and get them out. But try not to call too much attention."

"The cops already know you're in the city. The fire department not so much, but hopefully they'll know enough to keep their mouths shut. Just avoid being seen by anyone else coming out." Hopper coughed, waving away smoke. "It's too bad we didn't bring the 'shaving kit' to the meeting. Your civvies are gonna get burned."

"Actually ..." Tank pulled his collar aside, revealing Elodie's suit.

"Wait, you're already wearing it?" she asked. "How'd you know you'd need it?"

"I didn't. I put it on for something else." Tank stuttered. "It makes me feel brave."

Her face softened. "I'm glad."

"You ready?" Hopper called over the chaos.

"Ready." Tank snuck through the crowd toward the entrance, trying not to look like he was about to run into a burning building. Inside, he peeled off his street clothes, stashed them in the lobby and dashed through the stairwell door.

The stairs flew under his feet, four and a time. Too slow. The fire at the mayor's house roared through his memory. The heat, the flames devouring the house like an insatiable beast. Gerard unconscious on the floor. He had to go faster.

He crouched and leapt up the center of the stairwell, climbing over the railing to leap up another floor. On the twenty-seventh floor he skidded into the lobby.

"Who's in charge?"

"What the—Who let you in here?" a man in heavy firefighter garb bellowed.

Tank ignored the question. "Do you have those three people out yet?"

"You can't be here, get back outside." The firefighter made to drag him back to the stairwell, but Tank planted his feet. The man heaved like he was trying to move the building itself, then straightened, confused. Tank grabbed a fistful of his coat and lifted him off the floor.

"Trust me, you want me here. Have you reached the three people still inside yet?"

The man gaped at Tank before answering. "No, they're three floors up, man. This side of the building, but so much of the floor has collapsed we can't get to them."

Tank nodded and set him on his feet. "Thanks."

The smoke thickened in the stairwell as he bounded up the three flights. It flooded his lungs, acrid and searing. The pain was real, but he pushed through, knowing he'd be ok. The door to the thirtieth floor was already gone, eaten by the fire. Heat snapped at his face as he passed through the flaming doorframe.

Ten feet into the corridor, the floor was gone. The rooms that should have been on either side of the hall had collapsed into the inferno below, leaving a yawning hole between him and what remained of the next room. The fire reached up greedily through the empty space, like some movie scene of a pit in Hell.

Three more firefighters knelt several feet back from the pit, wrestling with some kind of extendable ladder. Across the chasm, three bodies lay sprawled on the floor, forms wavering in the shimmering heat mirage. Burn marks scored the metal of the ladder, like the crew had tried stretching it across but the fire had had other ideas.

Tank didn't waste time or oxygen talking, just tapped one of the crew on the shoulder, pointed to the ladder and shook his head no. He backed up, drew a breath and charged the gap. The flames snatched at him as he sailed across. He gritted his teeth against the blast of heat, landing as softly as he could. It wouldn't do anyone any good if the rest of the floor collapsed under his bulk.

Up close, the forms resolved into an adult and two children. A father and two daughters. The family was still breathing, if shallowly, and Tank sent out a swift prayer of gratitude to whatever part of the universe was listening. He scooped up the two girls first, afraid of trying to balance all three while he jumped. On the other side of the chasm, he passed them off to two of the crew members.

They ran with the girls for the stairs, and Tank rushed back for the father. The floor shook and a section to his right crumbled.

He leapt across with the father in his arms just as the rest of the floor fell into the abyss. The last firefighter grabbed the unconscious man, and all three tumbled into the stairwell.

The fire fighter gaped at Tank. "Who are you?"

"Um, new guy?"

"Yeah, no. Who are you, dude?"

Tank was about to sling both the father and the firefighter over his shoulders to get them down the stairs when his phone buzzed.

"Don't worry about it, just get him out." He handed over the dad.

The crew member threw one more look at Tank and piggybacked the father down the stairs. Tank whipped his phone out and started after him.

Elodie's voice came over the line as soon as he picked up. It sounded like she was driving. "Tank, Leona and Marlena are still inside." Panic leaked through her voice. "I left already, I was heading back to meet them at work, make sure they were ok, but then Leona called—"

"I've got it, El. Get back to Fashion Seeker, I'll get them out." He hung up, a small part of his brain noting that he'd just used a nickname for her.

He punched at the screen, calling Leona.

"If this is a robocall, I will hunt you down and end you," she growled through the phone.

Tank almost laughed. "Amherst. Where are you?"

"Tank. Thirty second floor, north side. I had a hunch our guy hadn't made it out after all, and I was right. We've got him, he's passed out. We've got oxygen masks, but the stairs are blocked above and below us."

"Ok, I'm on the south side, twenty ninth floor." He reversed direction, heading back up into the inferno. "It'll take me a minute to get to the other side of the building, but I'll be right there."

He found an intact hallway and ran through to the north wing, and up more flights of stairs. Halfway between the thirty first and thirty second floors, a section of ceiling filled the stairwell. Leona and Marlena crouched under the smoke on the other side, arms shielding their eyes from the heat, and the cause of the fire unconscious between them on the floor.

Tank heaved a sigh looking at the flaming chunk of debris between them. This was gonna hurt.

Heat seared through his hands and across his back as he dug his shoulder underneath the piece of ceiling and heaved. A twinge of regret passed through him. Elodie's suit was so beautiful, and now it'd be ruined. She said it was more durable than his former uniforms, but surely no fabric could withstand the flames so directly.

"Go, go!" He urged the Seeker Security team down the stairs. They sprung past, dragging the Abaddon arsonist, and Tank jumped back, letting the crackling mass drop back to the floor.

"Status?" Leona barked as they ran.

"Everyone's out," Tank said. "Fire crews working on the building. Cops outside. Elodie's driving to Fashion Seeker. The idea is to exit unnoticed and stay under the public's radar."

At the ground floor, they skidded to a halt outside the grand entrance lobby. Police officers already crowded the room. They pulled back around the corner.

"Correction," Tank stated. "Cops in the building. You need a different exit if El doesn't want the police knowing you're involved."

"El?" Leona raised an eyebrow.

"I mean, Ms. Seeker," Tank stammered.

"Sure you do." She looked like she wanted to say more, but one of the officers in the lobby called out orders about searching the lower floors for the culprit. Cops broke off into smaller groups and branched out down hallways and side doors. Outside the front doors, a growing number of news vans and reporters pushed against the barricade. Leona and Tank ducked into a side room.

"There's always a staff entrance in the kitchens, but there are too many cops in the hallway," Leona said.

"You need a distraction, something to gather them back in one place." Tank weighed the options. "I could hand this guy over to the police, then they wouldn't have to spread through the building to look for him."

Leona shook her head. "No good. He made me right before we lost him. If he identified me, it'd lead the cops back to Fashion Seeker. You could walk out the front door into the media circus. It might draw the cops off to the commotion."

Tank frowned. "If I go out the front, we blow keeping a low profile and violate the dispensation."

"Well, we have to keep Elodie's involvement out of the limelight." She gave him a look that dared him to argue.

"Same page there." Elodie had reasons for not wanting the cops to be in her business. He had no idea what they were, but he trusted her. And he wanted her to be safe. The feeling took root in his chest and spread. It must have shown in his eyes because Leona nodded in satisfaction.

"How about something in the middle. I'll call the cops back to the lobby and send them in the wrong direction after Sleeping Beauty here, and you can sneak out the back." A pang of guilt snaked through his guts at the idea of lying to the police. But Leona was right. He wasn't going to throw Elodie under the bus.

"That'll work. We'll wait here till you've got them out of the way." She clapped him on the shoulder. "See you back at Seeker. Thanks for the assist with the stairs."

Tank crept out of their hiding spot. In the lobby, he jogged up to a cop who was giving orders, and thirty seconds later, police officers were emptying the building and running in the opposite direction of Leona.

"What about you?" the cop in charge asked Tank.

He shrugged. "I'm not supposed to be running around the streets in uniform. Special Dispensation and all that."

"Right. Well, you better get yourself out of here quiet then. Appreciate the help." He paused. "You gonna find Slingshot?"

"I'm going to try, sir."

"I've got a couple kids at home who were devastated when the news broke this afternoon. Sure would like to get my hands on whoever leaked it."

Tank made a face. "Yeah, me too."

Tank recovered his street clothes from behind a sofa and slipped them back on over his suit. Outside, reporters clamored past the caution tape, hurling questions at the cops keeping them at bay. More news crews filmed in the street, the hotel in the back of their shots. Smoke still blackened the sky, but the fire crew's outdoor platform attack had the blaze in retreat. Across the street, paramedics cared for the evacuated hotel guests. The father and his two girls had oxygen masks on but otherwise looked unhurt. Tank kept his head down, making his way through the crowd till he reached Hopper.

It was odd, slinking away from a job like he'd done something wrong, like he hadn't just saved three people's lives.

*Of course, I did lie to the police about where the perp went.*

"Hey!" someone called.

Tank whipped his head up and groaned. The firefighter who'd carried the dad was running over to him, face determined.

"Who are you, man? How'd you do that?"

Tank shushed him, but the man made no efforts to keep his voice down. "You jumped like twenty feet over that pit and then jumped back carrying them." He pointed to the ambulance where the family was. "So I'm gonna ask you again, who are you?"

The man's questions attracted attention. People murmured and pointed, passing along his words. A reporter trotted over to investigate the commotion, then another, and another. Tank turned, searching for an escape route for him and Hopper, but the crowd was a wall of bodies around them now. Microphones popped up in his face.

"Is it true you rescued that family?"

"Do you have superpowers?"

"What do you know about Slingshot's disappearance? Is he being replaced already?"

"Hopper?" Tank looked to his manager.

"So much for a low profile." Hopper shook his shoulders out like a boxer prepping for a fight, faced the media and plastered on his public smile. "I can see you have many questions. We want to make sure we give our first responders plenty of room to work, so for right now we'll keep it simple."

"What are you doing?" Tank whispered, shaking his head. *He wouldn't. Hopper wouldn't.*

"Ladies and Gentlemen—" His manager gestured to him like a ringmaster in a circus tent.

"H, no—"

"This is The Tank."

The questions doubled in speed, coming at him rapid-fire and repeating. Tank forced himself to breathe slowly and stand tall, to look the part of The Tank like Hopper always told him to. Hopper would answer the questions. Hopper would deal with the press. And then they could get out of here and make sure Elodie and her team were ok.

After what felt like an hour, Hopper held up his hands. "Thank you all. No more questions at this time."

Tank followed his manager to the rental car, leaving the chaos, and the crowds, and the media behind, his heart sinking. That wasn't how things were supposed to go down. The plan was to follow the Abaddon psycho back to their headquarters, end their operation quietly and rescue Slingshot. Not burn up half a hotel, nearly get Leona and Marlena killed, and then announce his presence to the whole city on the news.

"I'm sorry, H. I blew it." He braced for a lecture.

But Hopper laughed. "Are you kidding? You did great."

"I did?"

"I can't wait to see the replay on the news. I think it was the Channel 5 camera—did you see it?" Hopper half turned to face him while he drove, grinning.

"I don't think so," Tank said slowly. This was not the reaction he'd expected.

"The angle the cameraman had it at, it was beautiful. A perfect low-angle shot of you, shoulders back, jaw strong, burning building behind you. I couldn't have framed it better myself." He cackled gleefully.

"Low-angle ...?" Tank stared at him in confusion. "But the special dispensation. We weren't supposed to let anyone know we were here. I had to talk to the fire crew inside," Tank hurried to explain. He hadn't meant to out them. "But I didn't think they'd call attention to it in the middle of the street. What happens now? Are we going to have to go back to L.A.?"

"No." Hopper waved away his concerns, still chuckling. "Delagarza already agreed to us being here, and Abaddon still needs to be stopped. I'll smooth things over with the AVA department. What do they expect you to do? Let people die because of red tape? It wasn't your fault we got found out."

"Of course I couldn't let people die, but I don't get it. Why aren't you upset? We weren't supposed to tell anyone I'm here, but—" Tank stopped short of saying *You told the whole city.* Hopper didn't appreciate anything that sounded like an accusation. *But he did tell. He didn't even really try to get out of it.* "If the Feds kick me back to L.A. we can't find Abaddon."

"Nah, nah. They're not gonna kick you out. If there are problems, I'll smooth them over, that's part of my job. Besides, you're already *here.* Possession is nine-tenths of the law, right?"

"Possession?" Tanked gaped at his manager. "What am I possessing? This is temporary. We stop Abaddon and find Slingshot and he goes back to working. This is his city."

"Right, right, of course we'll find him," Hopper said. "But in the meantime, trust me. I know what I'm doing. And, hey, at least we don't have to sneak around anymore, right? Tanks don't sneak. They roll on in wherever they want to go."

*As long as where they want to go isn't a library or a dating app.* Tank kept the comment to himself. Hopper was the AVA expert. And his manager. *I just can't see his plan yet.* "Right, H."

Thinking of dating apps reminded him of Grace's message. He pulled it up to read again.

*What brings you to Vegas? How long will you be in town? I'd love to meet up.*

Ice threaded through his limbs. Hopper didn't care that the people of Las Vegas knew The Tank was in town, but ordinary people weren't the only ones who knew. Abaddon knew. Whether they knew because they tracked his movements from L.A. to Vegas, or because the guy he'd stopped this afternoon let them know before starting the fire didn't really matter. They knew.

They knew he was here, they knew he was trying to stop them, and they were retaliating. Which meant anyone he was around was now a target.

He shut his eyes and saw flames. Flames around Gerard. Flames around the family in the hotel.

Dread balling in his belly, he read Grace's message one more time, letting himself imagine meeting her. Imagine talking about books in person, strolling someplace scenic. Imagine ending their first date with plans for a second and maybe even a kiss. Then he made himself compose a response.

*It's a librarian conference, believe it or not.* He grimaced at the lie. *I know, sometimes I have a hard time believing those are a real thing too ha ha. I'd love to meet up too, but so far, the schedule is pretty intense. I'll have to keep you posted on how it goes.*

He hit send before he could take it back.

Hopper turned north.

"Where exactly are we going?" Tank asked. "Did you make other reservations already?"

"Ms. Seeker said she has rooms at Fashion Seeker we can use. No one's getting back in that hotel for a while. Told me before she left."

Tank blew out a shaky breath. Grace wasn't the only potential victim. He glanced in the rearview mirror. "Make sure we're not followed on the way there, H."

# CHAPTER THIRTEEN

H and to her throat, Grace huddled around the TV with her co-workers, watching the news coverage of the hotel fire. The feed flipped from a news anchor to footage of firefighters carrying what looked like an adult and two children out of the building.

"Oh, thank goodness," she breathed. The women around her murmured their own gratitude. Grace paced between the coffee maker and the television. She'd given up caffeine years ago in her quest to keep her body as functional as possible, but prepping mugs for her co-workers kept her hands busy. Her own mug had coconut water in it.

The news anchor repeated the same information for several minutes in between shots of the hotel and the rescued family, until one of the firefighters drew attention to a man in the crowd. The camera zoomed in, and Grace's eyes widened.

A text came in from Dr. Oracion. *Are you watching the news?*

*Yes.* She knew what the doctor was thinking. They'd started their project by researching known, working heroes. The Tank was the only one they'd found that might have a kind of healing factor. They had no way of knowing if he had a true regenerative ability in addition to his invulnerability, or simply a power that shielded his person. Grace thought of it like the difference between a spaceship that had full power on its shields versus a spaceship that had its shields up but also had around-the-clock nanites repairing any damage as soon as it happened.

But since no one could get past The Tank's "shields," there was no way to know if he also had "nanites," let alone extract blood samples. No needles for The Tank. She sent another text to the doctor.

*It won't work.*

*He's here! We could at least ask him. Maybe he knows a way. There's always a way.*

*You know I appreciate your tireless enthusiasm, but let's keep looking for unknowns. There have to be more Alices out there, and Rene said she'd keep an eye out for her and try to convince her to change her mind.*

*Ok,* Dr. Oracion sent. *Then how about talking to him because he's cute ; )*

Grace sent a full line of exclamation marks. She knew Grace had been talking to Willard online.

*I'm just saying,* the doctor texted again. *A bird in the hand is better than ... another ... bird ... online. Or something like that.*

Grace snorted at the butchered proverb. *Yeah, I think that analogy could go bad real fast lol*

A different notification popped up on her screen and her heart sped up. She sent the doctor one more text.

*Speaking of the online bird, he's messaging right now. Talk to you later!*

She moved away from the TV to a quieter corner of the room and looked at the notification for a moment before opening it, savoring the anticipation. When the school called to tell her Willard had dropped by, she'd been flabbergasted. But pleasantly flabbergasted. She'd asked him what brought him to Vegas—surely he hadn't come only to surprise her, but she couldn't help indulging the thought of such a romantic gesture—and she'd asked him to meet up. And here he'd messaged back. Trying to suppress a grin—she loved her co-workers, but sometimes they could be nosy—she opened the message.

*It's a librarian conference, believe it or not. I know, sometimes I have a hard time believing those are a real thing too ha ha. I'd love to meet up, but so far, the schedule is pretty intense. I'll have to keep you posted on how it goes.*

The air rushed out of her like she'd been punched in the gut, and she fell back onto the couch.

*A librarian's conference?* she thought. Are *those a real thing? And "I'll keep you posted?"* What a brush off.

*You expect too much,* she chided herself. All they'd done is message back and forth a few times. There was no real relationship. No real reason to expect that Willard's heart beat faster when he received her messages the way hers did when he wrote to her.

A lump formed in her throat, but she swallowed it down. She hadn't gotten where she was in life by sitting and crying. She sent Willard a quick response.

*Sure, no problem. Enjoy your conference.*

There. Polite and brief.

Grace collected herself and rose from the sofa. There was work to do. The evacuees would need basic supplies to replace what they'd lost in the fire, places to stay. She'd make a few calls, put some things together.

*Librarian's conference.* Her heart stuttered once more, and a dull ache started under her breastbone. There'd be a new bruise purpling her skin that night.

# CHAPTER FOURTEEN

A half-moon kept watch over the city by the time Tank and Hopper parked in front of Fashion Seeker Designs. Tank tried not to grip the door frame too tightly as he pulled himself from the car. Physically, it took much more than what he'd done today to make him truly tired. But emotionally, the day had thrown plenty at him. His heart hurt. All he wanted was sleep.

Leona held open the front doors for them, looking no more nonplussed than if she'd spent the day minding the office. She let the doors close behind them and a click and blinking red light on a wall keypad indicated the security system had engaged for the night. Tank wondered again where Elodie had found someone like Leona and why she needed such a hardcore security team in the first place. Maybe the fashion industry was more cutthroat than he realized.

The head of Seeker Security led them through the plush lobby and downstairs to the basement. Elodie's tastes were reflected even underground, and despite the lack of windows, the space felt light and open. They passed through a lounge, complete with a flat screen on the wall, a pool table, squashy couches, and a kitchenette. Leona turned down a hallway, and Tank peeked into the rooms opening off it. Bedrooms, some with bunkbeds, some with a single bed, all with potted plants and grow lights and—Tank smiled—bookshelves. Small ones, only waist high, but full of volumes.

Leona showed them to adjacent rooms. "These are yours for as long as you need them. It's not a luxury hotel, but it beats smelling like smoke. Bathroom's down the hall. Help yourself to anything in the kitchen."

"This is great. Thank you, Ms. Amherst," Hopper said. She started to leave but turned back when Tank stuttered out a question.

"Leona, did Elodie make it back ok? Is she here?"

"She did, but she went home." She cocked an eyebrow. "Despite what it looks like, we don't actually all live here. She'll be back in the a.m."

"Yeah, no, right. Sorry." Heat crept into Tank's cheeks. "Morning's great. Goodnight."

He listened to the soft thump of combat boots on carpet as she strode around the corner before exhaling heavily.

Hopper slapped him on the arm. "'Is Elodie here?' Can I call it or what?" He grinned, hands on hips.

"What? No, that's not what I meant, H." Tank flushed deeper. "I, you know, wanted to make sure she was ok. That's all." He shuffled his feet in embarrassment but caught himself before Hopper could reprimand him. Feet shuffling was a Willard habit. A nervous Willard habit. He was supposed to be leaving Willard behind.

"You know, I like that Ms. Amherst." Hopper was still grinning. "She knows how to get things done."

"Goodnight, H." Tank retreated to his room. A bundle of clothes lay folded on the comforter on his bed. All of his own things had been lost in the fire.

*Not all of them.* He had the two most important things. Elodie's suit, which he was still wearing. And Grace's book, which he'd snagged from the back seat of the rental car on the way in.

He set *A Circle of Cats* down on the bookshelf and examined the clothes on his bed. Fresh clothes for tomorrow and a pair of flannel pajama pants plus a plain white tee for tonight. All the clothes looked like they would fit him perfectly—not an easy find on short notice. Tucked into the T-shirt was a paperback copy of *The Black Stallion*.

A smile snuck onto his face, despite his mental exhaustion. Elodie *had* been here before going home for the night.

A Post-it note was stuck to the inside cover.

*Thanks for getting my team out*

*—El*

*P.S. Dinner was great too : )*

Warmth spread through him, soft as sunlight. El. She'd signed it as El, the nickname he'd unintentionally used for her today. He shut the book, still smiling. He'd have to make sure Hopper didn't see the note; he'd assume it meant Elodie was flirting or wanted to go out again. Which she wasn't and didn't, because she was already interested in someone.

He cleared his throat. *So am I.*

He wiggled his toes out of his boots, peeled out of his suit, and put both in the closet. He sniffed ruefully at his beautiful, new suit. Maybe Elodie had some fancy way of removing smoke stench. Except ... He sniffed again. There was no smoke smell. And no scorch marks on either the boots or the suit, despite running straight through the fire. He marveled. What had she made them out of?

*Add it to the list of things to ask her, I guess.* For now, sleep. The pjs were like silk on his skin, and the comforter was the perfect weight. The mattress springs groaned as he laid down and he tensed—it'd be just like him to break the guest furniture—but the bed didn't buckle, and he slowly let himself relax. Tank drifted off, book and sticky note still in hand.

A faceless woman confronted him.

*I'm dreaming. This is a dream.* The lucid dreams had started when his powers began to manifest. He had no idea why. Other people with abilities had reported the same thing. As their powers developed, their control over their dreams grew.

He looked around the dreamscape. Aside from the woman, he saw nothing but blank fuzz. He concentrated, making his surroundings resolve into a room, a library. His library. That was better. He always found the blankness disconcerting.

The faceless woman clutched her arms across her middle, obviously distressed.

"Are you ok?" Tank asked. "Do you need help?"

"You don't have time to help me." She had no mouth, but Tank heard the words. Even lucid dreams didn't necessarily make sense. He tapped his fingers against his leg, thinking. What was his brain dwelling on?

"Willard," she said.

Oh. That's what his brain was dwelling on. He should've known.

"Grace, I'm sorry. I'm trying to keep you safe."

A familiar flicker of pain started in his stomach. Tank extinguished it with a thought. Banishing his reflux at will was his favorite part of lucid dreaming.

"You didn't have time for them either, Tank," another voice said. "Are you turning into a grownup?"

Tank turned. Gerard, a violent burn on his face, pointed to a group of five-year-olds sitting cross legged on a Storytime rug.

"No, I'm keeping them safe too," he said. "I'm helping them." The burn on Gerard's cheek glared at him. Tank touched his little friend's face and erased the wound. "See? I'm helping."

"Willard," Grace moaned and fumbled at where her face should've been.

Tank faltered. He didn't know what she looked like. How was he supposed to fix her face? The spark in his belly jumped back to life, and he frowned. *It's not supposed to do that here.*

"Willard," Grace called him again.

"I can try." He covered the featureless space with his hand, but when he pulled it away, Elodie's face smiled up at him. "No, that's not right."

His stomach flared. A ball of fire flew through the library. Books ignited and flames leapt toward the ceiling.

*No.* He pointed at them. *This is my dream. Go out.* Sprinklers sprouted from the ceiling, dousing the flames but another fireball crashed through the library. Heat crawled up his chest. The kids in the Storytime corner pelted him with flaming snowballs.

The burning snarled its way up his throat. The sprinklers petered out. The bookshelves lit up like torches. He was going to choke on this burn.

The dream wasn't working.

*Fine. Wake up.* The other advantage to lucid dreaming was escaping whenever he wanted to. He rolled off the bed and hit the floor with a boom. Hopefully it didn't wake Hopper.

His stomach was a volcano. Lava blistered his throat. Spiky fire clawed through his chin, stabbed his shoulders. Every exhale stung like gasoline fumes. No wonder the dream had gone haywire.

Tank curled into a ball, focusing on his breathing. Inhale. *It's not actually damaging me.* Exhale. *I'm fine, just need to calm it down.* Maybe there was yogurt in the fridge, if he could manage to stand up and get there.

He swallowed against the fire in his esophagus, forced his shoulders out of their hunched position. As the pain receded a touch, he climbed to his feet and made his way down the hall. A half-empty container of Greek yogurt hid behind take out boxes in the fridge, and he snatched it gratefully. The couch proved as squashy as it had looked, and he curled into a ball to polish off the yogurt.

Milky coolness smothered the burn. It was odd that something physical, like yogurt, helped even though there was no physical damage going on. Still, he wasn't going to complain. Whatever worked.

He laid his head back, reveling in the lack of agony.

Images from his dream swirled through his head. That had been a weird one. Usually, with lucid dreams he was able to do whatever he wanted—control the setting, the characters, the plot. He figured it was the closest he'd ever get to writing his own book. But this dream had slipped away from him.

*Stupid stomach.*

The microwave clock said 4:30 a.m. Not much point in going back to bed. He opened BlindDate, thinking about messaging Grace again. Maybe she hadn't taken his excuses as hard as the dream suggested, but he wanted to be sure she knew he wasn't blowing her off.

*Except, the situation hasn't changed.* He hesitated, fingers hovering over the screen. They couldn't meet up until Abaddon was no longer a threat.

On the other hand, he had promised to keep her updated. And they could still talk through the app, keep getting to know each other that way. *But you don't have any updates, genius. And it's 4:30 in the morning. You'll look like a nutjob.*

He closed the app. He'd try messaging again in the morning. The real morning, not this why-on-earth-am-I-already-awake morning. He snuggled deeper into the cushions. Maybe he'd be able to fall back to sleep after all.

The dream scene came back to him as soon as he closed his eyes. Gerard's ravaged face. The kids hurling fireballs. The void where Grace's face should be.

*Nope, not getting back to sleep.* He dragged himself off the couch and into the bathroom to beat back the dregs of the nightmare with a hot shower. Afterwards, he changed into the fresh clothes Elodie had left for him.

The shirt settled against him like butterfly wings, delicate and luxurious, but fit like a second skin. He checked in the mirror and saw the surprise on his own face. Usually, he avoided tight clothing for civilian wear. If he wore street clothes that emphasized his muscles, people skirted around him on the sidewalk, they avoided making eye contact. But this flattered his physique while simultaneously rendering him less intimidating. And it was soft.

He chuckled. Elodie really was a genius.

Tank grabbed his phone and the copy of *The Black Stallion* and headed back to the staff lounge for some reading, but before he made it back to the couch, a light at the end of the hallway on the other side of the lounge caught his eye.

*Huh.* Leona hadn't mentioned anyone else staying the night. If anything, she'd implied no one was. *Maybe someone's early for work? But who would come in this early?* He looked at his favorite book in his hand, felt the buttery softness of his shirt. *Of course.* He strode down the hall to thank Elodie for her thoughtfulness.

The door was ajar, and he poked his head through. "Hello?"

Elodie sat on a low, stone bench along one wall, her usual elegance marred by a grim expression. She looked up in surprise. "Tank, hi. Come in."

The room was a complete contrast to everything Tank had seen of her decoration tastes. Bare cement, bare light fixtures, bare walls. No plants. The portion of the room opposite Elodie's bench was walled off like a jail cell, complete with bars in the window of the door.

"You're up early. Couldn't sleep?" she asked.

He shook his head. "Mind if I sit?"

"Please."

"You either, I guess?" The cold of the stone of the bench seeped through his pants and he shivered.

"No, no sleep for me," she said heavily. "Even when I do, my dreams haven't been the most pleasant."

"I hear that." Tank held up the book. "Thanks for this. And the clothes and letting us crash here and all. I know we need to keep you off the radar, and the more people who know I'm in town, the harder that is. So, it's really kind of you. I'm sure Hopper can find us new rooms soon, so we don't—"

"Tank." She cut him off. "My friends can always stay here. And you're welcome. The outfit looks great on you, by the way."

He blushed, smoothing the flawless shirt. "Thanks. It feels amazing. I can't believe you had anything hanging around in my size, let alone this."

She shrugged. "I didn't have it hanging around. I made it."

"With everything that happened yesterday?" He laughed. "When?"

"Oh, you know, between this and that." She made a vague gesture. "I like solving design problems. It relaxes me." She turned her focus back to the jail cell. Tank took in the shadows beneath her eyes, the anxious set of her jaw.

"But not enough to sleep."

"No," she agreed. "Not this time."

A harsh voice snaked through the cell window. "Fashion. Filth. Pollution."

Tank nodded at the cell. "Your arsonist?"

She nodded, face haunted. "Not merely an arsonist. Leona said after I left for L.A., he burned everything in the cell, on his own. The rags and gasoline must have been props."

Tanked looked at the cell. "He's a firebug." Abaddon had people with abilities working for them. Made sense.

"Yes. He knows where they're at. I need to know—" She cut off and started over. "*We* need to know where they're headquartered. Leona thinks—But I can't—" She dropped her face in her hands.

Tank reached out a hand to rub her shoulder but thought better of it. She might take it the wrong way, and she was already interested in someone else. So was he. *Although I've probably ruined that.*

He went for a joke instead. "There are other forms of torture. All we have to do is read him something really boring and he'll be begging to give us what we want. But it'd have to be something truly awful like ..." He thought through the library shelves for something horrid.

"Moby Dick!" Elodie flipped her head back up. "Worst book of all time."

"Right?" Tank laughed. "Why is that considered 'great literature'? It's so depressing."

"Sooo depressing." Some color returned to her face. "It's so torturous, we'd likely be violating the Geneva convention."

He leaned in conspiratorially. "I won't tell if you don't."

She pretended to lock her lips and stow the key in her pocket.

"Honestly," Tank went on. "Ahab was so arrogant, the only good part of that book was when the whale won and got rid of the guys trying to kill it."

"Plague. Fire. Cleanse." More muttering came from the cell, and they both stared at the window.

Tank coughed. "I didn't mean that. Not like that." He pointed toward the voice rattling off death sentences for the human race.

"I know. Thanks for making me laugh." Elodie patted his knee, and he ducked his head. Maybe she would've been fine with his hand on her shoulder. *It was a pat,* he told himself. *Pats are friendly, not romantic. You pat a dog.* Not that he would have intended his touch to be romantic. *That would be stupid, because friends are what you want to be.*

She stood and stretched. "Enough brooding in here. Everyone is meeting to plan in a couple hours. I'm going to freshen up a bit and then how about a proper tour before the others get here?"

"Sure." Tank rose from the bench. "I'll meet you in the lounge in a few minutes." He lingered in the dungeon-like room after she left. The ramblings in the cell grew louder as Tank approached. Scorch marks scarred the walls, and the firebug sat hunched against the wall, knees to chest. His locust tattoo crawled past the collar of his shirt and up his neck, like it would bite off his earlobe. His voice rose and fell in a steady stream of near incoherence.

When he noticed Tank watching him, he stopped. He stared at Tank, laughed, and began rambling again with new words woven in.

"Pollution. Plague. The show. Chosen one." He cackled again. "Filth. Cleanse. Quite the show. Chosen one." Spittle gathered in the corner of his mouth.

Tank shuddered and tried to shake off the creep factor. "Hate to break it to you, buddy, but the Chosen One trope isn't in fashion anymore. It's been done too many times. And I'm not sure I'm buying this whole crazy act." He shrugged. "You got anything else for me?"

The man cut off his tirade, glaring at Tank. He twisted his neck and clawed at his tattoo, leaving violent red scratches on his skin. The locust seemed to waver and move, the folds of skin making it turn its head in Tank's direction and gnash its teeth.

Stomach churning, Tank recoiled and left the jail behind.

# CHAPTER FIFTEEN

W hen Tank turned the lights on in the lounge, the bright welcoming
colors belied the nightmare scene down the hall. He gulped down a
glass of water but immediately regretted it. With his stomach starting to roil
again, drinking was like splashing water on a grease fire. He found a loaf of bread
in the fridge and scarfed down a piece to soak up excess acid, then leaned against
the bar while his system settled.

His thoughts, however, didn't want to settle. What was with these people?
Weren't there enough thieves and con artists and stalkers and murderers to
protect people from already? Now he had to deal with some horror-movie
terrorist cult too. How was he supposed to fix this?

All of Hopper's lessons pressed down on him. Willard couldn't fix this.
Willard couldn't handle this situation. He needed to be The Tank, he saw that.
But he couldn't help the voice in his head from his past self, asking, *Where does
that leave me?*

"You ready?" Elodie entered the room in a drapey yellow blouse and
light-gray slacks. The brightness had returned to her eyes, and her dark hair fell
in a lustrous waterfall to her waist, a fresh plumeria tucked behind her ear.

"Wow," Tank breathed. "You look beautiful. I mean," he fumbled. "You
don't look like you didn't sleep at all."

She wiggled her fingers in the air like a stage magician. "The magic of eye
drops. Shall we?" She swept an arm toward the stairwell, and Tank followed her
up.

"This is our production floor." Elodie flipped a bank of switches on the ground floor, and lights rippled on through the large room. Sewing stations spread in rows before them.

"Stand-up desks?" Tank pointed to hinges at one of the stations.

"Yes." Her eyes lit up at being asked about the details. "Sewing is hard on the body, so we've made the stations as ergonomic and flexible as possible for what each seamstress's body needs."

"Genius designer *and* a good boss. Impressive. And your seamstresses, they're also your security team?" he asked.

"My seamstresses, my security team, my family." She strolled between the stations, trailing her fingers over the desks.

"I'm gonna be honest, I can't really picture Leona stitching up pants."

Elodie laughed. "No, being the head of security is a full-time position. But other than Leona and Sophia, they split shifts between production and other needs."

"How did that come about? I mean, is the fashion industry so nuts that you need this kind of security?"

Elodie pursed her lips. "Piracy *is* a very real threat. Counterfeit designs cost the fashion industry billions every year. My team keeps my business safe. But it's more than that. Where I was raised, community was vital. You work together; you work *for* each other. You depend on each other. You're a team, but more than that, you're family. Moving here took me away from that community. It was one of the most difficult things I've ever done, and I knew if I wanted community like that again I'd have to build it myself.

"Our arsonist downstairs? He's not wrong about the mess this industry makes. Fashion is the second highest-polluting industry in the world." She laid emphasis on the last word. "And it destroys and discards people as much as it damages the planet. When I got into design, I wanted to do things differently. No wasting resources. No throwing people away. I chose team members who shared those ideas. I found women who could help me build a community and who I could help lift. We were all misfits of one kind or another. All women rejected or exploited by toxic industries, or told they couldn't—shouldn't—reach for their dreams. We have all Fashion Seeker Designs facilities down to zero emissions and no clothing or raw materials are discarded. If we're overstocked or get returns, we donate the excess. And when I hire someone, they get the care they need to heal from whatever they've been through, and the resources to stay well. We even have our own medical wing upstairs that Sophia runs. It means I don't hire the numbers that other people do, but every one of us is invested in what we're doing. We take care of each other. We're a team."

Tank looked at the production floor with new eyes, seeing a place of growth and cooperative creativity. He felt a twinge of longing as well. Never had he been part of a community, a team, like that. "That's incredible, El."

She smiled at the name. "Maybe we need a nickname for you too."

"Not sure how we'd shorten Tank. It's already only one syllable." The idea warmed him all the same.

"I'm sure I can come up with something."

On the second floor, Elodie showed him a workspace much like the one in her house in Los Angeles. A smaller space housed a photography studio with various backdrops, props, and lighting equipment.

"This is for our in-house photographer, Danielle. She does her best to make my creations look fabulous in print."

"I can't imagine she has to try too hard. Your stuff even manages to make me look good." He struck a silly pose in front of one of the backdrops, trying to make her laugh again. It worked.

"That's not too hard either."

"I don't know," he said, motioning to himself. "You're working with a caveman canvas here."

Elodie tilted her head. "Oh, Tank. You really *don't* know, do you? Tell me the truth, before Hopper got it into his head to set us up, he was fending women off you all the time, wasn't he?"

Tank flushed. "That doesn't count. They were only interested in the superhero thing."

"I'm sure that's not all they were interested in. Come on, third floor."

At the end of the hall, past the conference room, Elodie pushed open a door with a flourish. "This is our study room."

"A library." Tank grinned at the sight.

Most of the books and magazines were fashion related—*100 Years of Men's Fashion, The Modern Kimono, Sustainable Design for the 21st Century*—but a smaller shelf cradled a collection of fiction titles. Tank knelt and ran his fingers across the spines. Judy Blume, Kwame Mbalia, Maurice Sendak, Madeleine L'Engle, Jason Reynolds, Sue Pickford Cheung.

Elodie knelt next to him. "Some familiar friends?"

"If I'm not at the meeting later, you'll know where to find me." He sighed. Hopper would kill him if he found him curled up in here with a book instead of showing up as The Tank. "But I will, of course. Be there, I mean." They were in Vegas for a purpose, and that purpose did not include curling up with book friends. He shoved to his feet and followed her back into the main corridor.

"Down the hall is my office, and our med wing runs the length of the north side of the building. It's Sofia's playground, she's always got a research project going in between treating employees." She went silent, half a frown forming.

"You alright?" Tank asked.

She sucked in a breath and brightened. "I'm good. I was just thinking, Sofia's going to tell us if she's identified that powder from the man you caught."

"Ah, right. I almost forgot, what with the fire and everything."

"There's one more thing I want to show you." She led him to the conference room and dragged two chairs from the glass table to the eastern windows. "This," she said, "is the best show in town."

Tank eased into the chair next to her, staring out over the desert. The velvet blue of predawn gave way to dove gray. Lavender trickled in like watercolors and brightened to pink, painting the few clouds in the sky like roses. Tangerine beamed through the pink until the curve of the sun broke the horizon. The peace of the sunrise spread over the freneticism of the city that never slept.

"Good morning, officially. Are you hungry?" She moved to the side table and started coffee.

"I could maybe eat a little." Tank inspected the platters next to the coffee maker. Coffee was a terrible idea for reflux, but a banana and a couple of pastries should be safe enough. They took breakfast back to the chairs by the window.

"El, why do you not want the police involved?"

"It's a fair question." She set her plate aside, eyes on the desert. "Slingshot's philosophies are not popular with everyone. The hero industry is new, growing, but it *is* an industry. Structures are already in place for people to profit from, which means there are people who stand to *lose* profit or power if those structures change. Before he disappeared, Slingshot was planning on firing his manager."

"Mr. Delagarza?"

"Yes. Slingshot found out a while ago that his manager was turning away requests for Slingshot's assistance because the cases weren't high profile enough to rate positive media coverage, or better sponsorships. They wouldn't have grown Slingshot's image."

"Whoa." Tank's eyes widened. Mr. Delagarza had appeared genuinely upset when Tank met him at Slingshot's apartment. He'd assumed Mr. Delagarza was worried about losing a friend, but maybe he was more worried about losing an asset.

Hopper had said possession was nine-tenths of the law. Since signing with him, Tank had considered his manager his friend, but suddenly he wasn't sure if Hopper had been referring to Tank possessing Las Vegas—*which would be bad enough and which I'm not going to do*—or if he'd meant Strickland Talent possessing Tank.

"Yeah. Slingshot started freelancing as many of those jobs as he could, but since they weren't through Delagarza's agency, they weren't covered under his permit. LVMPD started calling him a vigilante, but he was too popular to arrest outright."

"Vegas loves her superhero?"

"Exactly. And his bigger jobs *were* covered under Delagarza's license. So they didn't arrest him, but they didn't go out of their way to cooperate either. The cops would deliberately take forever to get to a scene to arrest whoever Slingshot caught. Or they'd lose paperwork and blame it on him, that kind of thing." Her cheeks colored and her jaw hardened.

"What kinds of jobs was he doing?" Tank asked. Anything that could be categorized as community service technically didn't need a permit—it made no sense to label someone a vigilante for picking up litter or adding benches to a park. But Slingshot had been researching Abaddon on his own. He'd helped Elodie on his own.

"Some violent crime, some smaller stuff. But it was all in neighborhoods that the people who make the rules don't care about. What do they care if someone is beating up the unhoused, right?" She closed her eyes and inhaled sharply. "Sorry, I get worked up."

"It's worth getting worked up about. I got into the hero business because I wanted to help people. Not 'the right people.' Just people. Although, after what you've shown me here," he circled a finger to indicate all of Fashion Seeker Designs, "maybe we need to redefine what counts as a superhero. You are doing fantastic things here, Elodie. You're taking your beliefs and your passions and turning them into action. And Slingshot. I understand why this city loves him. He's—" He stopped. *Oh. Tank, you idiot. You're so slow.*

He cleared his throat. "And I totally get how you and Slingshot would make a powerful couple."

Elodie's eyes bugged. "What?"

He shrugged and ducked his head. "You said you were interested in someone. Every time Slingshot came up, anyone could see you were upset. More upset than a fan, or even someone who had a working relationship with him."

"Oh my gosh." She hunched over, rubbing her forehead. "I've got to be more careful." She straightened and looked him in the eyes. "Tank, I know we haven't known each other long, but you are kind and honest and an absolute cinnamon roll of a guy."

"A what?" His hand went to his middle. Just firm abs. He didn't think he could get fluffy even if he tried; his strength was always there, whether he worked out or not.

"Nothing. The point is, I trust you, so I'm going to tell you something, because it will help things make more sense, and help us work together better. My team already knows, of course, but I need you to promise not to tell anyone else. Not even Hopper." She made a face. "Especially not Hopper."

Tank hesitated. His manager was *his* team and was supposed to be his friend. Keeping BlindDate a secret had already gotten him in trouble. But Elodie was his friend too, and she was looking at him so earnestly.

"Sure, El. I promise."

"Good. Slingshot is my brother."

"Your brother." An odd feeling swept through him. Like the blissful blankness when the pain in his stomach stopped. Like he'd been holding onto stress and had suddenly dropped it. Relief.

*Quit that.* Even if he'd ruined things with Grace, he still had feelings for her, and Elodie already liked someone else. *So it's not Slingshot, so what? It's still someone.* The dropped weight piled back onto his shoulders.

"Many of the women who find refuge with Fashion Seeker lack certain paperwork that the legal system cares way too much about." She quirked an eyebrow. "The police are already looking for ways to discredit Slingshot—they're probably dancing for joy that he disappeared. If they knew how closely we're connected, it could bring us under exactly the wrong kind of scrutiny. My team are like family. I'm not letting anyone take them away from me."

"Oh, El." He sat back in his chair and blew out a breath. "I completely understand. I won't say anything."

"Thanks." She paused, tilting her head. "Thanks, 'T'?"

"Eh." Tank bit his lip.

"You're right. That doesn't quite work."

"Hopper calls me big guy." He wrinkled his nose. He'd never put his finger on why the moniker made him uncomfortable but had let it slide, trying to find belonging in the fact that Hopper had a nickname for him at all.

Elodie shook her head. "That doesn't work either, and, while I'm airing all my opinions, I don't like it when he calls you that. It feels patronizing."

Tank blinked. Patronizing. There it was. Finger on it at last. "That's the word all right."

Elodie checked the time and unfolded herself from the chair. "The others will be here in a bit. I have a couple of things I need to take care of in my office. Feel free to hang out here or wherever you like."

"Sure, sure." Tank shoved upright and gathered their plates. "Thanks for the tour, El. And the company."

"Thanks for listening." She gave him a quick hug and slipped out the door.

Tank stared after her for two full minutes, standing dumbly in the middle of the room, breakfast dishes in hand, thinking that plumeria must be the most delicious smell in the world.

*Oh, I'm in trouble.* He stacked the plates in the sink and ran his hands through his hair. *Hopper called it.* Tank groaned. No way could he let Hopper know he was falling for Elodie.

He rolled his shoulders and jogged—lightly—in place to reset his thinking. Hopper wasn't going to know because there was nothing for Hopper *to* know. If he'd fallen, he'd simply get back up and move on. Elodie didn't have feelings for him, and he'd get rid of his feelings for El.

He yanked his phone out and opened BlindDate.

*Grace,*

*I think I need to apologize. My last message came out more brusque than I meant. I really do want to try to meet up when this conference is over.* He winced at the tiny lie. Taking down an apocalyptic cult wasn't exactly a conference. But even if he needed to get rid of his feelings for Elodie, meeting Grace had to wait till Abaddon was eliminated. He wasn't going to put her at risk. *Is it ok if we still talk here until then?*

There. Take that, feelings.

The phone buzzed in his hand, and he almost dropped it. She'd written back already. Unexpected. *But she does get up early.*

*Hi Willard,*

*To be honest, I didn't think I'd hear from you again. It sounded like you were pretty much blowing me off. But sometimes typed messages aren't the best for saying what you mean. Aaaand ... now that you wrote, I'm glad to hear from you again. So, yes. We can still message. How about this to start: Tell me three things about you. One thing you love (other than books, I know that one).* She added a winky face. *One thing you hate, and one totally random fact.*

Tank laughed out loud and read the message three times. He almost did a victory dance but noticed the security camera in the corner of the ceiling.

*Thanks for being understanding about it.* He added a smiley face. *Hmmm, good questions. One thing I love, other than books.*

He drew a blank. What did he love? His life was punching bad guys. He thought of what Elodie said about Slingshot taking jobs on the side. He thought of the dad from the hotel fire, squeezing his daughters tight in the back of the ambulance.

*I love helping people.* No, that was too serious. It sounded like a line. *And Moose Tracks ice cream in waffle cones,* he added. *Might actually be a toss-up between those two.* He hit send. It'd take a minute to type out answers to the other two questions and he didn't want Grace to think he'd disappeared in the middle of their "conversation."

*Ha! So if the proverbial Little Old Lady needed help crossing the street, but there were Moose Tracks in the other direction?*

Tank chuckled, pleased to find it was still easy to message back and forth, and sent a laughing emoji. *Yup, little old lady might have to wait. For the thing that I hate, grape jelly. Apricot jam, peach, blackberry, raspberry, apple butter. Those are all great. Grape jelly is gross.* "Shrug emoji and send," he murmured.

*The random thing: I've never been ticklish.* He stilled, wondering if that were still true. He wouldn't have felt it as a teen. Now, other than Hopper, people didn't touch him. Maybe for the same reason they never asked him if he was ok. *No, Elodie touched me. She squeezed my hand and patted my knee. And asked if I was ok.*

He shook himself. "Not thinking about that."

*How about you?* he asked. *A love, a hate, and a random thing.*

Her answer came a minute later. *I love my family. Sounds cheesy, but it's true. I actually still live with my parents. My grandma and my brother are in the same house too. (Well, he technically has his own apartment but he's here all the time.) I know that sounds weird to mainlanders, but it's different in Hawai'i. Aside from multi-gen households being cheaper—Hawai'i is crazy expensive ha ha—culturally it's not a stigma the way it is here. Extended family living together is pretty normal. So when we moved to Nevada, it wasn't really a question. We stayed together. Ok, sorry for the culture lesson ha ha. Back to the questions.*

Tank wrote back. *No, it's cool! I wish I had that kind of family.*

*Yeah, it'd be really hard for me to be as far away from your family as you are.*

Tank grimaced. As far as he was concerned, his uncle could stay away the rest of his life.

Grace continued, *For the thing I hate, I'd have to say SPAM musubi. They're so dry! You need like a whole bottle of shoyu to get it down ha ha. (Shh, don't tell.) And my random thing is that in the third grade, I won our school talent show by playing* Another One Bites the Dust *on a nose flute. It was epic.*

Tank sent three laughing faces. *That's two pieces of very blackmail-worthy information ha ha. I'm flattered by your trust.*

He laughed to himself but then remembered Elodie's words. *I trust you.* Grace's secrets were certainly less stressful to keep than El's. *Argh, you're not supposed to be thinking about Elodie right now. Knock it off.*

An AI voice floated over the intercom system. "Overnight system disengaged. Front door open."

Tank checked the windows overlooking the parking lot. A handful of cars had arrived, and women in Seeker Security uniforms were ambling into the building. Morning chatter and footsteps echoed up the stairwell.

*Looks like I've got to get back to work.*

*Yeah, me too.*

The chat went quiet, leaving Tank to wonder if that was it, or if he should say something else to end the conversation. Grace beat him to it.

*Willard?*

*Yes?*

*Message me again if you have time during your conference. This was fun.* A red heart followed.

Tank whooped quietly and spun his chair in a triumphant circle. The conversation from the stairs walked through the conference room doors. Elodie came back, retrieved her chair from the window and spun it to the conference table. As she turned, a lock of hair caught on Tank's shoulder and her plumeria fell into his lap.

He picked it up gingerly, afraid of squashing it. The fragrance swirled through his brain and Elodie's hair was like velvet across his neck as she pulled it free. Tank's throat went dry.

*So much for getting back on my feet.*

# Chapter Sixteen

S ofia's presentation was making Tank's brain spin. Literary analysis he was fine with. But this? This was all numbers and chemical formulas.

"This is not my area of expertise," Sofia said, "not being an entomologist. But I pulled in some opinions from friends, and they agreed." She held up the bag of powder they'd retrieved from the duffle bag. "This is formulated from the locust pheromone 4-vinylanisole, sometimes also known as 4-methoxystyrene ..."

Tank stared at Elodie's discarded plumeria on the table, thoughts wandering away from the science lingo. She'd taken the seat to his right, and he was aware of every small shift or movement. He shut his eyes, focusing on red heart emojis.

Someone kicked his ankle. Tank opened his eyes to find Hopper giving him The Look. The what-on-earth-is-the-matter-with-you look.

"Sorry," Tank whispered.

"Were you asleep?" Hopper hissed.

"Sorry. I didn't sleep very well last night." He pointed to his stomach. It was the truth, even if it wasn't why he'd tuned out of the meeting.

Hopper's mouth thinned but he nodded. "Just try to pay attention."

"Yeah, sorry," Tank repeated. If he could design a perfect day, aside from books, it'd be a day where he didn't have to apologize for anything. He worked to pull his focus back to the presentation, but he didn't understand it any more than he did before. His uncle's taunts resurfaced, despite the number of years it had been since Tank heard them in person.

*Dumb oaf. So far behind, you'll never catch up.*

"Hang on, Sof. It's made of locusts?" Elodie wrinkled her nose. "This guy was going to spray bug powder? All over the school?"

His uncle's words faded. If Elodie didn't get it either, maybe he wasn't so far behind.

"Not quite." Sofia's eyes were alight with discovery. "See, the 4-vinylanisole is the *swarming* pheromone. It's emitted by locusts in a group—you only need four or five together to start the process—and attracts other, solitary locusts to their group until it grows into a swarm."

"So why release it in a school? What does it do to humans?" Elodie asked.

Sofia shrugged apologetically. "I don't know yet. We aren't locusts. We don't swarm."

"Saturday night on the strip aside," Leona joked.

"And pop concerts." Hopper laughed.

The others threw out more examples of human swarming—football games, holiday shopping, rush hour traffic, overcrowded apartments—and Sofia took on a speculative look. She shifted the conversation away from jokes to hypothesize on the interaction of crowds and pheromones in their own species.

"Tank," she said. "Did he say anything when you encountered him? Any hint as to what they're going to do with the pheromone?"

"No, sorry." There was that word again. "He didn't say much of anything." *Especially not after I knocked him out.*

Leona rapped a fist on the table. "Maybe we should go ask him now."

"Is he here?" Hopper leaned forward. "What'd you do with him after the fire?"

Leona smirked. "He's here. We've got him in one of the holding cells."

Tank's eyebrows lifted. "*One* of the holding cells? How many do you have?" Leona shrugged. "Three."

"Three. And—" He started to ask the obvious follow-up question of how often they had used them, but Elodie gave a tiny shake of her head. *Right. They hadn't used them. Slingshot had, in his "on the side" work. Another reason why Elodie having such a hardcore security team makes sense.* He changed tack. "And I guess we better go talk to him."

They trooped down the stairs. Elodie happened to be in front of him and he worked on concentrating on the top of her head instead of the way her hips moved.

*What is wrong with me?* This wasn't a problem he'd ever had before. He'd had plenty of crushes in high school, but none of those girls had ever looked at him twice except to wonder what was wrong with him. After he left his uncle's and went to California, he'd dated some in college, but when his abilities began to manifest, he'd been too busy figuring them out and training to maintain a relationship. And not once during any of those times had he had feelings for two different women at the same time. What was his deal now?

He resisted the urge to thunk his head against the wall. It didn't matter whether he was attracted to Elodie. Didn't matter that his heart hammered when she smiled at him, or that she was a genius but didn't make him feel dumb, or that she was doing concrete work to make the world a better place, just like he wanted to.

She already liked someone else.

A vicious little flicker of hope sparked in him. Elodie had said that she was *interested* in someone else. Not that she was *dating* someone else. And she was wearing her plumeria behind her right ear, not her left, which meant she was technically available.

He smacked the little spark of hope in the face and sent it flying. If he couldn't definitively choose between them, then hoping to be with either Grace or Elodie was a selfish, jerk-faced thing to do. Besides, if he were honest with himself, the real problem wasn't that he was falling for two different women. It was that he couldn't be with either of them.

Because even if the threat of Abaddon suddenly disappeared, neither Grace nor Elodie knew all of him. And if he became who Hopper wanted him to be, they never would.

Hopper insisted that for Tank to really succeed in the hero industry, to really be able to help people, he had to leave his old life, his old interests, his old self, behind. Gerard's little body lying in the middle of a burning house had driven

Hopper's point home, but what was Tank supposed to do about the gaping hole that wrenching Willard out would leave behind?

Grace had connected with *Willard*. If he erased Willard, what was left for her to connect with?

And Elodie only knew Tank. Even if she decided she wanted to be with Tank, it wasn't fair to give her only the empty shell that carving out Willard would leave.

In the basement staff lounge, Leona swiped a key card in a door next to the firebug's room that Tank hadn't noticed last night. The interior was identical to the other holding room, but the cell had furniture in it and no scorch marks. Two Seeker Security women kept watch. Tank and the others gathered near the cell. Inside, the man Tank had caught lounged on the bed. He had two black eyes from Tank breaking his nose.

Leona leaned against the door like she was having a conversation with a neighbor across a fence and held up a baggie of the pheromone. "So, what's the plan with this stuff?"

The prisoner shrugged. "Why don't you ask NineEighteen?"

"That's a mouthful. Who's NineEighteen?"

He shot Leona a withering look. "Do I look stupid? NineEighteen never made it back to the car the other night. You've still got him here."

Tank leaned down to whisper in Elodie's ear. "The guy in Bronson Studios called himself NineSix, after Revelations chapter nine, verse six."

"Let's find verse eighteen." She did a quick search on her phone.

"'... *men killed by fire* ...'" Tank read. "He's a firebug, I guess that matches."

Elodie scrolled back to verse six. "If the verse is indicative of a power set, what does verse six mean?"

Tank shrugged. "He conjured up bugs at the studio somehow, which matches the tattoos, but this verse doesn't even mention locusts."

"There was a team of you sent to burn us out?" Leona kept questioning the prisoner. "Pity we couldn't meet all of you that night. I still don't know your name."

The prisoner rose from the bed and sauntered to the door. He leaned against it, mimicking Leona. "NineZero." He pointed to himself. "Not that it matters, there are plenty of NineZeros."

"Maybe NineZeros don't have powers?" Tank whispered to Elodie.

"Sounds likely."

"What's the powder for, NineZero?" Leona kept her face neutral.

He laughed and returned to lounging on the bed.

Leona turned to Elodie. "Give the word and I can start pulling fingernails."

"Just keep trying," she said. Leona turned back to the terrorist.

Elodie tugged Tank back from the group a step. "Ask NineZero about Slingshot." She spoke barely above a whisper and cut her eyes at Hopper.

Tank nodded and moved to stand next to Leona. "Where did Abaddon take Slingshot?"

"Where did we *take* Slingshot?" NineZero's face lit-up like a kid with a box of candy. He sat up. "Oh, man, I'd give my right eye to be there when you find him."

Hopper shot an I-told-you-so look at Tank, and his manager's theory that Slingshot had joined Abaddon rather than been kidnapped slunk uncomfortably into the space between his shoulder blades.

Nostrils flaring, Elodie glared at NineZero. Her hand was still on Tank's arm, and he took her hand in his and gave it a squeeze.

*A friendly squeeze,* he told himself. *Because that's what we are, friends.*

"He's trying to rile us," he whispered to her. "Don't listen to him."

She reined in her expression and nodded. "I'll be back in a bit."

As she slipped out the door, Hopper pointed at her with his chin and gave Tank another self-satisfied smirk.

Everyone had gone to lunch. Tank scuffed through the empty production floor, telling himself that he wasn't hoping he'd run into Elodie. Leona, muttering about needing to employ her own methods, had called an end to the day's interrogation while Elodie was still out of the room, and he hadn't seen her since.

*Which is fine. You don't need to see her right now.* He shook his shoulders out and pushed through the front doors. Maybe some sun would help.

Outside, Hopper's voice came from around the corner of the building, sounding agitated. Tank followed it.

"Everything ok, H?"

Hopper held up one finger while he paced, phone glued to his ear. Tank leaned against the building to wait. The warmth from the sun-warmed wall radiated through his shoulders and he slid down to sit against it, thoughts running in circles. Red hearts, plumerias, locust pheromones. He didn't know what to do about any of them.

Irritation laced through Hopper's words. "Initiative is good, but we're not to that point yet ... No. Rein it in ... Good." He hung up and sat next to Tank. "Hey, big guy, what's up?"

Tank frowned. Patronizing was still the word. Then again, maybe he deserved it. Elodie had talked about doing things on his own terms, but what would his own terms even be? Working at the library was incompatible with being a hero. Even if he could guarantee the kids' safety, there weren't enough hours in the day. Time manipulation was not in his power set.

"Trouble with other clients again?" He pointed to the phone.

"Oh, yeah." Hopper made a dismissive gesture. "Big ideas, this one's got, but their career's only starting out. I want to hit a couple milestones before I let them off their creative leash."

"Well, you're the boss, H." Tank couldn't keep the bitterness out of his voice.

Hopper narrowed his eyes. "What's eating you?"

"Nothing."

"Oh, no, no, no. You think I can't tell when something's up? Is it Elodie? Tell me how that's going."

Tank looked away. "How what's going?"

Hopper elbowed him in the ribs. "Don't give me that. You couldn't take your eyes off her this morning. Aside from when you were staring at the floor. Remember what I told you about that. Eyes up, confident gaze, steady—"

"Steady voice." Tank finished the mantra. "I know. Sorry. And it doesn't matter if I can take my eyes off her or not." It was the closest thing to a confession he was going to give his manager; he didn't want Hopper putting any more pressure on Elodie. "She already has feelings for someone else."

"So what?" Hopper shot back. "You're The Tank. Who's a better catch than you?" He shrugged like it was a no-brainer.

Tank flushed. "Plenty of guys, I'm sure." Guys who didn't have to excise parts of their identity. Guys who knew who they were. "And I can't make her feel something she doesn't."

"Sure you can."

Tank laughed incredulously. "It doesn't work like that, Hopper."

His rep rolled his eyes. "I mean, go after what you want. Roll on through, no matter the terrain, like a tank. Crush the competition. Who is he anyway?"

"I don't know, she didn't say."

Hopper scratched his chin, lips pursed. "That's ok, we'll outmaneuver him all the same. You and Elodie will be spending plenty of time together during this whole Abaddon thing."

Tank studied his manager. They were facing a genocidal terrorist cult and yet Hopper was focused on Tank's love life. "You don't seem too concerned about this 'whole Abaddon thing.'"

"At the beginning, I was scared, I admit it. But then I thought, 'Nah, Abaddon is facing my boy.'" He slapped Tank's knee. "We'll be fine. And when it's all over, Vegas will have an opening for a hero. You'll have the largest territory of any hero working in the States."

Tank sat up. "What are you talking about? We're gonna find Slingshot; he'll be fine." *We have to, for El's sake.*

Hopper shook his head. "Didn't you hear what that NineZero said? He practically admitted that Slingshot is one of them."

"No, H—"

Hopper held up a hand to stop him. "Opportunities are my specialty. That's why I'm good at what I do. Trust me, big guy, this is a golden one. Bigger region means bigger jobs and bigger sponsorships."

"Hopper, you are good at finding opportunities, but this? I can't ..." Tank trailed off. Even if—heaven forbid—Slingshot didn't make it through this fiasco for whatever reason, the impracticalities of trying to work such a large area were reason enough not to do this. But Hopper wouldn't listen. And he couldn't tell Hopper that taking over Slingshot's city would alienate Elodie because he couldn't tell him that Slingshot was her brother. Tank dropped his head in his hands, the weight of his growing stack of secrets grinding down on him.

*Can't talk to Grace about Tank, can't talk to Elodie about Willard, can't talk to the police about Elodie, can't talk to Hopper about Slingshot.* Maybe he should simply stop talking.

"Tell you what." Hopper stood and dusted off his hands, grinning. "I'm going to give you an assist."

"What kind of an assist?"

"Where's your suit?" Hopper started for the entrance before Tank could answer.

"My suit?" He scrambled to his feet and followed. "It's in my room, er, the guestroom downstairs." *Not my room. We can't get comfortable here.* Now that the public, and Abaddon, knew he was here, they had to be extra careful about connecting Elodie or Fashion Seeker Designs with The Tank and the mission. "H, we should find a new place to stay tonight."

"Are you kidding?" Hopper stopped outside the front door. "No, right here is perfect. You can spend more time together. Bond through adversity and all that. She's perfect for you; we just need to help her see that. Now, get your suit and meet me on the second floor."

"H, I really don't think—"

Hopper cut him off, reaching up to take him by the shoulders. "Am I your manager?"

"Yes," Tank said slowly.

"Ok, so I want what's good for you, right? What's good for you is good for me, buddy. Trust me. Go get your suit and meet me upstairs."

Tank sighed. Maybe Hopper should have named himself The Tank. "Fine."

He retrieved his uniform and marched up to the second floor. Hopper was sitting in Elodie's workshop, smug as the proverbial cat. Tank felt a swell of pity for the canary.

*Oh, wait. I'm the canary.*

Hopper jumped out of his chair and rubbed his hands together. "She'll be up in a second. Remember, ride over the terrain. Be The Tank. Kiss her if you can swing it."

"What? No, I'm not going to kiss her."

Smirking, Hopper slapped him on the arm and strode out the door, whistling. Tank made to follow him, to argue whether Hopper listened or not—this had gone too far—but Elodie breezed through the door.

"Hey, Strickland said there's a problem with the suit?"

Tank swallowed and glanced guiltily at the uniform in his hand. "He did?"

She set up an accordion style changing screen in the corner. "Go ahead and put it on and we'll take a look."

"You know, I'm sure it's fine." He edged toward the door. If he put on the suit, she'd see nothing was wrong, and Hopper's ruse would be clear. Worse, it would look like Tank was in on it.

"It's no trouble. I want to make sure the design is working for you."

"You've got a whole company to run, I'm good."

"Tank." She laughed and circled behind him to push him toward the changing area. "Let me see."

Her shoving did nothing, but the electric feel of her hands through his shirt jolted him forward. Determined to protest again, he turned and Elodie collided with his chest. She stumbled and Tank caught her around the waist before she fell.

"Sorry," he said, hating the taste of the word in his mouth. "I'm kind of a brick wall."

She gripped his arms, regaining her balance, and laughed. "Do we need to exchange insurance?"

He smiled and ducked his head. "Maybe." Her skin was warm beneath her lightweight blouse. He focused on not accidentally squeezing too hard to distract himself. He willed his hands to let go, but her eyes were laughing. And the scent of plumeria wrapped around him like silk, pulling his face closer to hers.

*How long have we been messaging? Is it too soon to kiss her?*

"Tank."

*Tank?* Why was Grace calling him Tank?

Elodie leaned back and clarity punched him in the face. He dropped his hands and escaped behind the screen.

"I'll get changed real quick," he stammered. He crouched on his heels, head in his hands. *What are you doing? What are you doing? What are you doing?*

Elodie. He was here with Elodie. Who, he was sure now, had been about to explain her lack of feelings for him again. Because he'd been standing like an idiot with his hands around her middle and his face inches from hers. When had Grace crept into his thoughts? *Stupid, stupid, stupid.* He tried not to groan out loud in embarrassment.

"Everything okay back there?"

"Yup." He yanked off a boot and dropped it to make dressing-room noises. "Almost there." He tugged on the suit and stepped out from behind the shield, intending to make something up about the fit to cover Hopper's horrible scheme.

"Sorry again. About tripping you." He tried to laugh it off. "Like I said, brick wall."

"No worries. Thanks for not letting me fall." She set to studying him in the suit, walking a full circle around him and sweeping her gaze from his feet to his hair. If his near-screwup was bothering her, it didn't show on her face.

"Yes, I see the problem," she said, chin in her hand.

He blinked. "You do?"

She nodded. "The design isn't quite you. I didn't know you as well, of course. And this is better than your old one, but still. It's missing something. Not quite reflecting who you are."

Tank pressed his lips together to keep the question inside. *Who am I?*

She perched on a stool and tapped a finger on her cheek. "It's a bit too harsh, I think. You have a certain gentleness to you, along with your strength, that this look isn't quite capturing."

"Oh." The word escaped like a breath. Elodie saw gentleness *and* strength in him. Saw them both, and yet hadn't fallen for him the way he could no longer deny he was falling for her. His heart sang. And broke.

"Don't let Hopper hear you say that." He went for a joke to keep his warring emotions off his face. "He thinks I'm better off tossing anything gentle to the curb."

Elodie didn't laugh. "And what do you think?"

He pulled up a stool next to her. "I think, I'm really trying to make the whole hero part of my life work. I want it to. I want to help people; I want to be their shield. But ..." He paused.

"But?"

"But I'm not sure I know who I am as *this*." He gestured to the suit.

Elodie pursed her lips. "Who do you want to be?"

Tank stared at her. Such a simple question. Willard carried so much pain from the past. Pain that he didn't want to carry anymore. But he didn't want to pick up the suave, tough-guy, smash-the-terrain persona that Hopper had built for him in its stead either. The weight of both identities challenged even his strength.

*Who do I want to be?* Such a simple question, but he didn't have an answer.

"Did people ever tell you that you had to be one thing or not be another?" he asked.

"They did." She turned her gaze over the desert out the windows. It was a theme in the building, windows anywhere a window could be. Tank found it appropriate. Open and illuminating, like the woman looking out of them. "I was told plenty of times that I was prideful, for wanting to excel and have my own line, my own business. Some people thought I saw myself as better than them. Some of those people were in my own extended family. But I knew who I needed to be."

"How did you know? How did you figure out who to be?" He kept his gaze on the floor.

"That's an answer that's different for each person. You have to find that path we talked about." Elodie's face softened and she gathered his hands in hers. Her fingers didn't make it all the way around his fists, but the protectiveness of the gesture settled around Tank like a hug. What would his life have been like if he'd had a friend like Elodie in high school? What could it be now, to call her more than a friend?

"But Tank," she said. "When you think you've found your path, you have to choose it. That can mean *unchoosing* other things, other paths. Letting go of things that are holding you back. You have to trust your chosen path will bring better things."

A throat cleared from the doorway. Tank jerked his head up, and Elodie slid off her stool, releasing his hands.

"Sorry to interrupt." Hopper shot Tank a genuinely apologetic look. "But Las Vegas Police just called. Abaddon sent you an invitation."

# CHAPTER SEVENTEEN

H opper handed him his phone, open to a text and photo from LVMPD. "They found this taped to the door of the station downtown. So far, no one's reported seeing anyone leave it there."

*For The Tank:*

*Container Park entrance plaza. Sundown*

*No police*

*Don't be early*

*If you empty the park ahead of time, we won't show*

A drawing of the Abaddon locust mascot served as a signature, needle-like teeth threatening the reader.

"Not exactly picture book material," Tank muttered.

"What?" Hopper asked.

"Nothing."

"You realize they'll have some kind of trap set up?" Elodie took the phone to examine the picture.

"Of course they will." Hopper shrugged. "But this is The Tank we're talking about. Nothing they have will be a problem."

"Everyone has limits, Mr. Strickland. And they've already abducted one superhero."

"No offense to Vegas, but Slingshot was small potatoes." Hopper folded his arms. "And it looks to me like he went willingly."

"You are out of line, Mr. Strickland." Elodie glared at him.

"H, we can't assume that." Tank tried to rein in his manager.

Hopper looked from Tank to Elodie and held his hands up in surrender. "Ok, alright. We can come back to that later."

Tank narrowed his eyes. Hopper never conceded a point that easily.

"But this is what we're here for, to stop Abaddon," his manager continued. "Trap or no trap, Tank has to go. I'm sure you could help us plan though."

Tank shut his eyes and breathed through his nose. Hopper hadn't conceded a point—he was working on a different one. *Always maneuvering, H.*

"Of course." Elodie shot off a text. "Let's get Leona and move this upstairs."

On the third floor, she turned down a short corridor to her office. More windows overlooked the same horizon where they'd watched the sunrise.

Tank sighed. That seemed like days ago. And days since he'd messaged Grace. *I suppose I should wait till tomorrow to chat with her again.* It didn't look like he'd have time tonight anyway.

Leona jogged down the hall. "What's going on?" Elodie filled her in while Hopper shared the photo of the note with her. The head of Seeker Security barked a laugh.

"Something funny?" Hopper asked.

"Container Park? Have you ever been there?" She put her hands on her hips. "Who knew terrorists would have a sense of humor."

Tank looked to Elodie for an explanation.

"Oh, I forgot." She pulled up Container Park's website. A photo of the entrance showed a giant metal statue.

"What is that?" Hopper leaned toward the screen.

"It's a forty-foot-tall praying mantis." Leona snorted. "At night, flames shoot out its antennae. Of course they'd pick there."

"A forty-foot-tall praying mantis statue," Hopper said slowly.

"What can I say? It's Vegas."

He shook his head. "And I thought L.A. was weird."

Tank stared at the metal insect, torn between wanting to laugh and vomit. Abaddon wanted to murder millions of people, and yet they picked a location on brand with their tattoos? It was unnecessarily theatrical. Like something out of Gerard's comic books, when superheroes were still fiction. Why did they want to meet anyway? What were they waiting for? Why not go ahead and put whatever their plan was into action? Something was off.

Elodie cleared her throat. "Container Park is a shopping center. It has a playground and an entertainment stage—it'll be full of people on a Friday night. There'll be families, kids. Abaddon is demanding that we not clear the park, so regardless of whether they have a sense of humor, they will have plenty of civilians to use as hostages. Leona, let's plant plainclothes Seeker Security throughout."

Tank tore his eyes away from the mantis. "If we're going to do plainclothes, maybe we should use the police instead? This is gonna be awfully public, and we need to keep your involvement under wraps."

"True," Leona said.

"But if there's other information ..." Elodie laid extra emphasis on the last two words. "I don't trust the police to catch it."

"What information?" Hopper asked. "Any details about where Abaddon is that the authorities learn from whoever Tank catches, they'll give us."

"I agree with Tank," Leona said.

"Le." Elodie widened her eyes meaningfully, but Leona shook her head.

"Your safety is my first priority. That's my job. We can't risk the exposure. Strickland, you can arrange it with the police, yes?" She pulled up a map of the area, and they started planning the best spots to place officers.

Elodie pushed out of her chair and paced the other side of the room, rubbing at her chest.

"El." Tank followed her. "What's wrong?" He faced away from the others so Elodie wouldn't worry about Hopper overhearing.

She squeezed her arms around her middle. "Once you apprehend someone and turn them over to police custody, that's it. You don't get to go back and question them or have access to them, correct?"

"That's right. But the city wants Abaddon stopped. If they get info that will help us—" He stopped, understanding her concern. "You think they'll withhold info about Slingshot."

She nodded tersely. "And if Abaddon is holding him somewhere other than a base, we still won't know where to find him. Leona is amazing and loyal, but like she said, she puts my safety first, even if that isn't what I want. But I need *my* team there, not the cops."

Tank reached for her hand. Stopped himself. Reached again. She'd held his hands when he'd been upset. "Elodie, you'll have someone there. Me. If there's any info about where he is, I'll get it before handing anyone over to the cops."

She squeezed his hand and pulled him toward the hallway. The office door snicked closed behind them, and she sagged against the wall. Her fingers were still twined in his. Tank loosened his in case she wanted to let go but she tightened her grip.

"When I left for L.A., he was fine," she whispered. Tank stepped closer and leaned against the wall too, facing her. "He dropped me off at the airport in fact. We'd caught NineEighteen the day before, and he promised me he'd have leads by the time I got back." Her eyes glistened. She closed the small distance between them, hesitated once, then laid her head on his chest. Tank wrapped his free arm around her, wishing he could block sadness like he blocked a punch. His shirt soaked up her tears, but Elodie's shoulders didn't heave while she cried and she made no audible sobs, not like when people cried in a book. He wasn't surprised that this was how she wept. Focused. With purpose. No unnecessary waste or fanfare. The same way she did everything else in her life, from designing clothes to lifting the lives of others.

"We'll get him back, El," he murmured into her hair. "Don't listen to Hopper's theories. I'll get him back. And I'll make sure whoever is responsible is behind bars. I promise." The words took root in his bones. He *would* find Slingshot and bring him back to his sister.

She sucked in a breath and lifted her head, cheeks wet. "Thank you." Her fingers wove themselves more tightly into his and she held his gaze. "Tank, what I was going to say earlier, in the workshop."

He dropped his gaze to the ground and braced for her to say he'd messed up, that this moment of closeness was strictly between friends. That he needed to keep his distance.

"Maybe it isn't fair for me to say." Uncertainty crept into her voice. "But part of me wishes I'd met you first."

Words left him.

She released his hand and wiped her eyes. "I know you already met someone too. And I'm not trying to interfere with that, but I've never been great at lying about my feelings." She rose up on tiptoe to brush a kiss on his cheek. "Just remember the world is full of possibilities."

Tank touched his cheek. *Part of me wishes I'd met you first.*

"I need to step out, but I'll see you before you leave this evening?"

He nodded, mute, and she strode down the corridor. Speech tumbled back into his throat, and he called after her. "Elodie?"

"Yes?"

"Part of me wishes that too."

His feet pounded the desert, raising puffs of dirt. With hours to go before sundown, he'd found some sweats in the dresser in his room and gone running to clear his thoughts. A mile north of Elodie's facility, he'd come across a slot canyon and decided on a little work out.

From the top of the canyon, he ran two steps, leapt across the crevasse, turned and jumped again, zigzagging his way up the length of the divide. *Yup, just a little work out. To work out the train wreck that is my head.*

The ghost of Elodie's kiss burned his cheek, and her idea of possibilities burned his mind. *Part of me wishes I'd met you first.*

*A Circle of Cats* waited in his room, and red heart emojis on his phone. *Message me again.*

He'd never seen Grace in person, but she was one of those possibilities Elodie talked about, while he'd spent part of everyday for the past four days with Elodie, and she wasn't a possibility. Because, by some cosmic joke, they'd met each other second.

Furrows split the rock beneath his heels as he slid down the canyon wall to the desert floor. All his doubts from that morning rushed back. Who was he kidding? Neither of them were possibilities because nothing in his situation had changed.

He hurled a chunk of rock along the canyon and out of sight, growling. *Get your head in the game. Focus on the job.*

Stomach burning like the sun overhead, he ran back across the desert.

# CHAPTER EIGHTEEN

G race's limbs ached with weariness as surely as they'd ever ached from a bruise. She eased herself onto the cot she kept tucked away at work for days like today.

The latest bruise showed up over her right ribs while trying to help situate the displaced hotel guests. Grace's line of work meant she had useful contacts in various industries in the city, and she'd been able to coordinate new lodgings and donations of the things lost in the fire.

*Most of the things,* she thought. One guest had spent two months hand quilting a blanket for a new grandbaby. Grace couldn't replace that. One of the kids lost their favorite stuffed animal. She couldn't replace that. And Las Vegas had lost her hero. And she couldn't replace that. No one could.

She was grateful for the efforts The Tank was making. Los Angeles was a lucky city. But the way The Tank's manager had introduced him on the news after the fire ... Hector Strickland, she wasn't so sure about.

Her side twinged, and she imagined what Dr. O would say. *Stop thinking about it and get some rest, Grace.*

"Right. Ok."

The cot was heated, like a massage table—she'd had it retrofitted special-ly—and her pillow provided just the right amount of neck support. Neither had been cheap, but they allowed her to rest when the pain was too distracting to focus on work. And tonight, she'd be working late again. A nap was definitely in order, although that wasn't the only reason she was trying to sleep.

The heat coaxed her muscles to relax, to melt into the bed, and after a few minutes of deep breathing, she drifted off.

Something shimmered ahead of her. A pond, or a lake.

*No, wait. I've seen this before.* It had appeared in her last lucid dream as well. Streaked pink and silver, the surface of it bubbled like a hot spring. Her bruises had all been hot lately—hot to the touch, hot under her skin—so Grace assumed whatever this mess spread before her was, it stemmed from her brain ruminating on her worsening condition.

*Speaking of.* She banished the boiling lake and turned the dream to what she wanted to focus on.

Rest wasn't the only reason Grace kept the cot at work. She found long ago that her lucid dreams gave her creative brain a place to work through an issue or a project free of the restraints of fully conscious logic, much like the space between sleeping and waking. Through practice, she'd learned to call up a lucid dream when she needed to, and she used them to analyze and dissect problems she was working on. Usually, it was a design problem for work, but today she called up the memory of her last visit with Dr. O and replayed it like a movie.

*"It's hot again."* She lifted her shirt to show Dr. O the new bruise over her ribs. *The doctor ran light fingers over the contusion, frowning.*

*"I feel that. Almost like a fever."*

*"It hurts deeper than usual too.*

Lucid-Grace watched her friend give memory-Grace a CT-scan. The doctor's well-furnished, self-sufficient facilities made that a simple procedure. There was no fussing with scheduling or insurance. The scan had shown internal bruising on Grace's liver.

That was new.

The bruises had never gone so deep, never affected an organ. They'd always stayed in the realm of skin and muscle, like bruises were supposed to.

Lucid-Grace slowed the memory, studying the images from the scan, before letting it play at normal speed again.

*Dr. O looked at her with concern. "You need to take it easy."*

*Grace snorted. "A terrorist group is threatening the entire city of Las Vegas. How am I supposed to take it easy? People are gonna need help."*

*The doctor took Grace by the shoulders and looked her in the eye. "You are unfailingly compassionate, my friend, and I love you for that. But you can't solve everything. And you can't help anyone if your organs start giving out. You need to rest and hydrate, and we need to keep an eye on you."*

Grace paused the memory and rewound it to look over the CT images again. She placed her hands over the bruise on her right side, where her liver should be, and pictured it healing. She imagined all the blood vessels whole and undamaged, the tissues laying smooth and unswollen, her skin clear and unblemished. She willed the healthy version of her organ to stick, to take, and woke herself up.

She sat up. Checked her side. The purple and green blotching was as violent looking as it had been before her dream.

"Worth a shot," she muttered.

Her phone buzzed with a text from work. *We're ready.* She sighed and dropped her shirt.

"Alright, keep going, Grace. Back to work."

# CHAPTER NINETEEN

Hopper was waiting for him in Tank's room. His manager brushed dirt off his sweatshirt. "Been throwing some rocks around?"

"Just a warmup." No need to tell him about trying to work out his feelings.

"Alright, suit up. I'll meet you in the car."

"I need to say bye to Elodie before we leave."

Hopper chortled and elbowed him in the ribs. "The extra fitting session helped, eh? You're welcome."

Tank blushed. "No, that's not what I meant."

Hopper rubbed his hands together and headed out the door. "What would you do without me?"

Tank watched him go. "Good question."

After he'd put on the uniform, he slipped the street clothes from Elodie over it and jogged up the stairs to the front lobby.

Elodie gazed out the south window, arms folded tightly across her chest. The gold of the lowering sun highlighted her cheeks and the edges of her hair.

*Focus.* Tank reminded himself. "We're heading out."

She turned and pinned a flat, metallic device to the neck of Tank's uniform and inserted a matching smaller version just inside his ear canal. "Take this. It's like an ear bud, but less obvious. The one on your collar picks up, the one in your ear is the speaker. Hopper has his already. Leona and I will be listening in on my office computer."

"Thanks." Tank checked the skyline. The light was fading. Time to go.

"This is full of unknowns, Tank. Be careful."

"I'll get whatever information I can." He took her hand briefly and went outside.

Hopper pulled out of the parking lot. "Why are you wearing civvies?"

"I've got the suit on underneath. I figured it'd be more discreet if I showed up in normal clothes first."

"No, take off the street clothes. Branding matters. Show the suit."

Tank shifted in his seat to look at his manager as they sped up on the freeway. "Sure, but keeping people out of harm's way matters more. If I go in with the suit on display it'll draw even more of a crowd than will already be there."

Hopper waved away his concern. "They'll be fine. We live in a world with superheroes, for crying out loud. People know that. They know by now to get out of the way when it looks like something's going down. But after the dust clears, they need to know who to thank. So you show the suit."

Irritation bit at Tank. "I'd rather people be alive than be thanking me."

Hopper shot him a severe look while weaving through traffic, and Tank was back in the principal's office. He sighed but took his boots off and started to wriggle his pants off from over his hero suit. The confines of the car didn't make it easy.

"Ok, listen up." Hopper cut across three lanes of traffic to their exit. "Plain-clothes police will be stationed throughout the shopping center, with cars posted a few blocks out. No doubt Abaddon will anticipate us ignoring their 'no cops' request, so keep your eyes open. The cops have orders to follow your lead. You and I will use the transmitter's from Elodie to communicate." He grinned. "Leona filled me in on them. They've got a much bigger range than typical earbuds, they're less visible, and they pick up everything. Your girl's a genius."

"She is a genius," Tank agreed. He shifted in his seat, wrestling with his clothes. There wasn't room to lift his arms fully and his shirt got stuck halfway off. The car hit a bump, slamming his elbow into the roof, but he managed to pull the shirt off. He folded it carefully, his fingers finding where Elodie's tears had dried. "But she's not my girl."

Hopper didn't acknowledge the comment. "The cops have their own communication. I'll be in one of the squad cars, so you keep in contact with me, and I'll relay what you need to them. Clear?"

"Yes, H." Tank laced his boots back up.

Hopper shot a look at the dent in the ceiling above Tank's head, eyebrow raised like a parent whose toddler had dumped dinner all over the floor.

"Sorry," Tank said. "I'll cover it."

Hopper sighed. "Don't worry about it, big guy. We don't know what Abaddon's plan is for tonight, so if there's a group of them, you focus on the leader, and I'll have the police corral the rest."

"H, NineEighteen is a firebug. They could have other people with powers there tonight too."

Hopper shrugged. "I'll let the police know, but that's why we've got you, big guy."

"But don't let the cops know how we know that. Right?"

"Right, right. We've gotta keep your girl safe."

"Not my girl," Tank insisted.

Hopper snorted. "I don't believe that for a minute, but if she's not yet, she will be after tonight. You know, they interviewed that dad you saved from the fire, had shots of him with his kids and everything. And I saw an op-ed calling for the city to officially invite you to work the region. Yessir, bring the cops an Abaddon crony tonight and you're in."

Tank stared at the glee on his manager's face, unsure whether he was talking about Elodie, or Las Vegas, or if Hopper even knew the difference. "And we'll be one step closer to stopping a terrorist cult that wants to murder millions of people," he said softly.

"Yes, yes. Absolutely. Priority number one." Hopper pulled up to the curb in front of a 24-hour prime rib place. "I'm gonna drop you here so I stay out of sight. You can walk to the mantis statue from here. Remember, everyone's filming everything these days, and the internet is forever, so shoulders back and voice steady."

"Yeah, I know, H." Tank climbed out of the car, trying not to think about cameras. Instead, he visualized the shopping center emptying of people, willing them to all go home.

The sidewalk wasn't overly busy. Maybe Container Park would be having a slow night. A few people eyed him as they passed, and he smiled and nodded. *Nothing to see here, keep walking.*

He wasn't worried about himself. In all the years since his abilities had manifested, he hadn't found anything that pierced, burned, poisoned or otherwise hurt him. But this was a busy outdoor mall full of families. And Hopper was looking at it as a publicity opportunity rather than the risk it was. Tank needed to make this go as quickly and smoothly as he could. There was always the possibility of talking these guys down and apprehending them without a fight. Not a big possibility, but Tank clung to it.

Across the street from the entrance plaza he paused, surveying the layout as the last sliver of sun slipped below the city scape. The mantis held court from the east side of the square, in front of a geodesic dome and some kind of tower. A smaller, heart-shaped sculpture was on the west side. In the middle, a long, blue shipping container had been repurposed as the entrance arch into the shops proper. The open area of the plaza wasn't large, but it was full. Tank's heart sank.

Half a dozen twenty-somethings in Las Vegas Health Challenge T-shirts milled about the square, handing out bottles of vitamin water. A banner flew over a display table to the right of the arch proclaiming tonight as the official kickoff of the challenge.

*You guys have rotten timing.* Tank crossed the street to the square, scrambling for a way to convince the health challenge people to move their activity without looking like he was clearing out civilians.

A hand tapped his elbow. "Excuse me?" A pack of teenage boys gaped at him. One of them wore a Slingshot tee. "You're the guy from the fire, right? The Tank?"

Tank ducked his head, but Hopper's voice rang in his thoughts as clearly as if he'd spoken through the transmitter. *Confidence. Steady voice.* He lifted his gaze and smiled at the boys.

"Yeah, I am."

"Sick. Can we get a selfie?"

"Uh, sure." He squatted to fit in the frame with them. "Hey, don't make a big deal or anything, but it'd be better if you guys got out of here for a bit, ok?"

They weren't listening, jostling each other to check the picture on the phone. "Thanks, man!" They disappeared in the crowd.

"Who are you talking to?" Hopper's voice came through the transmitter as if he were standing next to Tank.

"Just some kids. No Abaddon yet."

"Forget about kids. We're not doing Storytime here."

"They weren't—" Tank protested. "Never mind."

"Listen, once you find who's in charge, nab him quick."

Tank made a noncommittal noise. He had information to extract first.

A group seated themselves in front of the mantis statue and pulled hand drums out of cases. One of them started a rhythm and the rest joined in. Tank stopped a passing shopper.

"Excuse me, what are they doing?"

"Oh, that. They do that for fun to 'wake up' the mantis before the fire display." She pushed a stroller under the arch into the shops.

"Such affection for a man-made object," a refined, English voice said over his shoulder. "I wonder how they feel about real insects?"

Tank turned slowly to avoid calling attention. NineSix smiled benignly at him, wearing a custodial uniform with "Nick" embroidered above the shirt pocket. A small, blood-soaked rip marred the shirt below the ribs. Tank would have to let the police know to find the real Nick's body when this was done.

Only the head of NineSix's locust tattoo was visible, its mouth gaping open in the hollow of his throat. His pulse beat beneath the teeth, making the nightmare arthropod quiver like it was waiting to spring.

"Tank, what's going on?" Hopper asked.

A couple bumped NineSix from behind, and he waved at their apology. "Busy tonight, isn't it?" He pressed a button on a remote, and fire spurted from the mantis' antennae. The crowd whooped and drummed faster.

"Yeah, it is." Tank surveyed the crowd, copying NineSix's nonchalance. "I think some of them might love real insects, but I don't think they'll like your bugs."

"If that's an Abaddon guy grab him now." Hopper's volume kicked up a notch in Tank's ear.

Tank kept talking to the would-be custodian. "I'd like to hear more about them, though. Especially the part about what you plan to do with that cocktail you've been making out of your little friends. There's a ribs place down the street, walk that way with me?" There was nowhere empty of civilians, but if he could get NineSix away from the shopping center it would help. And he'd have a few more minutes before the police arrived to work on getting information about Slingshot for Elodie.

"Tank, did you hear me? Take him now!" Hopper insisted.

Nerves squiggled in Tank's belly. He'd never disobeyed a direct order from Hopper. Hopper was his manager, his rep, his liaison so he could work and help people. Tank needed him. But Elodie needed information. And none of the people walking through the plaza needed the violence simmering in NineSix to erupt.

*I heard you. I'm ignoring you.* Hopper would be furious later, but he was also Tank's friend. *He'll forgive me.*

NineSix tucked the mantis remote in a pocket and fingered the bloody hole in his shirt. "*Nick* ate at that ribs place once a week. Did you know it takes nearly 13,400 gallons of water to produce one pound of beef?"

While he spoke, a dozen people formed a circle around them. One of them rolled up a sleeve to expose a locust tattoo on her forearm. One removed a beanie to show the insect on his bald head. The boy with the Slingshot tee lifted his shirt to show the tattoo on his belly. He tossed Tank a wave.

At the health challenge booth, a woman climbed onto a stool and tapped a microphone. "Welcome! So happy to see so many of you here for our kickoff.

Raise of hands, how many of you have been enjoying the vitamin water this week? We still have extras up here for free!" Most of the crowd raised their hands, and a few shuffled forward to claim their freebie. A fresh influx of people came from the shops into the square after the water bottles. Tank almost swore. They needed to move this, now.

"I just want to talk for a minute. Your friends could come too, NineSix." Tank emphasized *friends* to let Hopper know there were more.

"Wait, NineSix is there?" Hopper sounded incredulous.

"I have nothing else to say." NineSix smiled.

"Here we go!" The woman with the microphone threw a round package in the air with a squeal.

A locust tattoo snarled on the back of her hand.

The package exploded in midair, raining a fine white powder over the crowd. Tank lunged for NineSix but found only air. He spun, searching, only to see the terrorist waving at him, halfway across the plaza.

"H, he's a jumper," Tank called. Hopper cussed in his ear and yelled at the cop with him to send in the plainclothes officers.

Tank stalked toward NineSix. At least his name made sense now. *Seek death and not find it.* Teleporters were tricky to deal with, but they all had a few things in common. A tell—some physical clue they were about to jump; a limit—the farthest jump Tank had heard of was one hundred and seven feet; a cool-down period—a length of time after jumping they had to wait before they could jump again; and a lock. Someplace on their body that, once broken or disabled, shut off their ability to teleport. In the two years he'd been working with Hopper, he'd only had to take down a jumper twice, but he knew what to do. Pinpoint the tell, hope NineSix wasn't breaking any records with his limit or his cooldown, and find the lock. Since their molecules reformed every time they jumped, any bones that Tank broke searching for the lock would simply heal the next time NineSix teleported, and he'd have to try a different spot.

Tank grimaced. He did not enjoy snapping people's bones.

NineSix jabbed at the mantis remote again and the flames sputtered out. A cloud of powder puffed out in its place, layering over the first wave of dust on the faces of the crowd. He blinked twice and flickered to the mantis' head, laughing. Tank launched after him. NineSix's laughter cut off as Tank slammed a fist into his side. Ribs cracked and NineSix wheezed. Tank hadn't hit him full strength, of course. He still needed him to talk.

"Where are you keeping Slingshot?" He grabbed the front of the terrorist's bloody shirt, nose to nose, not knowing how long he'd have to get answers before NineSix's cooldown ended.

The jumper grinned and pointed to his side. "Nice guess, but not quite." He blinked twice, vanished, and reappeared on the ground.

*Short cool-down. At least I've got his tell.* "He blinks twice, H. Tell the cops." Tank made to leap after him but froze.

The throng in the entrance plaza swayed from side to side as one, an eerie imitation of wheat stalks in the wind. Powder clung to nostrils, eyelashes, dazed faces. The Abaddon followers surrounded them, arms stretched wide, herding the shoppers closer together.

Two men knocked shoulders, and the dazed look gave way to bared teeth. They shoved each other, snarling and crashing into people until the whole square was a heaving mosh pit of fists and elbows and feet.

"Hopper, we need those officers," Tank said.

NineSix called up to Tank. "We don't need to kill you. You'll kill each other for us. In twenty-four hours, this city will be a battlefield."

Tank leapt, landed on top of NineSix, grabbed his leg and wrenched. A shriek and the jumper vanished from underneath him. He popped into view at the far corner of the plaza, perched atop the heart sculpture. Tank smashed a foot down, snatched up a piece of broken pavement and hurled it over the thrashing tangle of humans. It crunched into NineSix's shoulder, knocking him to the ground.

"Where are the cops, H?" Tank charged to the other side of the square, but the crowd swarmed around him, blocking his path. A gray-haired woman swung a shopping bag at his face, and he ducked. Teal fingernails flashed in the streetlight as she swiped at him again. He let the blow bounce off and carefully picked her up to move her out of the way. She rained kicks at his shins, thrashing in his hands. A kid tried to bulldoze him as soon as he set her down. Tank caught him before he crashed to the pavement, pinning his arms to his side. The kid couldn't have been more than ten.

"H?" he called again. "I'm serious. They gotta contain these people. They're gonna hurt themselves." Bodies sprawled on the ground, the mad press of people trampling arms and legs and necks. "*Are* hurting themselves," he amended. "What gives with the cops?"

"The plainclothes aren't responding," Hopper finally answered.

"What? None of them?" Tank immediately thought of Elodie, of how the cops refused to arrive on scene for Slingshot. *Maybe we should check the police force for tattoos.*

Sirens shrieked over the transmitter. "Cars are on their way. What's going on over there?"

Across the square, NineSix struggled to his feet, arm hanging from his shoulder like a broken tree branch. Tank shoved through the mob as gently as he could.

"They sprayed a powder over everyone. Guess what it looked like?"

Hopper's voice shot up in panic. "But humans don't swarm!"

"Tell that to these folks. I'm working on NineSix's lock, I can't hold these people back myself. I need back up, now." He broke free of the melee to where NineSix waved with a wild-eyed grin. He blinked twice and teleported across the street to the shadows between two buildings.

*Sure, now you leave the square.* Tank followed, hurdling cars that swerved around the riot spilling into the street. He slammed the jumper against the brick wall of a building and jabbed the heel of his hand into NineSix's clavicle, breaking it.

"Where's Slingshot?"

NineSix leered at him. "He doesn't want to be found."

"Liar." He broke his nose this time. *Come on, lock!* "Where is he?"

Two blinks and he popped halfway down the alley. Tank growled in frustration and pounded after him. The terrorist faced him, feet planted, the locust at his throat in a frozen snarl, and shot one arm forward.

A wall of insects collided with Tank's face.

Locusts battered their bodies against his face like a jet stream, their abdomens bursting on impact. Insect innards squirted into his eyes. Spiny legs filled his mouth. The chariot thunder of wings flooded his ears. He couldn't see, couldn't hear, couldn't breathe.

Asphalt cracked under his knees as he fell, spitting and swiping at his face. The swarm finally passed, and he scrubbed his eyes clear.

NineSix was gone, the alley empty.

# CHAPTER TWENTY

*No, no, no, no.* Tank sprinted to the end of the alley, heart in his throat. He spun, scanning the cross street. No sign of NineSix.

"H, I lost him."

Hopper made a strangled choking noise. "You what?"

Tank winced. "I know. Heading back now."

Hopper met him at the corner. Police cars and ambulances lined the street. Tank didn't see any of the other Abaddon cultists in squad cars or being detained. They must have fled after making sure the frenzy had taken hold of the crowd. The cops were thinning the mob. A pair wrestled a beefy man to the ground and held him while a paramedic injected something into his arm. He slumped, arms going limp, and the EMT set to inspecting the nasty gash on his forehead.

"Sedative?" Tank asked

"Her idea," Hopper said, showing him a text from Elodie relaying Sofia's suggestion. "I didn't tell them that of course, just made a few round-about comments so they came to the same idea on their own. Sofia thinks the pheromones will wear off by themselves, but she's not sure how long it will take, and we can't sit around waiting for them to get too tired to keep beating each other up." Hopper's jaw jutted out, his eyes tight. "Why didn't you grab him at the beginning, Tank? What was with all the chatting? This isn't Storytime. I told you to nab him."

"I—" Tank resisted the urge to back away. Yes, he'd delayed, for Elodie's sake, but Hopper's plan hadn't accounted for NineSix's abilities. "He was a jumper,

H. It wouldn't have mattered *when* I tried to nab him. He would've jumped and everything would've happened the same."

"You should've stuck with the plan," Hopper hissed.

Unsure what else to say, Tank took a step toward the melee in the square. "I better help with cleanup."

"You do that." Hopper poked a finger in his chest. "And make it look good. I have to go do damage control, try to find some way to spin this." Hopper jerked his head at the news crews converging west of the square.

"Hopper, I'm sorry—"

His manager raised a hand to cut him off. "Don't. We'll talk later." He stalked across the street to face the reporters.

Tank watched him go, acid burning like someone had rubbed a tube of IcyHot all over the inside of his chest. Something tapped his back, and he looked over his shoulder to see a skinny man in a white shirt and tie throwing punches at him. Or trying to. Blood dribbled from his nose and bruises darkened both eyes. His face sagged in exhaustion, but his arms kept flailing.

"Come on, buddy." Tank marched him to the paramedic with the syringes. He carried out a seventy-something woman next, who he suspected had broken her hip.

"Will she be ok?" he asked as an EMT strapped the woman to a stretcher.

"If her hip is broken, they'll set it at the hospital, but she's in for a long road. An injury like that is bad even when you're young. And she's not."

Tank swallowed bile and waded back into the fray, concentrating on retrieving whoever looked in the most danger or to be causing the most damage, and dragging them over to be sedated and taken to the hospital. They all aimed kicks and punches at him, two had knives. None of it affected him, but the officers were having a harder time.

And for many of the injured, their lives would never be the same.

His manager swept back into the square like a thundercloud. "Let's go."

Tank looked at the small knot of people still trying to fight. "We aren't done yet."

"The cops can finish up. If you want to get to you-know-where without being followed by some new-to-news-Nancy, hot for a story, we need to go while the cameras are still trained on the fracas here."

Tank gave a reluctant nod. "Ok, H." Near the edge of the square, one of the would-be combatants slipped on something and fell. The object rolled into Tank's foot—an unopened bottle of the vitamin water. The Health Challenge official had been Abaddon. Maybe she was just a plant, but maybe there was more to it. Tank scooped up the bottle and tucked it into his cargo pocket. Sofia could analyze the water back at Elodie's.

They didn't talk on the ride back; Hopper's anger was loud enough on its own. Tank stared out the window, stewing over what NineSix had said about Slingshot.

*He doesn't want to be found.*

Elodie's brother couldn't be part of Abaddon, that made no sense. They had to be lying, trying to confuse and misdirect. Tank scrubbed his eyes, pulled a locust leg out of his hair. NineSix was a terrorist trying to murder millions of people. Of course he was lying.

Faster than they should have—*Hopper must be speeding again*—they pulled into the Fashion Seeker Designs parking lot.

"You're sure no one followed us?" Tank asked.

Hopper arched an eyebrow.

"Right. Sorry."

As soon as they went through the doors, Hopper stormed downstairs. Elodie was pacing the lobby, hugging herself too tight, indentations showing where her fingers gripped her arms.

*Crap.* He'd forgotten she had a transmitter too. She would have heard everything NineSix said.

"Hey." He stopped her pacing, gently prying her fingers loose. "You're gonna bruise yourself."

"NineSix—you don't believe him. Slingshot would never. Sometimes he's reckless, even hot-headed, but he'd never—"

"No. I don't believe what NineSix said. He's lying."

Elodie took a shuddering breath and pulled her shoulders back. "Good. Mr. Strickland, I think, doesn't agree."

"H means well, but I think being in the image business for so long has jaded him. 'Everybody's got an angle' kind of thing, you know?"

"You don't need to defend him, you know. Maybe he needs to choose not to be jaded. Life shouldn't do that to you."

Tank thought of the scars on his back. *Life shouldn't be a lot of things.* He pulled the vitamin water from his cargo pocket. "I did manage to get this. The woman at the booth had a locust tattoo, I think the water might be connected. Can you have Sofia take a look?"

Elodie took the bottle, fingers brushing his. He ached to pull her close and banish the grief on her face, whether as a friend or something more. "El, I'm sorry."

She looked up at him, confused. "For what?"

He cast about, searching for the words. "I didn't find out where they're holding your brother. And all those people ... I don't know, maybe I should have listened to Hopper. He told me to nab NineSix at the beginning and I didn't but—"

She took his face in her hands. "Tank, I was listening the whole time. If you'd done what Hopper said and tried to grab NineSix at the beginning, he would've jumped. Everything would have been the same."

"That's what I tried to tell Hopper." An odd sensation swept over Tank. *Validation. This is what validation feels like.* Elodie understood what had happened. Why couldn't Hopper?

"And thanks for bringing this in." She held up the water bottle. "I'll get it to Sof. You should go have a break. I'm having dinner sent to your room in case you're hungry."

"Thanks." He didn't know if he'd be able to eat, but the gesture warmed him. She squeezed his hand and headed upstairs.

Hopper ambushed him as soon as he reached his room, shoving his phone in Tank's face. "Look at these." News clips played interviews with eyewitnesses to Container Park.

"My aunt went over for the Friday concert. She's in the hospital with fractured ribs and a concussion."

"I was looking out my hotel room." A young man pointed up to a second story window. "And people started freaking out. Like they just went crazy or something."

"After that fire yesterday, I was hoping that Tank guy was going to help until Slingshot gets found. But he wasn't a whole lot of help here." The interviewee turned away from the camera, disgust on his face.

"How about that last one, huh?" Hopper bit the words off, his sarcasm slicing into Tank as deeply as any knife in high school. "What's gotten into you, Tank? You used to be so easy to work with. You listened, you did what I said." Hopper paced, gesticulating. "Now you're all over the place. Dating apps, comic books, leaving your ringer on, running all over the city." He threw his hands in the air. "Why didn't you follow the plan? What were you waiting for?"

The support he'd felt from Elodie evaporated under Hopper's wrath. He'd already explained his reasoning to Hopper, and yet his manager was berating him with the same questions. Tank sank onto the bed, forgetting to check his bulk. The frame cracked and the mattress sagged. "I didn't want people to get hurt."

"Well people got hurt anyway, didn't they?" Hopper glared for a moment, then sighed and plopped onto the bed next to him. "You gotta listen to me, big guy. Follow the plan."

Tank rubbed at his throat, willing the acid to subside. He nodded, tried to agree, but couldn't speak. Follow the plan and he'd get to help people. It should be simple, but still the words wouldn't come.

Voice softer, Hopper patted his shoulder. "Get changed and see if you can eat. I think one of Elodie's girls picked up more yogurt today if that's better."

"Ok." Tank barely heard his own voice.

The door shut behind Hopper, and Tank dropped his head in hands, Hopper's demands and Elodie's advice battling in his brain.

*Follow the plan.*

*Choose your own path.*

The food smelled amazing. Seared and sizzling, the aroma of fajitas filled the room.

Tank couldn't eat it.

He replaced the cover. Still, his years of scraping by before signing with Hopper wouldn't allow him to waste it, and he left it in the staff lounge with one of Elodie's employees before escaping to the shower.

The scalding water helped drown out the heat in his belly. Steam soothed his throat and calmed his breathing. A large print of a beach scene hung on the wall of the bathroom. Tank tried to picture himself digging his toes into the hot sand, far from PR concerns, Hopper's criticism or Abaddon.

He failed. That picture—one free of responsibilities—wouldn't materialize. He switched the water off, the immediate drop in temperature raising goosebumps. These were his responsibilities. He'd taken them on, knowingly, willingly, to help others. To be the shield he wished he'd had. A shield was not allowed to crack. A shield was certainly not allowed to take a vacation.

In his room, he found another set of clothes on his bed and wondered again how Elodie had found time to make them. A note lay on top of the green tee and jeans.

*Thanks for trying,*

*El*

He traced the letters, smiling at the thought of her leaving him another present.

*Knock it off.* He cut off the smile, fisting his hands. Part of Elodie wishing she'd met him first was not *all* of Elodie wishing she'd met him first, and the fact remained that she hadn't met him first. *You gotta get your feelings under control.* He opened BlindDate.

*Hey, it's late, but I had a minute and thought I'd send a hello for you to find in the morning. So, hello! Today was ...* He paused, fumbling for a way to describe recent events that was truthful but nonspecific ... *brutal. Who knew librarian conferences could be so tough ha ha. When you get this, send me your favorite joke. I could use a laugh.*

He slipped into the new clothes on his bed, hoping for a message back in the morning, but the phone buzzed before he sat down. Voices—Elodie and Leona— drifted down the hallway. Tank took one involuntary step toward her voice but then gritted his teeth and made himself turn back to his room to read the message.

*Hello yourself. I'm sorry your day was so hard but glad I didn't have to wait till morning to find this : ) I'm working late, so that tells you about my day.*

For half a second Tank worried she'd mention something about Container Park—she lived here, she must have seen the news—but her next message said nothing about it.

*For my favorite joke, you have to help with it. Ok, here goes: Ask me if I'm a truck.*

Tank chuckled, thinking he saw where it was going. *Are you a truck?*

*No!* Six laughing faces trailed the word. *That one gets me every time ha ha.*

*LOL. Yeah, that's good.*

*Ok, my turn. Tell me your favorite fairy tale trope.*

Tank hesitated. His favorite fairy tale trope definitely did not fit Hopper's image. But this was Grace he was talking to. She called him Willard, not Tank. And she hadn't thought his favorite picture book was lame.

*Ok, but don't laugh. True Love's Kiss gets me every time. I know it's a little bit silly, but ...* He added a shrug emoji and sent the message.

Grace's answer came quickly. *That's not silly! I wish people didn't look down their nose at the idea of true love. The world is so cynical. But I think the idea that two people are so connected that they can heal each other is beautiful.*

*Wow, yes, exactly.* "It is beautiful," Tank murmured. *Do you have a favorite fairy tale trope?*

*You mean other than True Love's Kiss? ; ) I love it when the characters make something out of virtually nothing, like they grow a whole tree or a ladder out of*

*a knuckle bone or throw a walnut over their shoulder and it turns into a lake or*
*something like that. Always fun. I hope your tomorrow is better.*

*Thanks, yours too. Goodnight.*

*Goodnight xox*

Tank touched his cheek, imagining Grace planting the *X*s there in person.
The same cheek Elodie had kissed earlier.

He slapped the offending cheek. *Oh, I'm in trouble. Soooo much trouble.*
He closed his eyes, inhaling deeply. *Stop thinking about it. It's easy.* Someone
knocked and he opened his eyes.

"You need to come see this," Elodie said, worry lines furrowing her brow.

"What's wrong?" Tank followed her to the staff lounge, pretending he hadn't
just been thinking about her kissing him. Her hair swished as she walked, grazing
the top of her hips. He grimaced. How was he supposed to not think about her
when she was right there, determined and worried and beautiful? How was he
supposed to not think about the fact he had feelings for two different women
when Grace's attempt to cheer him up was still on the screen in his pocket?

In the staff lounge, Hopper, Leona and a knot of Seeker Security personnel
huddled in front of the flat screen, watching the news. Tank leaned against the
back of the couch, Elodie next to him.

"After the bizarre eruption of violence this evening at Container Park, we
received another message from the terrorist group known as Abaddon. Here,
on KTLV Channel 4, is that footage."

The screen flipped to a shot of NineSix. Night desert spread behind him,
and the light flickered and jumped off screen, like he was lit by a campfire. Tank
scanned the terrain behind the terrorist but didn't spot anything identifying.
A low buzz emanated from the video, and he shuddered, the feel of exploding
exoskeletons on his skin too fresh.

"Las Vegas, did you enjoy our little preview this evening?" NineSix spoke
with the same mild tone he'd used at the shopping center. "We even had a guest
star." His tone changed, a sneer rippling his lips. "Tank, we told you in L.A. that
we would no longer tolerate your interference. You failed today. These people
will tear each other apart, consume themselves like the parasites they are." Live

locusts crawled from under his shirt and up his cheek. "Destruction is coming for this city, and the beast is coming for you all. Make your peace and die."

He flicked his fingers, and the insects swarmed the camera lens, like they'd done in the video in Los Angeles. The feed cut off and the news anchors reappeared.

"They need to get another ending to their videos," Leona said, arms folded disapprovingly. "That one's getting old."

"Where do they get all the bugs?" Tank murmured. In the alley, a solid wall of locusts had purposefully crashed into him for a full thirty seconds. No way did NineSix have that many insects hanging out in his pockets waiting to get tossed at somebody. And there'd been no green screen, no tech to create a mirage. He rubbed his face where the locusts' spiky legs had snapped against his skin. That had been no illusion.

"Good question." Leona frowned. "I haven't come up with any working theories yet, so if you have ideas, I'm all ears."

Tank shook his head. "That's the second time they've mentioned a beast. They talked about it in the video in Los Angeles too."

"Probably rhetoric," Hopper said, eyes glued to the screen.

"It appears The Tank has some kind of connection to Abaddon," the news anchor said. Tank turned his attention back to the TV. "Did he bring them down on Las Vegas? We'll chat with an analyst after the break."

His mouth dropped. "Did *I* bring them down?"

Hopper's face went purple. His jaw worked back and forth, hands clenched at his side. Tank made to speak to his manager but thought better of it and shut his mouth.

"You ok, Strickland?" Leona asked.

"Those—they dare—ugh!" He threw his hands up in disgust, shot Tank an I-told-you-so glare, and stomped up the stairs.

Leona whistled. "I guess he doesn't like his clients being abused."

"At least not when someone else does it," Elodie, silent through the newscast, spoke up.

Tank shoved his hands in his pocket and stared after Hopper. "I think he's more mad at me for messing up tonight. He comes across as harsh, but he's not wrong that if people think this is my fault, things'll get a lot harder."

"Tank," Elodie said. "You're defending him again."

He didn't have an answer for that.

Heels clicked on the stairs, and Sofia hurried into the staff lounge waving a stack of papers. "Elodie, it's the water!" The vitamin water bottle stuck out of her lab coat pocket.

"What's the water?" She took the jumble of papers from the doctor. Several pages of chemical formulas and diagrams fluttered to the floor, and Tank crouched to help gather them.

"The missing piece." Sofia brandished the water bottle. "We thought the swarming pheromone in the powder couldn't affect humans—we aren't locusts, after all."

When she ushered them to the couch, Elodie sat next to Tank. A faint scent of plumeria lingered in her hair. Tank inched to the side—*Red hearts, favorite jokes*— but two more Seeker Security women squished onto the couch, listening to the discussion, and Elodie scooted closer to him.

"But I analyzed the water Tank brought back—thank you for that, by the way—and there's some kind of nanotech catalyst *in* the water." Sofia thunked the bottle onto the coffee table. "The nanites act like a virus, altering human DNA to be susceptible to the pheromone. You have to ingest the nanites for the pheromones to work on you. Which explains why neither Tank nor the terrorists tonight were affected by the release of the powder."

Tank worked to wrap his brain around the science. Sci-fi had never really been his thing, and Elodie's thigh pressing against his wasn't helping his concentration. "How long do you think it takes the nanites to do their job? Seems like altering DNA would take a bit."

"It does take a minute, but even so, these are fast. I'd say about twelve hours. No more than twenty-four." Sofia twisted her hair into a bun and jammed a pencil through it.

"What about all the folks from tonight?" he asked. "They only drank the water a few minutes before Abaddon sprayed the powder."

"True. But they've been handing out that 'vitamin water' downtown all week."

"It's been in hotel lobbies too." Leona sat in the chair opposite, heel bouncing.

"Ms. Seeker?" A petite blond girl leaning against the bar raised her hand uncertainly. She couldn't have been over seventeen, and Tank wondered what had happened in her life to make her one of Elodie's Lost Girls.

"You can call me Elodie, Claire, remember?" Elodie smiled gently at her.

Claire swallowed. "It's just, I was wondering, if it takes that long for the nanites to work, why were they still handing out water bottles at the park? Anyone drinking it for the first time—there wouldn't have been time for the nanites to kick in for the fight. The pheromone wouldn't have affected them, so why bother?"

"No, it wouldn't have," Elodie said. "But it will by tomorrow."

"A preview," Tank whispered, echoing NineSix's words in the video. His guts twisted in a spiky knot. "He said in twenty-four hours the city will be a battlefield."

Everyone was silent, staring at the deceptively innocuous water bottle on the coffee table.

Leona shoved out of her chair and paced, fingers tapping against her thigh. "If Container Park was the preview, their test run, they'll be trying to get the nanites to the whole city for the main event."

"They can't count on everyone drinking the vitamin water though," Tank said. "There are too many people in the city to get the water bottles to. It worked for tonight, because they were concentrating on the downtown area where they've been handing the stuff out for days, but it wouldn't work on a larger scale. They'd never get the nanites into enough people."

Leona shrugged. "So, the evil buggers have a two-part job. Get the nanites in the city water and deliver the pheromone."

"The pheromones won't be the obstacle," Sofia said. "NineZero was going to put it through the air duct at the school. They could have teams all over like that. Schools, grocery stores, casinos, malls. Anywhere with an HVAC system. And they could easily station people at high-traffic areas with powder bombs like the one they used tonight."

"Leaving the nanites." Leona nodded at the water bottle.

Tank heaved himself off the couch. Pacing didn't help, but sitting still was worse. "Where does Las Vegas get its water?"

"Hoover Dam," Elodie said. "Although I admit I don't know anything much about the path the water takes from there to here." She clutched her hands in her lap, back straight. The sight jarred Tank. Usually her movements flowed, free, easy. Her stillness made him fidget more. He needed to fix this. Stop Abaddon and get Elodie her brother back so she could flow again.

"I'll look into it." Leona took the stairs two at a time.

Claire timidly raised her hand again. "My brother works at the water treatment plant. We could ask him some questions. Maybe he could get us in if we need to go there?"

Elodie rose and took Claire's hand. "That would be very helpful, thank you, Claire. Go catch up to Leona and call him."

At Leona's name, Claire's eyes went wide, and Elodie leaned into whisper, "She won't bite, I promise."

The girl didn't look convinced, but she trotted up the stairs.

"Abaddon won't have to hit every single person in the city with the pheromones." Sofia took Leona's place, pacing in front of the TV. "Those affected will attack anyone, including those who didn't get the pheromones. We need to know how long the swarming behavior lasts." She looked at Tank. "Can you and Mr. Strickland check in with the hospital and find out if the pheromone is still in the victim's systems?"

Tank nodded but didn't move for the stairs. Hopper hadn't returned yet, and Tank didn't want to face him. But they needed to know how long the violence might last if they failed to stop it. *No. If I fail to stop it.* This was his job. This was what he'd come to Vegas to do. And he couldn't fail. "Yeah, I'll go talk to him now."

He found Hopper in the parking lot yelling into his phone, his irate gestures triggering the floodlight's motion sensor. The front door was unlocked. Leona must not have activated the security system's night protocols yet, what with all the people still here. Tank slipped through the door and gave Hopper a tentative wave.

"...NOT what we—" Hopper cut off when he saw him. "I'll call you back."

"Sorry to interrupt." Tank planted his feet and grasped his hands behind his back to keep from fidgeting under his manager's glare. "Sofia is wondering if we can talk to the hospital or the police or something and find out how long it's taking for the pheromone to wear off. We think we know what Abaddon is planning."

Hopper listened, heaving chest slowly returning to a normal rhythm, as Tank filled him in. "Good. I'll call them and let her know. I'm glad to see you're working on this. If we get on top of it now and cut them off, we can turn this fiasco around. But do you see now? Why I tell you what I tell you? The public, the media, they're fickle. They'll turn on you the first time something isn't perfect."

"Yeah, I see, H. And I get you were trying to protect me. You've done good by me. You plucked me out of nobody-ville, you believed in me, poured so much into getting my career going, but I—" He stopped, the words stuck in his throat. He was a teenager again, trying to confront his uncle.

*I need you to help change the bandages on my back. I need your help with school. I need you to stop calling me a dumb oaf. I need you to be an uncle.*

He cleared his throat, reset his stance. He hadn't been a teenager for years. He wasn't numb. He had strength. No one could hurt his body. He had the power to protect people. And if Elodie was right, maybe he could protect them on his own terms.

*Confidence. Steady voice. You taught me that, H.* "I want to have a say in that career. I want to have a say in my persona and how people perceive me. I want them to see it's possible to be strong *and* gentle. I want to be a shield, not a bulldozer."

Hopper stared at him, jaw hard and eyes stony. "You do."

"Y-yes." Tank broke eye contact.

"Look at this." Hopper jabbed at his phone and held it in front of Tank's face. "Look familiar?"

"It's the Strickland Talent Management application form on your website." He'd filled it out himself a little over two years ago, intentions pure and stars in his eyes.

Hopper stabbed at the screen again. "Yup. And these are all the applications that have come in. This month." He scrolled the page. Scrolled again. The list kept going. "Eighty-three, in case you're wondering. Eighty-three other people with superpowers, all wanting to do what you do. And they want me to help them do it, because I've got the license and the know-how to make it happen. But L.A. can't have more than one hero at a time, can it?"

Tank fought for words. Ice flooded his veins. Flames erupted in his stomach. "Are ... are you thinking of dropping me, H?"

Hopper stowed his phone. "Just remember this the next time you don't like what I've built for you." He stomped inside.

Tank stayed in the parking lot, motionless, staring at the closed door until the floodlights ticked off and darkness stole around him.

# CHAPTER TWENTY-ONE

C louds swept across the sky, eating the stars. Tank watched them disappear, watched the clouds cover the moon. They were still there, the stars and the moon, behind the clouds. Not erased but not seen.

Hopper's threat crawled across his skin, spiky as locust legs. Willard would have to go, be covered like the moon. He needed to help people. Whatever the reason behind humans suddenly gaining superpowers—cosmic plan or biological accident—protecting people who needed it was his reason for using those powers. But legally, he couldn't do it on his own, he needed to work through Hopper's license. At least until after Abaddon. If he left this job now, on bad terms with Hopper, no other manager would touch him with a ten-foot pole. No one wanted a client who was "difficult to work with." But if he proved himself here, perhaps he could apply to a different manager, in a different city. One who would let him uncover Willard.

The front door opened, triggering the motion sensors. Light flooded the parking lot, and Elodie ran to him.

"Tank, what are you doing out here?"

He set aside thoughts of a new manager. For now, he was stuck. "Nothing, sorry. Hopper said he'd call the hospital."

"Good. Claire's brother said the supervisor sent nearly everyone on the night staff home. It looks like Abaddon's going to hit it tonight, so we need to get out there fast. We can pick him up on the way, and he can get us in." She took his hand to pull him inside, but he didn't move.

She'd run out without a jacket, her arms bare. The light shone behind her, painting shadows and stripes on her skin. He couldn't tell if it was a trick of the light or if Elodie really had left bruises on her arms. Even if she hadn't hurt herself, she was breakable. Everyone was. Except him. And if he was going to cover up Willard, he might as well get it over with. Willard wasn't needed at the water treatment plant. The Tank was.

"Us?" He shook his head. "You don't need to go. And I don't need someone to sneak me in."

She hugged herself as the wind picked up. "It's always better to have a team."

"Elodie, I can do this. Or The Tank can do this. I don't need anyone else to come."

Her eyes narrowed, and she stepped closer. "That's Hopper talking. What did he say to you?"

"He didn't—"

"Yes, he did. What did he say?"

The clouds threw raindrops, fat and thick. They bounced off the asphalt and torpedoed the field, the smell a fight between ozone and dust. The exterior lights made it impossible to see into the upper windows, but Tank imagined he could feel Hopper scowling at him, hear his constant reprimand—*Be The Tank!* But Elodie waited for his answer, no hint on her face that she thought Tank wouldn't give her one.

"I brought up some of my own terms, like you talked about, and he threatened to cut me off. Drop me as a client."

"He what?" Elodie's voice raised an octave. She reached up to take his face in her hands and made him look at her. "That's ridiculous. You know that, right?"

Tank didn't say anything. He didn't know that. What he did know was that Elodie's hands were holding his face, her eyes were locked with his, and her body was close enough to feel her warmth. He knew, right then, that whatever Hopper thought, Elodie believed in him. And he knew he'd made her a promise.

He wrapped her hands in his. She didn't pull back. The rain came in earnest, subduing the desert's protests, and she shivered. His heart pounded, and his nerves jolted through his limbs like electricity.

But his stomach was quiet.

Tank wrapped both arms around her and drew her close, a shield against the storm. Elodie sighed and melted closer. Neither moved as the clouds spilled over them.

"You're right," he whispered. "A team is better. But tonight, the fewer people there, the better. I can fight Abaddon better if I don't have to worry about other people getting hurt. But if it's like this afternoon ..."

She raised her head. "I understand. But let's use the transmitters again."

He nodded. "Good idea. Then if I get anything out of them about your brother, you'll find it out with me."

She blew out a breath and laid her head back on his chest. His hand covered the whole of her lower back. She fit in the crook of his arm. Something shifted inside him, resistance falling away. Elodie said the world was full of possibilities. Maybe something would have been possible with Grace, if Tank had been able to get to know her in person. But Elodie *was* here in person. He couldn't help how he felt anymore, and he didn't want to. At least this was one decision Hopper would approve of.

"El?"

"Yes?"

He swallowed. *Steady voice.* "When I get back, could we pretend you did meet me first?"

She rose up on tiptoe and pressed soft lips to his cheek. "I'd like that."

The road was deserted. The water treatment plant lay east of the city, west of Lake Mead. Tank had checked the map before leaving, studying the layout of the plant. There was nothing else out here, which was a relief. Fewer potential casualties. He fidgeted with the pair of night vision googles Leona had given him as protection against more locust swarms while Hopper drove.

"It's too short notice to get a warrant," Hopper said. "The cops can't come out unless there's something going on, so as soon as you know Abaddon is there, you pass me the word." He hadn't said anything about his earlier tirade. Tank didn't bring it up either.

"I'll let you know the second I find something." He said it as much for Elodie's benefit as Hopper's. Close to fifty miles separated Fashion Seeker Designs and the Alfred Merritt Smith Water Treatment plant, but Elodie's transmitter carried across the distance easily.

They rounded a low hill, and a building complex lit up the distance. Hopper turned left down another empty road. When they reached a locked gate, he pulled off onto the dirt shoulder. Tank pushed open his door to proceed alone on foot, but Hopper grabbed his elbow.

"I don't have to tell you that Las Vegas needs these psychos stopped. But they don't need Willard, they need The Tank. This isn't Storytime. No stopping to listen, no coddling these guys, don't try to get them to talk, you hear me? Follow the plan, take them all down. Be The Tank." He waved his phone, with its multitudes of hero applications, in the air with his other hand. "And remember what I said." He released Tank's arm and stared at the gate.

"Yes, H." Tank shoved out of the car. The lives of an entire city were on the line. *And, oh yeah, let's add my career too, just for fun. No pressure.*

The plant proper lay a ways back from the fence. Figuring it would make less noise than peeling back the metal, he hopped the gate and settled into a quick jog. A couple of admin buildings cropped up on his left, but nothing stirred, and he saw no one.

Claire's brother had said Abaddon would have to add the nanites to the clear well, near the end of the treatment process—any earlier and they might be filtered out—so Tank had to navigate through the structures and machinery of the plant to reach it.

Still scanning, he passed an open basin. A woman with a tattoo on her forearm leapt from behind it and fired a pistol.

*A pistol? Really?* The bullet pinged off his chest. It took only seconds for him to carefully knock her out and lay her on the ground. Next to the locust on her arm was tattooed 9-0.

"Hopper," he spoke to the transmitter under his collar. "Looks like they're here. This one is another NineZero."

"Noted. I'll call the cops in. Keep going."

Tank hesitated, watching the woman. He adjusted her position to be more comfortable, double checking she was still breathing easily. Frizzy red hair haloed her face, smooth and devoid of violence in her unconscious state. He wondered what her story was, who she was before joining a cult and trading her name for a number. Hopper's warning brought him out of his musings. *No time for stories.*

An array of open pools lay ahead. Long buildings ran the length of the facility between him and his objective. According to the satellite images, the clear well should be to the left of the array.

Someone charged from behind a storage shed. One hit and the man slumped to the ground.

Tank huffed. So far he'd encountered just two woefully unprepared people. If this was Abaddon' big plan, where was everyone?

"Tank?" Hopper's voice interrupted his thoughts. "Everything ok?"

"Yeah, H. All good." He hurried along a path that cut between the buildings, the pumps and machinery muffling his footsteps. "Flocculation basin, filters ..." He identified the structures, picturing the plant map in his head. A cement reservoir loomed ahead. "Clear well."

Shadowy figures scurried on the top of the clear well, each hefting a bulky shape. One of them pried open a square shape from the roof. The access hatch.

"Hey!" Tank sprinted and launched onto the clear well, knocking two people off their feet. Another ripped the lid off a bucket and leaned over the hatch. Tank dove. The container clattered and spilled as he collided with it.

Something shattered across his back. He rolled, sprang to his feet and found the same kid from Container Park who'd been wearing the Slingshot T-shirt, crouched in a fighting stance, a broken baseball bat in his hands.

Baseball bats? Pistols? Abaddon knew who he was, they knew his abilities. Why arm their foot soldiers with useless weapons? Why send foot soldiers at all? Where was NineSix?

"Where's your boss, kid?"

T-shirt Boy's eyes flicked behind Tank. He threw a quick glance but saw no one. Two other cultists took advantage of the pause to rush the hatch, open buckets in hand. Tank beat them there, kicked the hatch closed, tore the buckets from their fingers and tossed them to the ground below. The nanite-laced water glugged harmlessly onto the pavement.

T-shirt jumped on Tank's back, arms flailing. The other two launched equally pointless attacks, and a minute later, Tank was stowing a roll of duct tape back in his cargo pocket, the three Abaddon kids—they were all teenagers—taped up in a neat bundle.

Tank knelt in front of T-shirt Boy. This made no sense. If tainting the water supply with nanites was Abaddon's objective, this was a pathetic attempt. There had to be more. "Tell me where the guys in charge are. You're just kids. If you cooperate, I can talk to the cops. Get them to go easy on you."

T-shirt blinked. Swallowed. Shook his head violently.

"Tank," Hopper said in his ear. "What's going on? I want to hear less talking and more punching."

"They're just teenagers, H. I'm trying to find out where the real bad guys are."

"Well, find out fast. The cops are on their way. The last thing you need is *Tank harasses group of kids* on the news."

Tank groaned in frustration and turned back to T-shirt. "Let's try something easier. How many more of you are there?"

"Just one," a voice called.

Something whizzed past Tank's neck and shot the transmitter off his collar. Another pebble zinged his ear, knocking out the speaker, and flew back out, like a horizontal yo-yo. The newcomer stood on the edge of the clear well roof, nonchalantly tossing a small rock up and down in one hand. He stared Tank down with eyes that looked too familiar. Eyes that looked like Elodie's.

Tank took a step forward in disbelief. "Slingshot?"

The other hero looked him up and down. "I thought you'd be bigger." He shrugged. "Oh well. Tag!" He made a flicking motion with his free hand, and the rock he'd been juggling ricocheted off Tank's cheek. Slingshot catapulted himself to the adjacent roof, but not before Tank caught a glimpse of a locust tattoo snarling from the inside of his forearm.

His heart dropped through his boots and crawled up his throat at the same time.

This was wrong. All wrong. Slingshot had an Abaddon tattoo. Elodie's *brother* had an Abaddon tattoo. The "missing" superhero was halfway across the other roof before Tank managed to leave his shock behind and pursue.

His stride ate Slingshot's head start, and he tackled him, caging his arms around him to cushion the blow. They rolled to a stop, Tank pinning both of Slingshot's wrists above his head and pressing a knee into his chest to keep him from wriggling free.

"What do you think you're doing?" He heard the confusion in his own voice, the hurt on Elodie's behalf.

"I'm—"

Shouts broke out from the clear well roof, and Slingshot snapped his head toward the voices. The kids had sliced through the duct tape, laid a plank across the gap and were storming across. Two of them threw themselves on top of Tank.

"What does it look like?" Slingshot quipped. "Trying to dump nanites in the clear well. I assumed you'd already figured that out, since you're here."

Tank transferred Slingshot's wrists to one hand and dragged him to his feet. The two would-be attackers slid off his back with a thump. Tank glared at them.

"Don't you have homework you should be doing?"

Slingshot twisted in a move meant to break the wrist hold. Tank arched an eyebrow. "Really? You were the one who told El to bring me to Vegas. I assumed you'd know what you were dealing with." He echoed Slingshot's sarcasm, blood pumping faster through his veins.

Slingshot smirked and twitched his mouth side to side. Bits of roof gravel careened into Tank's goggles, splintering the plastic into a web of cracks and obscuring his vision. He ripped them off and jerked Slingshot closer to growl in his face. "You weren't kidnapped. You're a traitor."

Slingshot cut his eyes to his younger counterparts. "Seems that way, doesn't it?" He jerked his head sideways, and a debris-filled mini tornado shot straight at them. Dirt and gravel stung Tank's eyes. Out of reflex, he dropped his hold on Slingshot to cover his face. He shook his head, scrubbing at his eyes. Tears washed the grit out, turning the night scene to a drippy watercolor picture. Slingshot was half a roof away, firing a steady stream of rocks and bits of asphalt at Tank.

T-shirt Boy jumped in Tank's path, brandishing the broken end of the bat. Tank knocked it aside, scruffed the boy like a naughty puppy and set him aside. "Quit it. The grown-ups are talking."

Back on the clear well roof, Slingshot had the hatch open, throwing glances at his companions. Tank ran and launched himself over the gap, heart breaking and raging at the same time.

Elodie had called Tank on it when he'd tried to defend Hopper, saying the business had made him cynical, and he'd wanted to believe it when she'd said cynical was a choice. He didn't want Hopper to be right.

But here was a hero gone rogue, working to destroy the very people he was supposed to defend.

The cement of the roof cracked under his feet as he landed. He dove and rolled Slingshot a second time.

"People have been searching for you," Tank shouted. "Worried about you!"

"I'm doing this for them!" Slingshot struggled, and Tank tightened his grip.

"You joined a terrorist cult bent on wiping out humanity 'for them'? Tell me how on earth that works. You're supposed to be a good guy!" His pulse pounded. This man was betraying his city and hurting Elodie. The pain on her face each time she talked about her brother seared through Tank. "Your sister is distraught! She is *grieving* you."

"She'll be fine once this is all over. I'll expl—"

"Your new pals tried to burn her business down." Tank's mouth twisted in rage.

Slingshot stopped struggling, his face paling. "They were supposed to leave her alone."

"Well, they didn't." Tank's fist trembled from the urge to pummel Slingshot into the gravel.

"Where's the last package?" T-shirt Boy called from the clear well roof.

"You have to let me go," Slingshot hissed. "I've got to get that package in the water, so I don't blow my cover. No one's gonna get hurt."

"Ho-ho!" Tank feigned amusement. "So now you're undercover? If you were undercover, now would be the perfect time to flip, don't you think? And I *saw* people get hurt. All those people at Container Park, so don't you tell me no one's going to get hurt!"

Slingshot shook his head, flipping his gaze between Tank and T-shirt Boy. "Listen to me you big oaf—"

Tank hit him, punctuating his words—"I'm. Not. An. Oaf."—before pinning him again. Even with rage snaking through his veins, he held back, for El's sake, not breaking anything.

Slingshot glared at him, his cheek starting to swell. "I switched—"

"Sides," Tank finished. "That's obvious. If you're really undercover, prove you're still a hero. Tell me where Abaddon's holed up."

"Dude!" T-shirt hopped up and down, waving his arms like he expected Slingshot to pass him a football. "Where is it?"

Slingshot shot Tank a desperate look. "Listen, there's more than tonight. Catch!" He flicked one finger, and dozens of fist-sized rocks tied to a bundle soared up to the roof. T-shirt snatched it out of the air and sprinted for the hatch.

Growling, Tank yanked Slingshot up and launched the both of them at the teenager. All three tumbled off the roof, Tank breaking their fall. No way was he letting them break their necks and get out of being held responsible. T-shirt scrambled up against the wall, eyes wild.

Tank pointed a finger at him. "Stay." He turned back to Slingshot. Sirens sounded in the distance. "Cops'll be here any minute. Care to flip now, Mr. Undercover?" Sarcasm soured his words, and he hated how much he sounded like Hopper. But not as much as he hated how crushed Elodie was going to be.

"No." Slingshot's feet slipped and slid on the pavement, trying to run. "You don't know the whole story."

Tank glared at him, Hopper's words pounding in his head.

*This isn't Storytime. No stopping to listen, no coddling.*

He remembered his promise to Elodie that whoever was responsible for Slingshot's disappearance—for her pain—would be behind bars. He remembered the old woman at Container Park with the broken pelvis, and all the other victims whose lives would never be the same.

Tank had thought he could be both strong and gentle. He thought he could have both. But Hopper had called it all along. Slingshot was responsible for Elodie's pain. And Tank couldn't be both.

*Be The Tank.*

"You're right," he said. "I don't know the whole story. But I'm not here for Storytime."

# CHAPTER TWENTY-TWO

Sirens broke closer, red and blue lights strobing on the walls of the water treatment plant. A pair of cruisers screeched into the open area between buildings, and Hopper and the Point for Las Vegas police got out.

The Point rushed forward, relief on his face. "You found Slingshot?"

Tank clenched his jaw and flipped over Slingshot's arm, revealing the locust tattoo.

"No," the Point whispered. Apparently not all of LVMPD had it out for Slingshot. Tank's heart broke all over again, but he knew it wouldn't be the last time that night. He still had to tell Elodie what her brother had done.

The Point's expression hardened as he motioned two officers to take Slingshot off Tank's hands. "Don't bother being gentle."

Tank jerked his head to the roof. "There are two more up there. And one there." He pointed to T-shirt Boy, laying dazed on the ground. "You'll want this too." He scooped up the bundle tied to Slingshot's rocks from where it had rolled across the asphalt. The buckets had been filled with nanite water, but this package was a round bamboo frame with a thick paper membrane. Some of the paper had torn away, showing a thick bundle of glass vials strapped together and a timer. "Looks like they had a couple different delivery methods."

The chief nodded. "We'll have evidence round it all up."

Slingshot cast a desperate look at Tank. "Tank, this isn't the end of it. You have to—"

The Point cut him off. "You may want to wait till you have a lawyer. And that was the most cliche villain line ever. 'This isn't the end'? Please." He grabbed Slingshot by his shirt collar and marched him to a car.

Hopper whooped and clapped Tank on the back. "You did it, big guy! I'll admit, I was a little worried when Slingshot showed up, but you did it. You stopped them."

Tank looked at his manager, confused. Hopper had been worried? Why? Slingshot's betrayal aside, if anything, this had been too easy. "Pistols and baseball bats and kids," he muttered.

This attempt had been so poorly orchestrated—why hadn't Abaddon planned for the eventuality that he'd figure out their plan? Even if they didn't think he'd be here, this was the hinge point of their plan. Yet they'd sent only a handful of people—most of those teenagers—and Slingshot? Elodie's brother stared at him from the back of a cruiser as it pulled away.

Hopper was still talking. "… news crews lined up outside the gate. We can tell them all about how you stopped Abaddon on the way out."

Tank ripped his gaze away from the fallen hero. "I don't think that's a good idea, H."

"What are you talking about? You just saved the city. People need to know."

Tank almost shuffled his feet. *No, you were being exactly what Hopper wants you to be, don't backslide.* "But I don't think we're done. A couple of kids with baseball bats? There were more of them at Container Park, and NineSix wasn't even here. The rest of Abaddon is still out there, including whoever's in charge."

Hopper waved away his protests. "Slingshot was probably the leader. It makes perfect sense. He's got powers; he's got experience. And he wouldn't be the first hero to turn traitor. That's part of why they made the AVA in the first place. Now that he's in custody, the cops'll get him to talk, and we'll track down the rest of them, including NineSix."

"There's gotta be more," Tank said, aware he was echoing Slingshot's words.

"Tank, there's no more. Slingshot flipped sides, and you caught him. You stopped Abaddon." Hopper leveled his gaze at him. "And you need this win, remember? Come on. The cameras are waiting."

"Yeah, he flipped sides ..." Nausea swamped him, a cold sweat breaking across his forehead. Slingshot had turned villain, and Tank had to tell Elodie. "Hopper, I can't. I can't talk to the reporters tonight."

His manager sighed and scrubbed his face but shrugged. "Alright. You stopped an evil terrorist band from sending Las Vegas into full-Purge mode, I'll cut you some slack. I'll talk. You just stand there and look imposing."

*Imposing?* The word ran through his thoughts on a loop as he followed Hopper to the main gate. News vans and cameras and microphones filled the space like a roadblock. Hopper stepped up to take questions, and Tank planted his feet beside his manager, arms folded across his chest, the word still blaring in his head like a siren.

*Imposing.*

He ran through a thesaurus list for the term. Formidable. Awe-inspiring. Threatening. Scary. Intimidating, Powerful. Striking. Impressive. Commanding.

A cameraman met his gaze. And immediately stepped back. *That thesaurus list is how these people see me right now.*

They saw his strength, his physical prowess. And most of all, they saw the persona Hopper had crafted. The Tank—a badass who trampled whatever was in his way. All in the name of helping people weaker than him, of course.

The persona hung on Tank like a cape, while the cyclops eyes of the cameras immortalized the image. He'd resisted putting on that cape for so long, but tonight, in his fury at the pain Slingshot caused, he'd donned it completely. It chafed at his neck and tangled in his legs, but he'd worn it like Hopper wanted, and if his manager was right, he'd broken the backbone of Abaddon. The remnants would be swept up and disposed of, and people would be safe. They'd won.

The Tank had won.

He found the same respect and awe on the faces in the crowd as the cameraman had shown when he involuntarily retreated from Tank's gaze. A small part of him thrilled. If he had been capable of commanding this kind of respect back in high school, his life would have been vastly different.

He exhaled quietly, remembering toddler faces at Storytime and the smell of well-loved books. Maybe his life would have been too different. Maybe Elodie wouldn't have called him a cinnamon roll like it was a good thing.

His gut clenched. Yes, tonight he had been The Tank, and Abaddon was nearly finished. *But El's going to be heartbroken.*

It was all so unfair. He'd kept his promise—the person responsible for Slingshot's "disappearance" was going to prison. But how could Slingshot do this to Elodie? Bad enough he'd betrayed the people and city he claimed to love, but how could he do this to his own *sister*? And then have the gall to act upset that Abaddon had tried to burn Fashion Seeker to the ground. Tank had no siblings, had no experience with that kind of bond, but he could imagine. He was grateful Slingshot had shot out the transmitter, so El hadn't heard it in real time. At least now she'd learn it from Tank. He could break it to her gently, explain everything that happened.

"Is it true that The Tank captured Slingshot tonight?" one of the reporters asked. "That he was behind Abaddon?"

Panic rippled through him. What if El was watching the news? He shot a warning look at Hopper, but his manager wasn't paying attention.

"Yes." Hopper adopted a mournful expression. "I'm afraid Las Vegas' beloved Slingshot was not the hero he pretended to be."

Tank's heart sank like the Titanic. He wanted to smash every last camera. She couldn't find out like this.

"Thank you, everyone, for your support." The microphone squealed as he grabbed it away from Hopper. "But we need to go, no more questions at this time." He tossed the mic down and cut a path through the crowd to the car, hoping Hopper would follow him for once.

"What are you doing?" Hopper hissed in his ear. He still had his media smile plastered on his face.

"Just get in the car." He snatched the keys out of Hopper's jacket pocket and slid in the driver's seat. Hopper managed to keep his grin on until he was in the passenger seat, but his shock was visible in the tense set of his shoulders.

Tank broke his hard and fast rule of no texting and driving to send Elodie a message.

*El, transmitter got damaged. I'm ok. Please don't watch the news. Need to tell you about it myself.*

"What is wrong with you?" Hopper dropped his smile as soon as the news vans were out of sight. "That press conference was the start of your future in this city—of expanding your reach from L.A. to here."

Tank gripped the wheel too tightly, and it started to buckle under his fingers. Maybe Hopper didn't know Slingshot was Elodie's brother, but he didn't have to sound so smug that he'd gone rogue. "You wanted me to be The Tank. I was. I took charge. Or don't you like it when I'm The Tank with you?" He dropped the question like a gauntlet.

Hopper's eyes bugged, and his face purpled.

"Besides," Tank added the truth. He didn't really want to fight with Hopper right now. "I need to get back to El."

"Is that what this is about?" Hopper sank back in his seat, color returning to normal. "Fine. I told you she was good for you. But talk to me first next time. We're supposed to be a team."

"Yeah, sure, H," Tank gave his rote answer and hit the accelerator.

Hopper nodded. Sniffed. Adjusted his seat belt. "I'm glad to see you finally employing my strategies, just make sure you remember who made you The Tank."

Tank glanced at his phone, devoid of any response from Elodie. "How could I forget?"

Tank scrambled out of the car to find Leona waiting at the front door. El still hadn't texted back.

"Thanks, Leona," Tank said. She stared at him, eyes like granite. When he tried to enter, she stepped back only one pace, making him squeeze past her.

"Where's El?" he stuttered. "I have to talk to her."

"*Ms. Seeker* is busy dealing with a family matter."

"No, Leona, you don't understand. Was she watching the news? Where is she?" He sprinted to the basement without waiting for an answer. A knot of Seeker Security women were gathered around the TV, the news blaring.

"As word spreads of Abaddon's defeat, crowds are gathering downtown to celebrate. And it looks like Vegas has a new hero!" Masses of people churned behind the anchorwoman, waving signs with Tank's name on them like flags. Other signs bore Slingshot's name, crossed out with harsh red Xs.

Clair turned to him, hurt plain on her face. Elodie wasn't with the group, and he took the stairs four at a time. Her workshop and the library were empty. The conference room was dark. Finally, voices reached him from the med-wing lobby. It sounded like the same anchorwoman.

"No," he groaned. The door was locked. He knocked, barely resisting the urge to punch it down. "Elodie? El, it's me, are you in there?" The door dented under his fist, and he paused. *Stupid, Tank, stupid.* He should have texted her sooner, before the press conference. Why hadn't he thought of that? She was in there, devastated, and it was his fault. He knocked again. "El, I didn't want you to find out this way, I'm sorry. I left as soon as they brought it up."

The handle turned, and he backed up. Sofia slipped into the hallway, locking the door behind her.

"Sofia, please I need to talk to her. I need to explain what happened."

She glared at him. "You should leave."

He blinked, shocked. "No, I can't leave. I need to help her." Elodie needed comfort. She needed support. She needed a shield from the pain her brother had inflicted on her. It would've been difficult enough hearing what really happened straight from him, but finding out second hand from the news, with no details or explanation, like it had nothing to do with her? Like she had no relation to Slingshot? And who knew what kind of spin the media was putting on it. As Hopper constantly reminded him, there was nothing the evening news liked better than a fall from grace.

He tried to move around Sofia, but she pushed against his chest. "You. Should. Leave."

The Willard part of him wanted to retreat under the fire of her stare, but all he could think was that Elodie was hurting.

"No." He moved Sofia gently to the side and broke the doorknob. He'd buy her a new one later.

"Elodie?"

She hunched in front of a computer screen, her back to him, hair gathered in a messy knot, a fuzzy blanket around her shoulders. In the dim light of the lobby, Slingshot's face glowed bright onscreen, showing through the back window of a cop car as it drove away from the water treatment plant. She scrubbed the video back ten seconds and watched his face again. Scrubbed it again, watched again.

"El," he whispered. "I'm so sorry. I didn't want you to find out this way."

She laughed darkly but didn't turn to face him. "Yes, I got your text. I imagine you wanted to tell me yourself."

"Of course I did. You shouldn't have to—"

"Why?" She cut him off. "Why tell me yourself? So you could spin it like your boss taught you to?"

He froze like she'd slapped him. "N-no. I knew it would hurt you. I wanted to—"

"You knew it would hurt me if you arrested my brother, but you did it anyway." She did turn then, throwing off the blanket.

His heart spasmed at the grief on her face. "I didn't want to. But I had to, El. He was working for Abaddon. He was going to hurt people."

"How do you know? What if he was there to help? What if he knew something you didn't, Tank? *You* can charge through obstacles like they're not even there, but other people have to be more subtle. They have to find ways to work around problems."

Tank retreated a step. "Charge through?" he whispered. "You know that's not how I want to operate. But I had to." He swallowed. Charging through was Hopper's strategy, not his. But he'd used it at the plant. "I had to tonight. To stop people from getting hurt. The whole city would be at war otherwise."

"You were supposed to find him, not arrest him!" She squeezed her arms across her chest, fingers finding the bruises they'd left earlier.

"I was supposed to stop Abaddon." Tank kept his words soft. She was angry, she was hurt, she was mourning. She wouldn't stay mad. She couldn't. Tank had done his job. "And I promised you I'd catch whoever was behind your brother's disappearance. I did both. He wasn't kidnapped. Slingshot was working with them—he had the tattoo. He may even have been in charge, we don't know yet."

"No!" Her face crumpled, tears smearing her mascara. "You threw away the transmitter. What didn't you want me to hear, Tank?" She stalked forward. "Guess what? I heard anyway. That was *my* design, remember? Picks up everything near it!"

"I didn't throw it away, El. Slingshot shot it off my collar and out of my ear." She shook her head in denial.

"And if you were still listening, then you heard what happened."

"Yes!" She threw her hands in the air. "He tried to tell you the truth and you wouldn't listen." She rushed him, hitting his chest, his arms. "You listen to everyone's story—"

"Elodie—" He caught her wrists, worried she'd hurt herself.

"You listened to my story. You should have listened to his!"

"I tried. I gave him a chance to flip, Elodie. I did."

"He's not a terrorist," she screamed, struggling against his hold. "You should have listened!"

"El!" He gathered her close, pressing his cheek against her head. She sobbed into his chest, knees buckling. "I'm so sorry, El. I gave him a chance, but he passed the nanites to one of the others to get in the water. I'm sorry. I'm so sorry. I had to arrest him. He was trying to kill people."

Her sobs cut off with a gasp, and Tank let her go when she wrenched away. "I don't believe it. He wouldn't." Her nostrils flared, and her eyes tightened. She pointed at the door. "Get out."

Tank's mouth dropped. "Elodie, please."

"Get out!"

Her words shot through him, making up for every bullet that had ever failed to pierce him. For the first time in years, he felt vulnerable. Unprotected.

Sofia spoke from the gaping doorway. "We'll send your things. Your associate is already in the car outside."

A lump hardened in Tank's throat. He tried to call Elodie's name once more, but no sound came. She turned her back on him and fled into an office off the lobby.

"I'm sorry," he whispered. The words turned to ash on his tongue.

# CHAPTER TWENTY-THREE

D igital numbers flipped, changing 8:14 a.m. to 8:15 a.m. Tank lay in bad, staring sideways at the clock. He wished it would leave him out of its stupid forward-march through time, but Hopper would be knocking on his door any minute to go talk to LVMPD about mopping up the rest of Abaddon. He wanted to stay burrowed in the covers forever. He missed Lint, missed his reading nook, missed his city—who was Hopper kidding? Vegas wasn't his city—and he missed Elodie.

After she had kicked them out last night, Hopper had found them last-minute hotel rooms. It was Vegas after all. Tank passed the night watching the glowing red numbers on the clock radio, still dressed in the uniform Elodie had created for him.

Hopper maintained rounding up the rest of the terrorists would be a piece of cake, but Tank wasn't so sure. The ease of the water treatment plant events didn't sit well with him. NineSix was still out there. Tank tossed the blankets off and sat up, rubbing his eyes. He'd need new goggles to shield his eyes in case of another locust wave.

He snorted. *He* was supposed to be the shield.

*No.* He thunked his skull against the headboard. *I'm supposed to be The Tank.* He raked his fingers through his hair, biting back the urge to scream. Fat lot of good acting like The Tank had done—Elodie never wanted to see him again. He didn't blame her, but what else could he have done? Abaddon wanted to turn all of Las Vegas into another Container Park, and once they were done with Vegas, they'd go after other cities. He couldn't stand by and let millions of people die or be horribly injured because one woman—*one amazing, genius-level, caring, proactive, beautiful woman, who for some unfathomable reason thought she had feelings for me*—didn't want to believe that her brother was capable of being radicalized. Tank had given Slingshot a chance to come clean, and instead, he'd proved he was on the wrong side.

*Hadn't he?* Looking back, Tank knew he hadn't exactly exercised patience with Slingshot's claim of being undercover. And the disgraced hero's face in the patrol car had been desperate. Not angry, not crazed. Desperate.

"But it's not like I had heaps of time to figure things out," Tank muttered to himself. And Slingshot hadn't switched back to the right side when offered the chance. Why stay undercover? The pheromones and nanites had been Abaddon's plan. It had already been shown to work, so why would they have some other plot waiting in the wings? What "more" could Slingshot have possibly meant? None of it made sense.

True to her word, Sofia had sent their things early that morning. Surprisingly, the copy of *The Black Stallion* from Elodie had been included. Tank thumbed through the pages morosely. Alec had never had to worry about things like this. Never had to determine if Henry Daly was a good guy, or a bad guy.

*Or a good guy pretending to be a bad guy so he could eventually go back to being a good guy.* Tank dropped his head on his knees. Alec definitely never had to worry about being in love with Henry's sister.

"You up?" Hopper knocked on the door.

Tank groaned and heaved himself off the bed, wondering what would happen if he said no. But however Elodie felt, or didn't feel, about him now, NineSix and others were still out there. The Tank had a job to do. He yanked his street clothes over his uniform.

Hopper rubbed his hands together as Tank stepped out the door. "Ready?"

"Close enough."

"I've got good news." Hopper called the elevator. It dipped as Tank stepped in after him. "We've had a sponsorship offer already. Seems cutting the Q&A short last night didn't hurt anything after all. Good move, big guy."

"An offer?" Tank caught his own lost expression in the mirrors lining the elevators. Hopper's reflection was smug. "From whom?"

"Lucky Strike Casino. They want a series of commercials. Something along the lines of 'Thanks to The Tank, we're the safest casino in Vegas' yada, yada. I'm meeting with them later today."

"But I can't take a sponsorship—Vegas isn't my territory."

"Relax. The mayor of Vegas is the casino owner's brother-in-law. You'll get the offer to take over Vegas, it's in the bag."

Tank gaped at his manager. "No. We're not even done cleaning up Abaddon yet, and I don't know about being the face of a casino, H." In truth, he did know. He knew exactly how it would look to Elodie if he arrested her brother and then added Slingshot's region to his own. "We shouldn't even be looking at offers in Vegas at all. How am I supposed to work two cities anyways? I can't be in two places at once. There's already not enough time to handle everything that goes on in L.A."

"You're right."

Hopper had his full-speed-ahead planning face on, and Tank took a step back, instantly wary. "I am?"

"You don't have enough time. Which is why people will be willing to pay more for it. Simple supply and demand. We can handpick which jobs you take. No more messing around with convenience store stickups, eh?"

The conversation with Elodie about Mateo Delagarza turning people away came crashing back. Tank told Hopper the same thing he'd told Elodie. "H, you know I got into the hero business because I wanted to help people. Not only people with money, but whoever needs my help."

The elevator doors opened to the lobby, and Hopper marched through the jingling obstacle course of slot machines. "Listen, buddy, your intentions are noble, and I love you for that, I really do. But there's a time to think with your 'noble hero' hat, and a time to think with your 'business' hat." He pushed through the door to the parking garage, Tank following. "Look at it this way. Top detectives—they focus on the hard cases, right? The things that require their level of skill. They don't waste their time writing parking tickets. Let other people handle the small stuff." He waved a hand dismissively and unlocked the car. "You need to think about your career."

The sun lanced through the windshield as they turned onto the street, and Tank squinted against the light. Hopper's detective argument almost made sense, but Tank gritted his teeth against the temptation to take his manager's word for it, like always. While it was true that, superhero or not, Tank was only one person and would never be able to help everyone, the comparison didn't quite work. A cop writing tickets was rule enforcement, not protecting people from danger when they couldn't protect themselves. And both detectives and traffic cops had teams. They had co-workers, all handling different aspects of the job. No one expected one cop to do everything on their own.

*I need a team. I need other heroes to work with.* Before discussing it with Elodie, Tank had never noticed how limiting the AVA was. He'd merely accepted it as the way things were. But now the restrictions felt like a straitjacket. She was right. The hero industry was young but already had structures in place for people to profit off of, like Mateo Delagraza had been doing, and like Hopper was now suggesting. The Anti-Vigilante Act may have started out with the good intention of not allowing powered people to run amok, but by not allowing heroes to work in a team, or to work without a licensed manager, it propped up those structures.

Hopper pulled into the police station. Inside, the head detective presented his plan for finding the rest of Abaddon. A few FBI agents were there as well, to help coordinate cleaning up Abaddon out of state, Tank supposed. He fidgeted in his seat, unable to stop thinking about how the system was broken. And Elodie's face wouldn't get out of his head. Once he thought he smelled plumeria through the open window.

The meeting room felt sterile, lacking the welcoming design elements of the Fashion Seeker conference room and Elodie's ubiquitous plants. There were a couple of female officers in attendance, but male energy dominated the room, and the detective was giving orders, not asking for input. Tank missed the sense of collaboration that had marked the planning sessions with Seeker Security.

Hopper gave him a pointed look, and he tried to focus.

"We've assigned teams to each of these potential targets." The detective handed him a file. "These are yours."

Tank leafed through the papers, working up the courage to ask a question. "How's Slingshot? Has he said anything?"

"Actually, yes." The detective pointed at the files. "All of these names we got from him last night. He's being surprisingly cooperative."

"That's ... good," Tank said, once more seeing Slingshot's desperate face. Was he handing over information he'd learned from undercover spying, or was he cooperating because he hoped to cut a deal? "Which prison are they holding him in?"

"West Desert. Why?"

"Is he allowed to have visitors?" Tank looked through his file as he asked, feigning nonchalance. Elodie needed some closure. Maybe if he got her in to see her brother, it'd help.

"No," the detective said slowly.

"What's going to happen to him?" Tank asked, still not looking up. He didn't want to see the look Hopper was surely giving him right now. "Does he have legal counsel yet?"

"Tank." The detective gave him an incredulous look. "He's a hero who went vigilante, then villain. I'm sure the trial will be swift, and the sentence, what you would expect given the terms of the AVA."

"You're gonna execute him?" Tank jumped to his feet, tipping over his chair. Several officers drew back. One laid a hand over his gun. Tank gave him a flat look. "Really?"

The detective moved between them, arms outstretched. "Ok, everybody relax. Winston," he pointed at the officer with the gun. "Don't be insulting." He sighed. "Tank, I understand it's difficult, having to bring in another hero. Or at least someone we thought was a hero. But you did what needed to be done. Let us worry about Slingshot from here on out."

"What about the nanite water from that night? What did the lab say about them? I mean, you have to have proof before they'll sentence him to death, right?"

The detective's face hardened. "Are you suggesting I don't?"

"No, I just—"

"Tank," the detective cut him off. "Let it go. It's out of your hands." He pointed to Tank's chair where it had fallen. "Take a seat so we can continue."

Tank left his chair on its side and leaned against the window, arms folded.

"Now," the detective went on. "All teams are to apprehend their suspects simultaneously. We don't want these guys getting any more advance warning that we're coming for them than last night already gave them. We're waiting on a few more warrants, but it looks like we'll be good to go tomorrow."

He gave a few other instructions that Tank tuned out—Hopper could fill him in later. When the detective finished, Hopper ushered Tank out of the building and to the car.

"Got more details from the casino," he said. "They'd like some shots of you as a guest for the commercial spots, at the restaurant, in the pool."

Tank stopped short of the car. "Did you just attend the same meeting I did?"

Hopper kept going like Tank hadn't spoken. "I like that idea. Your fan base has skewed toward the seven- to ten-year-old demographic in the past. Some shirtless hot tub pics will help boost the adult-female demographic."

Elodie's brother was going to die, and Hopper was working demographics. "H, what are you talking about?" Tank asked tiredly.

Hopper leaned on the roof of the car. "Well, I'm thinking Elodie is no longer a contender."

"A contender? I wasn't aware we were running a competition."

Hopper shrugged. "You said you were lonely, so I'm looking out for you. That's what I do. And people love a good eligible bachelor story." He shut the driver's door and paced the sidewalk, painting a picture. "See, they already love you as a hero, so they want to see you rewarded, so to speak. They want to see their hero happy. And then the women who are looking for a man, they start to think, 'Why couldn't he be happy with me?' Because at some point you'll settle down with someone, and even the realistic ones nurse this secret hope that, because they live in the same city, they'll bump into you at the grocery store or a club or whatever and strike up a conversation. And then who knows? It could be them. And so they pay attention. And sponsors pay attention to who consumers are paying attention to, see?"

"Sooo, you're leveraging my marital status for contracts and publicity?"

Hopper rounded the car to pat Tank on the elbow. "Come on, don't be like that. I get that you're stressed right now. The idea of a superhero being executed is uncomfortable for us all. But that's never going to be you. I mean, I'd like to see them try."

It wasn't often Hopper acknowledged stressors. *Maybe the whole Slingshot thing is affecting him too, more than I realized.* "Sorry, H. What about Elodie though? It was your idea to date her, but you seem to have moved past her as a match awfully fast." *Faster than me.*

Hopper shrugged one shoulder. "She could have been a good match. Your careers would have benefited each other. But she's not the only one. We'll find someone else. Don't worry, big guy. Do you want me to drop you at the hotel before I go to the meeting with the casino?"

All Tank heard was his patronizing nickname. Elodie hadn't found a better one for him before everything exploded. He supposed now she never would. He shook his head. "I think I'll take a walk."

"Ok. I'll see you back at the rooms this evening."

Tank wandered for nearly an hour, past glitz and dirt and locals and tourists, till the crowd of pedestrians grew so thick he didn't have to think about where to go. The tide of people shepherded him along, in between buildings and down walking paths. The crowd deposited him at a railing overlooking a canal that ran through an outdoor shopping mall. Gondolas ferried couples under bridges and down the canal, gondolieri serenading them. He tried to find comfort in the fact that these people were alive and unharmed and going about their business today because of what he'd done last night. But Hopper was ready to auction him off to the highest bidder, and Slingshot was going to die.

Maybe he should chuck the whole hero gig in the canal and go back to being Willard.

He sank into a chair at one of the café tables lining the walkway. The chair creaked, and he sat straighter, supporting more of his own weight. *Sheesh. Tank the walking destruction derby.*

Another pair of lovers floated by, all smiles and handholding. Tank scrolled through his camera roll for something else to look at.

Lint's whiskered face too close to the camera, a beach picture he snapped on a walk back home, Lint chasing a catnip mouse, a screenshot of a book to add to his TBR, Lint curled in a doughnut shape on his bed. And one of him and Elodie from their picnic at Red Spring, the sun highlighting her hair and a goofy grin on his face.

*Yeah, not helping.* He was about to shove his phone in his pocket when a notification popped up.

BlindDate: 1 new message

*Hey Willard,*

*How's the conference going? I'd still like to meet up if you're game.*

*—Grace*

His breath left him. Grace. Meet Grace. After everything that had happened?

He skimmed through their past conversation, surprised to find the red heart emojis and book talk still sent nervous thrills through him.

*Tank, you big dummy.* How could he feel this way reading her messages when he knew he was still in love with Elodie? Even if he wanted to meet—and part of him did—it wouldn't be fair to Grace.

On the other hand, he'd had feelings for Grace when he chose Elodie. El had also been interested in someone else, but she'd chosen to try things with Tank.

He grimaced. *At least we would have tried things if her brother hadn't forced me to arrest him.*

Either way, they had chosen. Perhaps that was all love was. Finding sparks with various people and then simply choosing one to nurture to a full fire. Maybe there was no one right answer, no one right person. No one magical destiny to lead you to your true love. No True Love's Kiss.

Maybe love was a matter of choice.

Elodie's words replayed in his head. *The world is full of possibilities.*

He'd found a spark with Grace, a possibility. And he'd found it on his own, not through his hero reputation, or Hopper's machinations. If El was choosing not to nurture their spark further, maybe he could nurture a different spark.

He held his breath and typed a response. *Actually, I have most of today free. Would that work?*

He stared at the message for a full minute, heart racing and eyes watering from the glare of the sun off the canal. And hit send.

The single-story stucco house with the palm tree in the yard matched the address Grace had sent him. He'd been surprised when she suggested her house for their first meeting, but she'd said her grandmother wanted to meet him too.

*Besides,* she'd written. *I trust you.*

A volcanic bundle of nerves, Tank stared at the house from across the street, fingers drumming on *A Circle of Cats*. The house sat sandwiched between other normal, single-story, stucco houses on a normal, suburban street. This was Willard's world. None of the penthouse-press-conference vibes from the world Hopper had built for The Tank here. Tank's world had had an intense few weeks, Grace's messages having been the only moments spared for Willard, and the transition between his two worlds pummeled him from all sides like rapids smashing him against rocks. Even his clothes—Elodie's suit underneath, civilian shirt and pants on top—pulled in different directions.

A tiny dog sprinted out of a side gate and across Grace's front yard, yapping shrilly. An older woman in a loose, flower-print dress huffed after the dog and shepherded it into the house.

*That must be her grandmother.* A multigenerational family where people genuinely cared about each other. The concept was both alien and appealing.

Unbidden, Elodie's face swam before his eyes. Her family was broken now.

He shut his eyes and went through a round of box breathing, stilling his fingers. "Come on, Tank ... Willard. Whoever you are. You're here. Go meet this spark."

Keeping his breathing deliberate, he crossed the street and climbed three steps to the porch. The front door was open, a screen door shading the inside of the house from view. He rang the doorbell. Switched the book from hand to hand. Tried not to shuffle his feet.

Footsteps clicked in the entryway, and someone opened the screen.

Everything he wanted to say, all the words that could fan the spark between him and Grace, that could lead to shared stories, jumbled in his brain and froze in his throat.

Elodie stood in the doorway.

"Tank?" Surprise morphed to anger. "What are you doing here? How did you even get this address?"

He couldn't talk. Elodie, here. In Grace's house. In Grace's doorway. In Grace's place. His heart thundered in his ears as he understood.

Grace had told him the morning after the warehouse fire that she had a work trip. Elodie had arrived in L.A. from Vegas for the mayor's party that evening.

Grace said she was working on a tricky client project. Right when Elodie would have been designing his hero suit.

Grace got his message at the charter school the same afternoon Elodie returned to Vegas.

He'd never fallen for two different women in the past. And he hadn't fallen for two different women now.

Had he thought love was a choice? That he could simply pick one out of many?

*Not a choice.*

"Grace," he said, barely a breath. "Willard." He confessed his name like a sin.

Her eyes grew wide, traveled to the book in his hands. "Willard?"

Pain and elation knifed through him at his name on her lips, and his throat clogged with tears he refused to shed. *Not a choice.* "How ...?"

"Grace is my middle name. I use it with my family. Seeker was my maternal grandmother's last name. She taught me to sew." She clutched one arm around her middle and the other across her chest, fingers digging into her shoulder. He nodded at her explanation, the story of her name, but read another story in her eyes. She'd trusted him, as both Elodie and Grace. And he'd betrayed her as both Tank and Willard. As Tank, by keeping his promise. As Willard, by being himself. And how *could* he? How could he do that to her?

*Not a choice.*

He lifted her hand from her shoulder—she was leaving marks again—and gently pressed the book into her arms. "I fell in love with you twice. I'm sorry."

The line of stucco houses blurred as he walked away as fast as he could without running. He swiped at his eyes, footsteps echoing like gunshots on the quiet street.

It occurred to him that if he were in a romance novel, he'd hear another set of footsteps behind him at any second. Her voice would call his name—he didn't care anymore which name, all of him loved all of her. She'd run after him, say she loved all of him too.

But this wasn't a romance novel. It wasn't any novel. This was real life, and he couldn't find his place in it.

The street behind him stayed silent and empty.

# CHAPTER TWENTY-FOUR

G race clutched the book to her chest, her thoughts in shambles. It was a used copy of *The Circle of Cats*, with a plastic library cover. Used copies were better. They already had love in them.

*Whose love?* The cover crinkled under her fingers as the shock started to melt. Twice.

Tank—*Willard?*—had fallen in love with her twice.

He turned to leave, and a flash of green peeked from his shirt collar. He was still wearing his hero suit under his street clothes. *Because Tank is Willard, and Willard is Tank.*

She'd made that suit. And she was holding a picture book her keiki would love. *Because I'm Elodie, and Elodie is Grace.*

Both of them, Grace and Willard, had used BlindDate to hide parts of themselves. In the real world, Tank and Elodie hid parts of themselves too.

*Virtual or real, none of us have shown our whole selves.*

Willard—*Tank?*—had reached the end of the driveway. The man who'd listened to her stories online and who'd given her a book the way other men gave flowers, his gentleness unseen by the world. The same man who had fought off a terrorist threat, his strength seen and celebrated. The man who, seen or unseen, tried his best to make the world a better place with the circumstances and information he had. And the man whose story she'd refused to listen to when it conflicted with the one she wanted.

The book cover crinkled under her fingers again. Grace—*or am I Elodie right now?*—stared at her hands. The hands of a designer, a seamstress, an activist and a kid from Kahuku who most people thought would never make it. These hands had put her in the spotlight of the fashion world—*seen*—and these hands worked to lift people out of impossible situations—*unseen*. Seen or unseen, she did the best she could with the circumstances given.

"Tank?" she whispered. He was at the end of the block now and didn't hear her. An ache throbbed in her throat, tissues swelling the way they did when a bruise formed.

"Will—" She tried to call louder but the ache cut off her voice, her breath. The pain stretched to her ribs, shoved at her chest cavity. Her heart thumped out of rhythm, like it didn't have room to beat.

She managed to stab the doorbell a frantic five times before the world faded and her head hit the porch.

# CHAPTER TWENTY-FIVE

Tank trudged through the hotel lobby and up the stairs. Stairs were better. Stairs were empty. Elevators equaled people to smile at and pretend for. Hopper wouldn't be back from his meeting with the casino yet, a small bright spot of relief. Tank didn't think he could handle talking to him yet.

Numbness coated his soul the way it used to coat his body. Like someone had been carving slices out of his heart this whole time, and he'd only just noticed.

He cringed, remembering the horror on Elodie's—*Grace's?*—face. Horror at who he was. He couldn't blame her. Her brother was in prison because of him. Tank had sliced up her heart as surely as anyone had ever sliced up him.

Humiliation burned indistinguishable from the fire in his belly. He squeezed his arms across his middle and clenched his teeth to keep from screaming, wishing the numbness in his heart would move to his stomach. When he reached his room, the air was too close, his body too restless. *Maybe some air.* He opened the sliding glass door—slowly, he didn't want to break anything in his current state—and stepped onto the balcony. The balcony door to Hopper's room next door was ajar.

"You're sure?" a man asked from within Hopper's room.

"Yeah." Hopper's voice answered. "He's not back yet, probably won't be for a while."

They were talking about him. The casino rep must have met Hopper here. The man's voice sounded familiar, but Tank hadn't ever met him, didn't even know his name. Hopper always dealt with those details.

"Not too bright, is he?" the first voice scoffed.

Tank sucked in a breath as the numbness in his heart faded under the insult. He immediately wished it'd come back. *I should be so lucky.* Heart raw, he waited for his manager to defend him.

"Nope," Hopper said. "But he brings home the bacon."

Tank hadn't thought it possible to hurt more than he already did. He turned to go back inside, not wanting to hear anymore.

"Speaking of money," Hopper continued. "I transferred the last payment to your account."

Tank paused. If this was a sponsorship negotiation, why was H paying them?

"Although I'm not sure you deserve it." Hopper's voice again. Footsteps and ice cubes clinking into a glass.

"I'd like to see you find someone else who could have done it."

Impatience leaked out of Hopper's words. "I paid you to create a believable and worthy threat that only *my* client could defeat. A supervillain for my superhero. Something so horrific that, not just L.A., not just Vegas, but the whole country would fear for their lives. So the whole country would rejoice and lift Tank up on their shoulders when he saved them."

The balcony tilted underneath Tank. He grabbed at the glass door, his breath coming in short gasps. *I heard him wrong, that's all. The A/C is muffling their voices or something. I must have heard wrong.*

Hopper kept talking, the ice cubes banging against the glass like he was waving his arms as he spoke. "As it was, it didn't drag out nearly long enough for the whole country to be invested. And I had to bust my ass to turn around that Container Park fiasco—what was up with the wall of bugs, anyway? You actually keep those things in your clothes?"

"No," the voice said mildly. "Merely one of our tricks, all part of the service."

"Service." Hopper snorted. "You were supposed to let Tank have a win that day—bring in one of your compatriots, build up a back and forth for a few weeks. *You* weren't even supposed to be there. And I wanted the final showdown someplace flashy, visible, but instead we had to rush the ending at that water plant. Even *Tank* noticed it felt off."

The other speaker stayed calm in the face of Hopper's onslaught. "It's hardly our fault if your boy can't handle a few insects. And he got the credit in the end anyway."

The fire in Tank's stomach crept through his chest, a thousand needles in his ribs. This wasn't happening. This couldn't be true.

Hopper wasn't finished. "And what was all that with Slingshot? You were supposed to take him out before we got here, not let him join up. He was sticking his nose in everywhere. He could have blown it for all of us!"

An edge finally crept into the other voice. "But he didn't. And now he's better than dead, he's discredited. And Las Vegas is perfectly primed for your boy to take over. You ought to give me a bonus."

The volcano in Tank's gut exploded. His knees buckled.

Fake.

It was all fake. Abaddon, the locusts, the nanites, all of it had been staged. *A supervillain for my superhero.* Everything he'd worked for. Every box he'd crammed himself into. Every name he'd hidden himself inside of. All those people in danger, Gerard in the hospital, the woman with the broken hip, Elodie's heart ripped out.

All so Hopper could rake in fatter contracts.

Part of Tank wanted to be angry. Wanted to leap to the other balcony, storm into the room, beat Hopper to a pulp and turn what was left of him over to the police. If this were an action story, that was what The Tank would do.

But this wasn't an action story. And he wasn't The Tank. He never had been. The Tank was a fabrication of Hector Strickland. A fake.

Right now, he was high-school Willard all over again, drowning in shame and lava, bleeding and flayed open by the person who was supposed to be on his team.

Willard staggered to his feet, and for the second time that day, he fled.

He wasn't careful with his running, and his feet left cracks in the sidewalk. People stared and dodged out of the way, but he didn't stop. He wove through traffic and billboards and back alleys, industrial complexes, strip malls and residential streets. Red cliffs shimmered past the last line of artificially green lawns, and he realized his feet were dragging him west toward the park where he and Elodie had picnicked.

He veered north. And kept running.

He ran under the burn of the sun, arms pumping like mad. His breath came like a tug-of-war. Inhale—*Willard*. Exhale—*Tank*. He ran despite the flames his own body tormented him with. Inhale—*Willard*. Exhale—*Tank*. He ran through the scorch of the desert, hating both his names. Inhale—*Willard*. Exhale—*Tank*. He ran through the sunset, and the pounding of his feet began to jostle the two identities loose. Stars appeared, thousands of them, cold and distant. He didn't know any of their names. Maybe they had no names. Maybe they wanted no names.

Still running, he examined the name Tank like a thing outside himself. Choking, strangling, chosen for him by someone else, it had never fit him. He dropped it like a cockroach, and the rhythm of his feet crushed it into the dust of the desert.

The name gone, he found his strength remained, and he remembered. The strength had been there before the name.

Willard, he looked over with more compassion, like an old man who'd been sick for years and was ready to lay himself down. He peeled away the numbness, let go of the pain, scraped out the insecurities. Under ten thousand unknown stars, he laid Willard to rest beside a boulder, along with his now-shredded street clothes—they served no purpose out here, and he wasn't hiding himself any longer—and laid a hand over his heart. There he found a gentleness, and he remembered. The gentleness had been there before the pain.

Cutting out the names left him hollow and raw, his insides scraped out by failure and betrayal and heartbreak. He was free of names that didn't fit, but he knew he needed more—more work, more healing, more time. He also knew he couldn't do anymore on his own. For now, he was Nameless, and for that, he was grateful.

He took up his run again. The moon shadows shifted from his left to his right as the night waned. His stride slowed. His breath grew ragged. Even he couldn't sustain this pace indefinitely. Shapes grew out of the desert. Vaguely human, they hovered above the horizon. He stumbled to a walk. A billboard materialized near the hovering figures, welcoming visitors to the Goldwell Open Air Museum Gift Shop and Visitor's Center. A plaque reading *The Last Supper, Albert Szukalskis* identified the amorphous, hovering shapes as an art installation on a raised wooden platform.

He walked a circle around the statue, letting his body cool down. The sculpture mimicked DaVinci's *Last Supper*. Christ and each of his disciples were present, but unlike the original, each was represented by only a hollow sculpted fiberglass robe. No faces, no names. Like standing shrouds, or cloaks with no bodies to cover—the shapes of Christ and his followers scraped empty by Judas' fake devotion and betrayal. By the heartbreak of the apostles at the death of their hero.

The hollow spaces ached. He was Nameless, and he was grateful, but he was empty. Under a million unknown stars, he sat between the shrouds, laid his head on his knees, and sobbed.

# CHAPTER TWENTY-SIX

Nameless knew he was lucid dreaming again. Some kind of boiling lake stewed in front of him, pink and gray, but other than that, the landscape was blank, as it always was at the start of his lucid dreams.

He put himself right next to the lake and looked in. An impossible paradise gazed back at him. Green, verdant, peaceful. He ached for the peace of it.

But his chest was raw, empty—his identity carved out of him and discarded in the desert. He didn't want to lucid dream right now. Didn't want to dream at all, didn't want to be reminded that he existed. He darkened the blank dreamscape, like turning out the lights, and pulled his mind away from dreaming to simple unconsciousness.

Tires on gravel woke him. He blinked against the morning light, his eyes dry from tears, and wind, and grit.

"Been there all night?" A man wearing a veteran's cap and a dark, bushy beard peered at him from next to a dusty sedan. He eyed the green and black suit Nameless wore, eyebrows raised. When Nameless offered no explanation, he pointed at the shrouds. "They ain't going nowhere. No need to line up overnight." He chuckled at his own joke.

Nameless didn't answer.

The man shrugged and scuffed over to the gift shop to unlock the door. "You want some breakfast? It's not exactly a café, but we've got gas station food."

Nameless followed the museum caretaker inside the shop. He hadn't eaten since the morning before, when Hopper had made him drink a protein shake on the way to the police station. He hadn't had an appetite then and he didn't now, but he'd run for twelve straight hours last night, and his body needed to refuel.

Nameless bypassed the bell pepper-laden breakfast burritos, and the reflux-inducing hotdogs the caretaker had fired up, and laid a fistful of protein bars, three water bottles and a green juice on the counter. When he reached for his wallet, he realized it was buried, along with his phone, in the desert beside a boulder. They'd been in his pants pocket. "Um ..."

The caretaker shrugged one shoulder, bagged his items and handed them to him. "On the house. Looks like you need them more than the gift store does."

"Thanks." He ducked his head and noticed the Sunday paper stacked on the side of the counter.

SLINGSHOT EXECUTION DATE SET

"No," he breathed.

The caretaker shook his head. "Sad, ain't it? You know, he came out here once. Seemed like a real nice kid. I guess you never really know about people, do you?"

Nameless shook his head. He certainly hadn't really known his manager. "No. But I think they've got the wrong guy." Hopper had said Slingshot was supposed to have been "taken care of" before they arrived in Vegas. He'd been angry Slingshot had been involved. Which meant Slingshot wasn't part of Hopper's plot, or part of the fake terrorist group. When he'd said he was undercover, he'd been telling the truth. But if he'd been spying, he should have discovered that it was all a sham, so why try to stay undercover?

*I don't know.* Nameless shut his eyes and pinched the bridge of his nose. He didn't know because as Elodie—*Grace?*—had told him, he hadn't listened. And now an innocent man was going to be killed.

He grabbed the paper and scanned the front page. Tomorrow. The execution was tomorrow morning at 6 a.m.

Briefly, he thought of trying to call the authorities—the museum caretaker would have a phone—and explain about Hopper's sham and Slingshot's innocence. But he had no proof. It'd be his word against his manager's. And there'd been zero mercy in the detective's eyes when he'd told Nameless to drop it.

No. No phone calls.

But Slingshot wasn't going to die. No one else was going to be hurt because of the farce Hopper had constructed. Grace—*Elodie?*—might never want to see him again, but he could give her brother back to her.

"You don't happen to know where West Desert Prison is, do you?" he asked.

"Sure, it's along this same highway, south and a little east. Wouldn't recommend trying to walk there though."

"Not planning on walking. Thanks for breakfast." Nameless stepped out into the morning light and began the run south. He had a prison break to get to.

When he'd fled Las Vegas, Nameless hadn't had a destination other than *away*. He'd crisscrossed the mountains and the desert until ending at the *Last Supper* shrouds. This time, he knew where he was going. Following the highway, he made quick work of the miles, and the walls of the prison materialized on the horizon four hours after leaving the museum. He found a Joshua tree and settled in to wait for dark.

His plan wasn't subtle.

The walls were mere walls, the barbed wire mere barbed wire. The bullets, just bullets. They meant nothing. He may not be The Tank anymore, but he was still bulletproof. Tonight, he'd be a battering ram.

Cloud cover blew in shortly after sunset, muting the moon and turning the texture of the desert flat. Nameless crept toward the outer wall of the prison, dodging search lights. A leap took him halfway up the wall. He climbed the rest by punching his own handholds in the stone as he had at Bronson Studios back in L.A.

He paused, hanging from one hand. *Was that really only a week and a half ago?* How little time it took to rip a life out from underneath someone.

He resumed scaling the wall. Not very many prospects for a new life waited for him after this escapade was over. Breaking out Slingshot would label him a vigilante; he'd be on the run. He chuckled. *As if anyone could catch me.* Canada sounded nice, or maybe Alaska. He'd live on his own in the middle of nowhere, like in *Hatchet*, or *My Side of the Mountain*.

A pair of guards paced on top of the wall. Nameless heaved himself over the ledge and followed the one on the right. It didn't take much to disarm him.

He clamped one hand over the guard's mouth, gripping the back of his neck with the other. "Take me to Slingshot."

The guard trembled, wide-eyed. But surprised was good. It meant no one had expected a rescue attempt, which meant, while Hopper might be wondering where Nameless was, his manager had no clue that he had overheard that conversation.

The doors slid open with the guard's ID badge. Down one hallway. Right turn. Footsteps. He dragged his captive into an empty office and waited for them to pass. Another right, past the communal cells and left into a corridor built entirely out of plastic. No stone, no cinderblock. Nothing for Slingshot to use as a weapon.

Nameless couldn't help thinking of X-Men and Magneto's plastic prison. *I wonder how Gerard is doing.* A pang twinged through him. He'd never see his little friend again. Or Lint—he wouldn't be able to go back for the cat after this. Maybe he could find a way to get a note to Gerard and ask him to look after Lint.

A thick-looking resin door locked the only cell in the hallway. "Does your badge work on that?"

The guard shook his head.

"Sleep well, then." Nameless cuffed him on the side of the head and laid him on the floor. He drew in a breath, released it, and punched the door in.

Slingshot startled awake and jumped off his cot. "What are you doing here?"

Nameless held up a hand. "Do you want to go see your sister or not?"

Slingshot stared at him, eyes narrowed. "Yeah, let's go. I got things to say to you though."

"Fine." Nameless knocked out the back wall of the cell, exposing the night sky and the perimeter wall. "We can talk on the way."

The prison alarm shrieked from over the hill, echoing through the empty scrubland. Dogs barked, and giant searchlights swept over the brush. Nameless steered their path into a wash farther out of sight.

"Here, let me carry you, it'll be faster." He motioned for Slingshot to hop on his back.

The other hero made a face but climbed on. "Anything that gets us away from here faster."

Nameless picked up the pace, Slingshot's weight on his back negligible. The alarm call faded behind them, and they left the searchlights behind. The moon-shadowed shapes of the desert watched them flee. Nameless jostled a bush coming around a hill, and a jackrabbit spooked and zigzagged away.

Slingshot hadn't said anything yet. Nameless concentrated on running and breathing, figuring he'd speak when he was ready. The miles passed in silence until the glow of the city showed over the next hill.

"Are we headed back to Vegas?" Slingshot's voice bounced as he spoke.

"Your sister's there."

Quiet for a moment, then, "Why'd you break me out?"

Nameless didn't answer at first. Slingshot sounded suspicious. He couldn't blame him. He hadn't exactly been understanding the last time they met. "I found out what you were trying to tell me that night. About Abaddon being fake."

"Fake?"

"Yeah, fake. Why didn't you just tell me that? What was the point of staying undercover? You could have exposed Hopper and been done with it. Granted, I probably wouldn't have believed you about H at the time." The slimy feeling of forcing himself to "be The Tank" came back, and he cringed. "Or did you not have real proof yet? Is that the 'more' you were talking about?"

"Hold up, brah." Slingshot squirmed until Nameless had to stop running and put him down or risk hurting him. "What do you mean, 'fake'?"

Nameless threw his hands up. "I mean fake, what do you think I mean? Hopper orchestrated Abaddon as a way to—to make me look ..." His lips twisted. He hadn't had to say it out loud yet. "He fabricated Abaddon as a foil for me, to make me look good, to get better-paying sponsorships and all that."

Slingshot's eyes grew huge, and Nameless hastened to add, "I didn't know about it. Hopper tricked me like he tricked everyone else." He paused. "Well, maybe not everyone else. El ... Grace—" He swallowed. *First time saying those out loud too, since they became the same person.* "She never trusted him, although I don't think she suspected this. Anyways, I guess that night at the water plant was their 'grand finale' or something." The words tasted bitter in his mouth. "So, they're done. And I'm done with Hopper, even if he doesn't know it yet. And I believe you about being undercover, so there's no way I'm letting them execute you. I'm taking you back to your sister. The two of you can disappear or lawyer up and go after Hopper if you have evidence of his involvement, but I'm done. After I drop you off, I'm leaving."

Slingshot stared at him, mouth agape. "Ho!" He smacked both palms on the sides of his face. "I can't believe I didn't see that!" He paced, talking to himself. "But that's it, yeah? Gotta be. No one else. Plus, they had to wait for the key to be fully wicked before it could open the portal. And that's gonna hurt like jellyfish on a sunburn." He stopped and looked at Nameless. "The key is your boss, brah!"

Nameless put his hands on his hips. "He's not my boss. And he's not the key to anything, he's a manipulative sicko."

"Ok, but listen. Abaddon is only a set up to a point."

"What do you mean 'to a point'?"

"When I went undercover, all I knew about were the parts they wanted people to see—the attacks, the propaganda. After I went undercover, I found out somebody contracted them for the public-facing stuff, but I hadn't figured out who yet, before you arrested me."

Nameless ducked his head. "Yeah, sorry about that."

Slingshot waved it off. "But the rest of it isn't fake. They used the resources and exposure your boss gave them to recruit people for their real purpose."

Nameless clenched his teeth. "Not my boss."

Slingshot rolled his eyes. "Fine. Your former rep. All those videos about destroying humanity and cleansing the earth? They were being paid to say that, but they weren't faking it, brah. Their whole goal is to purge the earth of humans. In all their little evil-villain meetings, they were constantly preaching this part from Revelation about a beast—that's where their name comes from, yeah?—that's supposed to come wipe out humanity. Like a giant, freaky version of their locusts. And they've got this, like, portal to the underworld. They call it the pit."

"The 'angel of the bottomless pit.'" Nameless scrubbed at his face in disbelief. "The pit is a real pit?"

"So real. The pit's like a cocoon for this boss-demon, and when it's done incubating on the other side, they open the portal-cocoon, and the beast takes vengeance on humanity. But they need a *key* to open the portal—a person they have to physically throw in the pit. It has to be someone cold-hearted; I mean one fully wicked, selfish guy for it to work. When I was spying, I heard them talking about how the guy who hired them was the key, but they never said his name. It's your manager, brah. When did you see him last?"

Nameless shifted, uneasy. "At the hotel, yesterday, when I overheard him talking to whoever his contact is with Abaddon about how it was all a set up."

"His contact?" Slingshot resumed pacing, a circle of pebbles whirling around his fingers like a fidget spinner. "That's NineSix."

Nameless smacked his forehead. "That's why his voice sounded familiar. The accent must have been fake too."

"Oh, yeah. NineSix is from Florida. He started this after his house got flattened by a hurricane. But the plan was to grab the key as soon as the charade was over. I'd bet Grace's poodle that no one's seen him since you did. And that demon's gonna be done cooking any day now, so if they have the key, people are gonna die. We still have work to do, brah."

Nameless shut his eyes, a hand over his stomach. "Are you telling me that in order to save humanity from a vengeful demon, I have to rescue the one person in my life who *deserves* to be thrown down a pit to hell?"

Slingshot shrugged apologetically.

Nameless ran a hand through his hair. He'd broken a man out of prison, the one person he wanted to see never wanted to talk to him again, the one person *he* never wanted to talk to again needed saving, and he didn't know who he was anymore. "I need a book."

"You need a book? Like ... a guidebook? Or ...?"

"No." He laughed at himself humorlessly. "I need a book. Like how other people say, 'I need a drink' or 'I need caffeine.' I need a boo—" Slingshot was staring at him, baffled.

Nameless shook his head. "Never mind." He stared at the stars. He could start running again. Leave all of this behind and head up north, live alone like a grizzly bear. *What do I care if the world burns? I've tried to save them all every day for two years and look where it's gotten me.* Rejected, betrayed. Nameless. There wasn't enough of him left to give to saving people anymore.

"No. I can't. Hopper—I can't." He tossed Slingshot on his back again and resumed running. "I'll drop you at Grace's but that's it."

"Ok," Slingshot said slowly. "How about you and me and Grace all talk about it together?"

"I can't talk to Grace." Nameless crested a hill. The northern edge of the city was in sight now.

"Why not?"

Scree skidded down the slope as Nameless slid down to the rocky expanse separating him from Fashion Seeker Designs by a handful of miles. "She doesn't want to see me."

"Why doesn't Grace want to see you?" Slingshot wriggled down from his perch again, forcing Nameless to stop at the bottom of the hill. "What'd you do?"

Nameless threw up his hands. "You mean besides put you in prison?"

"Ok." Slingshot made a face. "She'd be pissed about that. But you're bringing me back."

"Yes, but—You don't—ungh!"

Nameless turned and kicked a boulder. It shattered, scattering a handful of beetles. He'd forgotten that Slingshot didn't know anything that had happened. He didn't know how Nameless had fallen in love with Grace online, or how he'd fallen in love with Elodie in person. Or that he'd broken her heart twice.

His throat closed, and he had to spit out each word individually. "I didn't turn out to be ... who she thought I was."

Slingshot's face darkened, and a fist size rock flew up to smack Nameless in the face. "What'd you do to my sister?"

Nameless mashed his lips together. "You know my skin is impenetrable, right?"

"You know she's my sister, right?" Slingshot echoed. He swirled his fingers, and a group of pebbles circled his hands. "What'd you do?"

"What did I do?" Nameless barked a laugh. "I fell in love with her—*all* of her. And I kept a promise."

Slingshot stared at Nameless a moment before answering. "Must have been some promise. Grace don't fuss over men. If she's mad, brah, that means she actually cares." He sighed and let the rocks fall to the earth. "I guess I'll let you live."

Nameless snorted. "Gee, thanks." He gazed across the open desert. So close to Elodie. But he'd leave without seeing her. Didn't matter what Slingshot said, he hadn't been there. Hadn't seen her face when she'd kicked him out. Or Grace's face on her front porch. "Come on, Slingshot. Let's get this over with." He bent down for Slingshot to climb on, so they could finish the run, but the other hero didn't move.

"You can call me James."

"James." Nameless straightened. *James, Slingshot. Grace, Elodie. Willard, Tank. We're all so many people, how do we even keep track of our own self?*

"What do I call you?" James asked.

Nameless shook his head. "I don't know yet."

"You don't know? How do you not know your own name?"

Nameless groaned and sat heavily in the dirt. He could see headlights on the roads from where they were. *So close.* "It's complicated."

James settled next to him, waiting. For a moment, Nameless could see Elodie in him, her patience, and how safe it felt talking to her.

"I gave one name up. The other was never mine to begin with. I haven't replaced either yet."

"I get it." James nodded, swirling a pile of pebbles into a miniature tornado while he spoke. "Listen, I know the AVA has given people like Hopper a stranglehold on people like us, man, but it's wrong. It isolates us, tells us we have to be everything to everyone, fix everything on our own. But we need each other. No one can do it all on their own."

A tendril of hope sprouted in Nameless. He'd tried to be too many people, and now he didn't know who he was, didn't even have a name. All the times he'd wished for a team came back to him. Maybe with a team he wouldn't need either Tank or Willard. Maybe he could find a new name.

"You really think El, er, Grace, cares? You think she'll talk to me?"

"I do."

Nameless took one more look at the open desert between him and Grace. *Just a couple miles.* "Let's go then."

# CHAPTER TWENTY-SEVEN

E lodie twisted a rolled-up newspaper between swollen fingers, staring at NineEighteen through the cell-door window. The world had people with all kinds of powers now. Why couldn't she have the ability to pluck thoughts out of others' heads? An IV tube tangled in the blanket wrapped around her shoulders as she shifted positions, and she shoved the rolling base to the side.

"Don't. You'll dislodge it again." Sofia adjusted cords and tubes, checked the portable heart monitor, and replaced the oxygen mask that Elodie had removed. "Glaring at him isn't going to make him talk. You should go back to bed, Elodie."

"I know." She squeezed Sofia's hand. Sometimes she called her friend Sofia, sometimes Dr. O. Sometimes Sofia called her Grace, sometimes Elodie. She'd told Tank—*Willard*—that her family called her Grace. But some of her family called her Elodie too. The women of Seeker Security weren't just employees. They were friends. They were a family that she'd started but that they'd all built together. In the short time she'd known him, she'd come to feel that close to Tank too. But she'd destroyed that.

*I fell in love with you twice.*

*And I sent him away twice.*

Her heart shuddered, sluggish, stealing her breath for a few seconds. Sofia bent over her, face taut. But it passed, and Elodie breathed normally again.

*Normally. Ha.* Stupid word.

Leona entered from where she'd been standing guard outside the room and looked Elodie over, lips pursed. "She should be in bed."

"That's what I told her," Sofia said.

Elodie knew they were right. Everything hurt. She should go back to bed, but she'd already spent most of the day and a half since hitting her head on the porch in bed, much of that unconscious. She'd woken not just to the usual bruises on her skin, but on nearly every major organ. Sitting here hurt. The beating of her heart hurt. *Breathing* hurt. Yes, she should go back to bed, but if she went back to bed, she'd only think about Tank, and there was the matter of what to do with NineEighteen now that Abaddon was finished.

*If Abaddon is finished.* The newspaper from yesterday proclaimed it so, featuring pages of coverage and analysis of the events at the water treatment plant. Elodie didn't buy it. There was no way her brother had truly been a part of Abaddon. The real terrorists were still out there.

Regardless, she couldn't hand the firebug over to the police—there'd be too many questions—but neither could she release him on the street. If Tank were still there, he could take him into custody and make it look like he found the terrorist on one of the mopping up missions the police must surely be running.

But he wasn't there. And NineEighteen might still have answers for her.

Leaning on Sofia, Elodie labored to her feet and shuffled close to the cell door, IV drip trailing behind her. Leona stepped close, a hand out in case Elodie stumbled.

"You know Abaddon has lost." She held up the newspaper for her prisoner to see. NineEighteen didn't need to know that she didn't believe it. "There's nothing left for you to protect. Tell me. What were you holding over Slingshot?"

He giggled. "Have we lost? Is it done?"

"El." Sofia gently tugged on her elbow. "You're not going to get anything out of him. Come away."

"Slingshot shot his rocks, but at whom did he sling?" NineEighteen pressed his nose to the window. "I never liked him. Too sniffy."

"What does that mean?" Elodie pressed. "Where did you see him?"

"At the pit," he whispered. He shot a look at the doctor, a gleam in his eye. "Doesn't matter if I tell, doesn't matter if you know. It's too late to stop it. It's all done." He pointed at the newspaper. "So now we can get on with it."

"Get on with what?" Elodie's heart spasmed again, and she pressed her lips together against the squeeze of it.

"The key is ready, plucked in his ripeness. The chosen one." He found a dead locust in his beard and made it jump across the window like a child with a toy. Elodie and Sofia recoiled. Leona glared at him. "Chosen to be the key. No compassion. Nothing penetrates his heart. His heart is like that other one's skin."

The mention of Tank stung, and Elodie's breath caught. "Whose heart?"

"Slow, slow." NineEighteen shook his head. "Slow like the other one, like Tank. He didn't see it was always about the mean one. I tried to tell him, for fun. But he was too slow. And now the key's already taken. *Hopped* along." He giggled again and made the insect hop across the window.

"Hopper?" Elodie's legs went shaky, and she leaned on Sofia and Lenoa. "Hector Strickland is this key?"

"What does the key open?" Sofia asked.

NineEighteen gave her an exasperated look like she wasn't keeping up. "The pit. Time to open the pit."

"Sof, the pheromones, the nanites. They weren't the real plan. They were just extras." A coughing fit wracked through her, like a paper shredder on her lungs, and Elodie retreated to the bench.

"So easily distracted, humans," NineEighteen sang.

"What happens when the pit opens?" Leona asked, jaw hard.

"The king comes." NineEighteen smiled. "You all die, the earth is clean." He curled up on his bunk, done talking.

"Let's go." Elodie held out her hands, and the doctor and her head of security helped her into a wheelchair. Two Seeker Security women nodded to her from their posts in the hallway. Most of the building was empty, only the Sunday crew was on duty. "We have to get a hold of Will ... Tank."

Leona called the elevator. "Are you sure you want to do that?"

Elodie bit her lip. She wanted—needed—to see him again, but who knew if he'd be willing to speak to her. "If what NineEighteen said is true, then it's not

about him and me. And he won't turn his back if there are lives on the line."
She hit call before she could talk herself out of it.

"Grace." Sofia steadied the chair as the elevator climbed to the third floor.
"You don't even know what name to call him. How can you know who he is or
what he'll do?"

Elodie supported her head with one hand, listening to the phone ring on
speaker. Her voice hurt from forcing words around the bruises in her throat. "I
know him." *The real question is does he know himself yet?* "I just don't know if
he'll answer for me," she muttered.

His voicemail picked up. "This is Tank. Sorry I missed you, um ... go ahead
and leave a message. Oh, for matters of representation contact Strickland Talent
Management. Hope you have a great day."

His voice stabbed through her like a new bruise. She hung up without leaving
a message and dialed again. "Leona, prep the teams." The elevator opened. Sofia
pushed her chair and the IV pole toward the med wing while she kept trying to
get Tank on the phone.

"Yes, ma'am." Leona strode down the hall in the opposite direction to
Elodie's office.

"This is Tank. Sorry I missed you ..."

"Prep them for what? We don't even know where this pit is." Sofia backed the
wheelchair into Elodie's suite, then pulled back the blankets on the bed. Elodie
pushed herself out of the chair with a grunt, agitation growing.

"We don't know how many people Abaddon still has. We can meet Tank
there, be backup." She stabbed at the phone for a third time. "Come on, Willard,
pick up."

"Again, we don't know where to go, so we can't 'meet him there.'" Sofia
snatched at the phone. "And what 'we'? *You* can't go anywhere."

"This is Tank. Sorry I missed you ..."

"Sofia! Give me the phone."

"Don't you 'Sofia' me. You have contusions around your liver, your spleen,
your lungs and your *heart*, El. And not even normal, medically recognized

contusions—'bruise' is just the closest word we have for these. Your body is *shutting down*."

Elodie stole the phone back.

"This is Tank. Sorry I missed you ..."

"Where is he?" She texted him, *I need you*, and pushed call again.

"Do you understand me?" The doctor's voice rose. "You could die, Grace."

"This is Tank. Sorry I missed you ..."

Elodie's heart spasmed like a dying fish, all frantic bursts and last-chance flailing. The heart monitor screeched a warning.

"Sit down. Now." Sofia led her to the bed, and this time, she didn't resist. She sank into the pillows, but the room was blacking out like she'd stood up too fast. She couldn't breathe. An odd, flat sensation filled her chest, like her lungs were empty balloons.

The security system came over the P.A. "Front door open."

# CHAPTER TWENTY-EIGHT

When he'd left Fashion Seeker Designs, the door had locked behind him as he'd walked into the dark. Now, Nameless left the darkness behind and jogged into the pool of light in front of Elodie's hub. He set Slingshot down at the front door.

"I hope she hasn't changed it," James said, punching a code into the keypad. The red light switched to green, and the door unlatched. Booted footsteps rushed down the stairs as they stepped into the lobby. Leona swung around the corner, handgun raised.

"Ho, Leona." James flashed her shaka. "Howzit, howzit?"

"James?" She lowered the pistol. "How are you here?"

He shrugged and hooked a thumb at Nameless. "This guy's a wrecking ball."

"You." Leona raised the gun again and shot Nameless in the chest. The bullet bounced behind a potted fiddle-leaf fig. "I thought Elodie told you to clear out, Tank."

He sighed and smoothed out his suit. "That's not my name anymore."

"Fine, *Willard*. She told you to go."

Slingshot turned to him. "Brah, *you're* Willard? The same Willard Grace was writing to on that app?"

Nameless winced. Grace must have filled Leona in about BlindDate. "That's not my name anymore either."

"Ho! No wonder Grace was all upset." Slingshot laughed and moved toward the stairwell, but Leona cut in front of Nameless, eyes flinty.

"Well, what is your name?"

"I don't know." *Team building is going great so far.*

"That's kind of a thing with him," Slingshot said. "But let him pass; we need to talk to Grace."

"*Let* me pass?" Nameless asked.

James ignored him. "Actually, you come too, Le, we're gonna need backup. You're not going to believe this, but Abaddon has this—"

"Hellish pit to raise a monster? We know."

James blinked. "You do?"

"We do. But we don't know where."

"I know where, come on." He took the stairs two at a time. Nameless dragged his feet after him, uncertain, now that they were about to see Elodie. *Grace. Both of them.*

"James, wait." Leona hurried after him.

"We don't have time to wait. Where's Grace?"

Leona glanced between Nameless and James. "She's in the med wing."

James stopped, face paling. "How bad this time?"

"Bad."

A falling sensation pulled at Nameless' middle. His arms went weak. Fear jolted through his spine like electricity. "How bad is what?"

James ran down the hall and into the med wing without answering. Nameless followed him to a hospital suite. His feet ground to a halt.

Elodie lay in the bed, face swollen, eyes closed, and bruises mottling her neck and arms. IV tubes and monitor cords snaked from her body to beeping machines. Sofia was sitting next to her, checking her pulse.

"Grace." She switched to chafing her arm. "Grace, wake up."

Slingshot hurried to her side. "What happened?"

Sofia started. "James?"

"He broke me out," he explained again. "What happened?"

Sofia took in Nameless, eyes wide, before turning back to Grace. "Right now? She lost consciousness. On a bigger scale?" She shook her head helplessly. "They're everywhere this time."

"I don't understand." Nameless hung back, afraid of knocking into vital machinery. Fire crept up his chest, up his throat, made his voice rough. "She was fine. I saw her two days ago, and all last week. She was fine. What happened?"

"It doesn't have a name." Slingshot rubbed his sister's hand. "Come on, Gracie. The doctors never figured it out. When she was a kid, she'd get bruises all the time. They thought she had anemia or something, but it got worse as she got older."

"Stress makes it worse," Sofia said. "When she's hurting, or when people she loves are hurting. And she loves too many people."

"Stress." Nameless moved into the room, carefully, checking his shoulders didn't bump anything. He'd arrested her brother and shocked her at her front door. Too many of those bruises would be his fault.

"It's like her body takes all the pain in the world personally," James said. "Everything gets in, she's like your opposite." He straightened. "Hey, Sofia, what if we try him?"

"I kept telling El to ask him, but she wouldn't. She said it wouldn't work."

"Try me for what?"

Sofia explained to him their search for someone with a regenerative power that was transferable to others. "But she knew it wouldn't work, so she never asked."

Nameless crumpled inside. Elodie—*Grace*—had needed this from him all along, and it was the one thing he couldn't give. "I wish it would work. I'd give her everything if I could."

Leona rolled her eyes. "Sure."

Nameless rummaged in a drawer, found a syringe and jabbed it at the crook of his elbow, like he had to prove he wasn't holding anything back from her. The needle bent in half.

Leona cleared her throat, arms in a stiff at-ease position. "James, if you know where the pit is, we should take the teams and go now before she wakes up. You know she'll try to come with us if she wakes up before we leave."

"Go where?" Elodie's swollen eyes cracked open. Nameless moved forward, hand outstretched, but caught himself and shoved his hands in his pockets. Her gaze fixed on her brother. "James?"

"Howzit, sis?" He pulled a chair close to the bed and took her hand.

"James? How are you here?" Her voice croaked, and Sofia put a straw to her lips.

"Your boyfriend busted me out. Literally busted, it was killer." He pointed to Nameless, and her eyes widened as far as the swelling would allow.

"You got him out? What about Hopper and the police?"

Nameless couldn't keep back anymore. He knelt by her bed, stumbling over all the words that wanted to come out at once. "El—Grace, I'm so sorry. I screwed up everything. Hopper set all of it up, but Abaddon's real, and they're gonna kill so many people, and if I'd listened—"

She put a finger on his lips, and he stilled. Her hand trailed down to his collar of his hero suit, and across his shoulder. "You still have it?"

He nodded. She struggled to sit up, and he slipped a hand behind her back to help. Grace reached behind her pillow and pulled out *A Circle of Cats*. "Me too."

"Oh," Nameless breathed. The flicker of hope that had started in the desert grew a little brighter.

"As much as I'd love to stand around and watch all this sentimentality," Leona said, arms crossed. "We still need to go. Elodie, we know where Abaddon is, the teams are meeting us on the way. Tank, or Willard, or whoever you are, I fully intend on shooting you in the face a few more times later, but we'll need you for this, so get off the floor and get moving. James," her voice wavered, "give your sister a hug and let's go."

Slingshot held Grace gently, kissed her forehead, and followed Leona out of the room. Nameless didn't move.

Elodie touched his face. "We'll talk when you get back."

He glanced at Sofia. She gave a tiny shake of her head, and he understood. Even if he did pull together enough scraps of himself to help Slingshot and Leona, Grace might not be there when they got back.

"I'm not going anywhere," he said.

She shifted, her face spasming. "You have a job to do."

The hollow spaces in him stabbed, and he shook his head. "I don't. I can't."

"Tank—"

"No." If he never heard that name again it would be too soon.

"Willard," she started again.

"I'm not either of them anymore."

She frowned at him, confused.

"El," he whispered. "I failed as The Tank. I failed as Willard. I can't even help you with this." He gestured helplessly to the mass of cords and tubes. "I can't do what they need me to do. I can't help anyone. I don't know who to be."

Elodie placed a hand on his chest, over the insignia. "I didn't fall in love with Hopper's Tank. I fell in love with *your* strength." She held up the book. "And I didn't fall in love with Willard's pain. I fell for *your* gentleness."

He sucked in a breath. "You fell in love with me?"

She smiled. "Twice."

She pulled on his collar. Or tried to. He barely felt the tug, and her loss of vitality shredded him. But her eyes were still her own. Elodie's eyes that lit up with delight and creativity. Grace's eyes that had read all of his messages with understanding and compassion. He leaned where she guided him and kissed her.

He kept it soft, gentle, letting her lead. She'd have no more bruises because of him. Her lips moved over his and the broken pieces inside him knit. The hollow places filled. The ever-present burn in his stomach extinguished, and the label "Nameless" slid off him like a sigh.

She rested her forehead against his, lips a breath apart. He wrapped his arms about her closer, supporting her worn-out body. Something golden warmed in his chest, radiated out, as if every cell was reaching for her. The darkness behind his closed eyes lightened until it was so bright that a part of his brain wondered if Sofia had turned on extra lights. Then Elodie kissed him again and no part of him thought of anything else.

She pulled back but kept a hand on his chest. "I know who you are. And so do you." She brought both hands up and pressed her fingertips into his suit. Color seeped from her hands, a glossy, iridescent black, and spread through the fabric, replacing the green. The insignia on his chest melted away and reformed in the shape of a warrior's crest.

"Be the shield you've always wanted to be, Will. Be you."

# CHAPTER TWENTY-NINE

*W*ill.

The name reverberated down his spine, shot through the fibers of his muscles. He had a name again. It wasn't fake, and it wasn't pain. It was his.

The name came with a purpose. Not to trample, or to hide, but to shield. To protect, and lift, and support, so others could live their names.

The jeep bounced over a rut as the desert flashed by outside the window, the rest of Seeker Security following in cars behind them. James directed Leona down a barely-there dirt road.

"They're using an old abandoned mine," he said, adjusting the spare Slingshot uniform he'd grabbed from Fashion Seeker. "Choke of 'em out in the desert."

Leona nodded tersely. "I suggest just us three go in after Strickland. More than that and we'll be too easy to spot. The others can cover the entrance. Get in the glove compartment, James. There are ear buds in there."

Slingshot handed out the transmitters, fitting one into Leona's ear so she could keep her hands on the wheel over the rough terrain.

"Anything from Sofia?" Will asked. James flicked a glance at Leona's phone in the cup holder between them.

"Not yet." Two words and his lips pressed together, but Will knew exactly how he felt.

He had a name again, but the woman who gave it to him lay dying. To have found this identity, to have found himself—to have found out Elodie loved him—only to be losing her. The thought clawed through him, rending and ruthless. It pried open his mouth and crawled down his throat, more vicious than any acid ever had been.

Will shut his eyes, focusing on breathing, and cast about for a way to distract himself. "James, Grace changed my suit just by touching it."

"Oh, yeah, she does that. Turn here." He pointed Leona off the dirt road to a cluster of low hills. "She changes fabric, creates fabric, in whatever shape too. Powers run in the family, I guess."

"I guess so." No wonder she whipped up street clothes in his size so fast. *She didn't have to sew it.* He remembered the fit and how the clothes made him feel. *She's still a genius.* The specter of losing her loomed closer. *More talking.*

"What about the nanites?" Will asked. "At the plant?"

"Ah, brah, I was trying to tell you. I switched the containers out for plain water. No nanites."

Will nodded. "Sorry again."

"You were doing your job. I would've done the same thing."

The caravan parked half a mile from the entrance, behind the hills. All of the Seeker Security women donned night vision goggles.

Leona handed a pair to Will. "For the bugs too."

"Thanks." The memory of spiky legs on his skin made him shudder.

So many things made sense now. Elodie's clothes; why "defeating" Abaddon had been so easy; how NineSix and the others summoned all the locusts—if the pit and the beast were real, so were the terrorists' supernatural powers—Slingshot and the nanites. So many things made sense now that the things that didn't make sense stood out all the sharper. The peace of the desert in the face of the upcoming battle. How long he'd put up with Hopper's treatment. *And El in a hospital bed. That will never make sense.*

His breath stuttered. *Focus. The faster you get this done, the faster you can get back to her.*

He army-crawled next to Leona to the ridge of the low hill. Two figures in desert camo squatted near an opening in another hill. A silencer pinged next to him twice, and both figures keeled over. Leona nodded in satisfaction.

"What was that?" Will pointed at the guards. "You didn't have to murder them! I could've knocked them out, or Slingshot could've done it with a couple rocks."

She shrugged. "Relax, I only hit them with tranqs. Besides, the point is to be quick and quiet, at least until we get Strickland out." She swapped the tranq gun for a more-lethal variety and motioned the rest of Seeker Security to spread out to cover the entrance.

"Well, no more 'murder' until then."

She smirked. "Murder *after* then?"

He rolled his eyes and ducked into the tunnel behind James. Red lightbulbs hung from extension cords every ten feet. Four bulbs in, the passage branched. Slingshot led them to the right.

The ground sloped down, long enough for Will to count seven more light bulbs. As the floor leveled out, the left wall fell away, and the tunnel became a walkway overlooking an enormous cavern. The lightbulbs continued their pattern down the walk, with HVAC grates fixed into the ceiling at the same intervals. The roof domed so high that Will had to crane his head to see the top. He hadn't played any football since high school, but he remembered the field dimensions. Abaddon's hideout put stadiums to shame.

The walkway circled the entire perimeter of the cavern, and Slingshot indicated the doors set into its rock wall at even intervals. "Guard stations and weapons storage. The ones patrolling the floor should be changing shifts soon."

Will counted a dozen armed guards pacing the floor below. They concentrated around a raised cement circle fifty feet wide with a platform over one end. Something about it niggled at his memory, but he couldn't place it. "Is that ...?"

Leona leaned past him to look. "Sweet mother ..."

Slingshot's voice was heavy. "That's the pit."

It seethed. Chunks of gray bubbled in a pink liquid, like a vomitous stew. A patch of fog materialized in the middle of the pit, like breath on a mirror, and Will squinted to make it out better. Something covered the disgusting mess, flat as glass, that kept the spurts of demonic amniotic fluid from splashing over the sides of the cement walls.

Slingshot nudged him. "Hopper's the key, yeah? That's the door. See that platform? All they have to do is get him up there and toss him in the pit. Door evaporates. Demon comes out."

A pale shape rose through the muck and bashed against the barrier. A tremor ran through the cavern, shaking loose a spray of dirt and pebbles from the walkway ceiling. Slingshot diverted it away from the group.

Hinges squealed as one of the guard room doors opened. Will and the others squished back to the edge of the tunnel, out of sight.

"Abaddon's restless. Almost time." A woman with a screaming locust on her left cheek sauntered out of the guard room and leaned against the railing.

A man joined her. "Just heard from command. It's not almost time, it is time. We're supposed to take the key out now."

Leona swore. Slingshot flung two of the fallen rocks and downed both guards.

"Hurry. They'll have Hopper down this way." He sprinted for a staircase leading down into the rock wall.

Will followed, eyes on the guards down below. Resentment bubbled in him like the pit on the floor. *Not only do I have to rescue Hopper, I have to do it in a hurry.*

At the bottom of the metal stairs, the hallway forked. Slingshot ran left, past an archway that opened onto the main cavern floor, and down a cramped corridor covered in violent graffiti. Thick, metal doors lined the hallway, each with a tiny window.

"What is this?" Will asked.

"They never built a prisoner-holding area—they don't take prisoners. But these are the quarantine rooms for new recruits. If Hopper's here, they'll have him in one of these little puka rooms."

"You two find him. I'll keep a watch on the floor." Leona headed back to the archway.

Slingshot pointed to himself, then at the row of doors on the right. Will nodded and took the row on the left.

"They might as well be cells," he murmured, looking through one of the tiny windows in the doors. Maybe ten feet long, with nothing but a cot and a bucket latrine each, Abaddon's recruits wouldn't get a luxurious welcome.

He checked two more. *There.* Hopper huddled against the back wall of the third cell, face buried in his knees, trench coat dirty and rumpled.

A tremor rocked through Will. A hollow place, screaming and silent, fought to reopen in his chest, a knife-sharp ice cave in the space where he'd held Hopper's supposed friendship. His feet froze to the floor.

James was at his elbow. "You find him?

"I don't—" Tank swallowed. "I don't know if I can face him."

"Nah, brah. You got this." James' voice was gentle. "The things Grace said about you—you half the man she says, you can do this."

*Grace.* He shut his eyes against the screaming hollow. Filled its emptiness with the memory of Elodie's kiss.

*Get him out. That's all you have to do right now.* Breath shaky, Will nodded to James. "Thanks."

"Anytime. Let's get this B-52 out of here."

"B-52?"

"Yeah, giant cockroach back home. B-52s because they're so big."

"Ah, I see what you did. Locusts, cockroach."

James clicked his tongue with an exaggerated wink. "Cock-a-roach." Will chuckled and realized the cheesy joke had swept away the rest of his nerves.

*This is what having a real team is like.* He punched the lock plate, and the door swung open.

"Tank!" Hopper clutched the wall, scrambling to stand. "You're here!"

Will grabbed Hopper by the collar without answering and hustled him out of the chamber. His former manager kept babbling.

"I am so glad to see you. It's NineSix. He nabbed me—the cops hadn't found him yet— and brought me here, but I don't know what ..." He quailed under Will's glare.

"I can't believe you're trying to play innocent. No, I take that back. I can believe it."

"Play innocent?" He tried to laugh. "I'm the one that got kidnapped here." Hopper's eyes darted over Will's face, and Will knew he was picking up on the difference in his tone, his bearing. No feet shuffling, no mantle to trip over. Nothing in the way of being himself. Part of Hopper's job was reading people. *Of course he'd notice.*

Leona trotted around the corner. "We've got movement out there. Looks like they're all gathering around the pit."

"What's the pit?" Hopper whispered.

"Oh my—" She threw her hands in the air. "Are you kidding me?"

"Let me fill you in." Will pulled Hopper along with him to peer around the corner of the archway and pointed at the crowd growing around the cement walls of the pit. "The terrorist group that *you* hired, kidnapped you—a prime example of how selfish and wicked people are—so they could throw you in a portal to the underworld and raise a demon to wipe out humanity. We're rescuing you so they can't. When we get back to town, you're under arrest. All caught up?"

Leona snuck to the far side of the archway. "And any minute, they're gonna realize the people they sent to get you are missing. So, we need to get back up the stairs and out of here, now."

Hopper paled but found his voice again while Will half carried, half pushed him up the stairs. "That I hired? Come on, big guy, do you hear yourself? It's me, I'm your manager, your friend."

"My friend?" Will spat. "Gerard almost died because of you. All those people at Container Park were hurt because of you. I arrested the wrong man because of you."

Slingshot gave a little wave. "And let's not forget the part where I was discredited and nearly executed either."

"Exactly." Will hugged the wall at the top of the stairs, the group keeping to the shadows. "Elodie never wanted to see me again because of you."

"Come on," Hopper said. "I'm the one who matched you up with her in the first place. You never would've made a move if it hadn't been for me."

"You lied to me. You manipulated me." Will's grip on the back of Hopper's collar tightened. "You made me think I was stupid, that I couldn't get by without you."

"No, no, feeling stupid, that's you projecting your issues with your uncle onto me. I was giving you honest feedback to make you better."

Will halted and glared at him.

Hopper shrank. "Ok, yes, fine. I may have ... arranged a few things with Abaddon, but I was doing what was good for you. Because what's good for you is good for me, right?"

"What would be good for you right now is to shut up," Leona hissed. "Unless you want the mob of cultists intent on killing you to realize you're escaping?"

A stir moved through the crowd on the cavern floor, and a small knot jogged to the quarantine chambers. On the opposite walkway, Abaddon lackeys trickled out of the guard rooms and down another set of stairs to the main floor, on their way to see the portal open.

Will pulled Hopper closer to the cave wall. Less than halfway along their own walkway, they still had two guard anterooms to pass—one ten feet away and the other near the tunnel—and he didn't know if they had emptied or not. "Let's hurry it up."

"See?" Hopper's toes barely touched the floor as Will dragged him toward the exit. "Look at you, taking charge. *I* did that. *I* made you a hero. You don't really want to arrest me when we get out of here."

"I'm not in charge," Will shot back, keeping an eye on the quarantine entrance. "We're working as a team, something you know nothing about."

"But you're here, you came for me. *We* can be a team, Tank."

"No, we can't." Will's anger with his former manager still burned. The betrayal still stung, and Hopper's pathetic attempts to win him over were grating on his nerves. But his stomach was quiet. The holes inside him were filled. The pressure his manager's words used to exert on him was absent, the need to please him, evaporated. Tank had never really existed, and Willard had grown into someone new. He would save Hector Strickland from Abaddon, because doing so would save others. And because whatever else Hopper was, he was still a person and Will's strength—the gift Hopper cared about—and his gentleness—the gift Hopper disdained—existed to help other people. But his identity, and his worth no longer depended on this man's approval. "And that's not my name anymore."

Shouts came from below, and two men ran from the quarantine quarters waving their arms and pointing to the walkway. A third pulled a switch on the wall, and an alarm screamed through the cavern.

Leona swore as shots pinged off the railing. Ahead, a group surged out of the farthest guard room, already firing. Will shoved Hopper and Slingshot against the wall and covered them with his body, shielding them from the bullets. Shards of rock splintered from the cave wall as Slingshot made a fist. He mimed a throwing motion, aiming the rocks at the shooter's eyes.

Leona tucked into Will's side and reached around him to return fire. "Marlena!" she called over comms. "We could use some help."

Will heard Marlena's affirmative answer in his own ear bud, but they couldn't wait where they were; he had to get his team out of the line of fire. No one had come out of the closer guard room.

"Move with me." He sidestepped, covering the others until they tumbled into the antechamber. Hopper scrambled on hands and knees through the cache of weaponry to the back of the room, face white.

"Ho-ho!" Leona crowed triumphantly and snatched up a rocket launcher.

"Keep an eye on him." Will nodded at Hopper. "I'll clear the path to the tunnel."

He charged out the door, Slingshot and Leona taking up posts at the opening. Bullets sprayed him from below and ahead. He ignored them. Five Abaddon guards formed up near the farthest guardroom. Will snapped five guns into useless pieces. Employing the minimum force needed to incapacitate them all, he stashed the unconscious guards in the antechamber and waved the others forward.

Leona, Slingshot, and Hopper dashed out of the antechamber toward the tunnel, but the HVAC grates along the corridor burst open, raining angry, locust-tattooed cultists. One swung his legs around Leona's neck, throwing her to the side and landing on top of her. Another dropped on Slingshot. Will charged.

He crashed into the swarm of guards like a bull. A hand shot out of the melee and ripped off his goggles. A jet of walnut sized rocks pummeled the guard's face, knocking him back. Will jumped to his feet in time to kick away a guard with a pistol aimed at Slingshot's back. James spun, took in the shooter laying on the floor, grinned, and fist-bumped Will.

A pair of men seized Hopper, and he screamed, "Tank!"

Will jumped and planted both feet into one of the men's chests. "I told you, that's not my name."

Hopper twisted out of his trench coat, wriggling out of the other man's grasp. "Fine, you want to rebrand? We can discuss that."

"There's nothing to discuss." Will swept the guard's leg, choked out another, and knocked out a third. The wave of attackers from the HVAC grates slowed, and Will took the chance to stare his ex-manager in the eye, glad someone had stolen his goggles. He didn't want anything in the way for this.

"Hopper," he said. "You're fired."

Hopper gaped at him, speechless.

"Ha! I wish I had a camera right now. Look at that face." Leona shut Hopper's mouth with one finger. "Come on, we're not out yet." Footsteps and yelling echoed up the staircase.

Hopper didn't move. Will grabbed the back of his shirt and hustled him toward the tunnel. "You two ok?"

Blood ran down the side of Leona's face, but she dashed it away. "I think James is limping."

"I'm fine. Sofia can fix us up when we get back."

*When we get back.* Adrenaline surged. They had Hopper and they were almost there. Three light bulbs and a tunnel away from getting out and getting back to Elodie. Leona could take Hopper the rest of the way to the police and lead them back here—Will was going straight to Fashion Seeker and El. He refused to allow himself to think that she might not be there when he returned.

A heavy, metal door dropped out of the ceiling like a portcullis, slamming shut over the tunnel entrance.

"No!" Leona growled, grinding to a halt. "Marlena, how far out are you?"

Movement flickered ahead. Will caught a glimpse of NineSix before there was a rush and a roar and a wall of locusts slammed into him. Serrated legs and crunchy exoskeletons blocked his view. He fought the reflex to bring his hands to his face—he couldn't let go of Hopper.

The jumper materialized next to him. Will shot one fist into the cloud of insects, found fingers, and snapped them all.

NineSix shrieked, then laughed. "Nothing so obvious."

Will growled. "How many bones do you have?"

"More than you have time for."

The locust swarm cut off. Will shook the remaining insects out of his face, tossed Hopper to James, and leapt for NineSix. He jumped back twenty feet.

"Leona!" Will charged, hoping she'd know what he meant.

"Got him!" She fired both pistols, blowing out NineSix's kneecaps.

He howled and went down but jumped again right as Will reached him. Will spun. A flash of NineSix next to Hopper and Slingshot, and then Hopper was gone.

Will dashed to the railing, heart pounding. "No!"

NineSix smirked at him from the platform over the portal, an ashen-faced Hopper next to him. The jumper gave a little wave. And shoved Hector Strickland in the pit.

# Chapter Thirty

H ot sand squished between Grace's toes. Salt air kissed her cheeks, and the sun's brightness made her squint.

She recognized her favorite childhood beach and the fact that she was dreaming at the same time.

As a test, she traced a curlicue in the sand, then drew it up from the ground, transforming the shape into a deep-blue silk scarf. She could have created the scarf in waking life but wasn't capable of changing sand into silk. Create fabric, yes. Alter existing fabric, yes. But turn something else into a textile, no.

The shimmering fabric slipping through her fingers told her this was a lucid dream.

With a thought, she swapped her slacks and blouse for a tankini top and board shorts and moved from the beach to the water. A swell splashed up to her hips and she shivered.

*Let's make that a bit warmer.* The temperature altered to that of a comfortable bathtub, and she dove in. Her breathing continued unbroken under the water, and the salt didn't bother her eyes—no snorkel or mask needed in a dream.

Clouds of color swept past her. Unless they were part of one of the reserves, the beaches near the North Shore were mostly fished out, but dream-schools of parrotfish, manini, and tangs bustled around her. She twirled under the water, the yellows, and oranges, and purples of the fish shining like merfolk. A honu glided through the waves farther off, and a pair of lauwiliwilinukunukuʻoiʻoi chased each other through a hole in the reef. The sunlight refracted beneath the surface of the water, illuminating the gentle ripples of sand on the ocean floor. Grace floated, peaceful, relaxed.

A wave jostled her sideways, pushing her into a tower of rock and old coral. Pain stabbed through her leg, and she looked down to see a purple splotch bruising her calf. She frowned.

This was her dream—her *lucid* dream—so if she didn't want the ocean to play rough, it wasn't allowed to.

She repositioned herself a safer distance from the rock, feet planted in the sand, water hip deep, and started over again, floating on her back, face to the sun.

*Float, relax.*

Something beeped. She stood up. It wasn't any kind of bird call.

*Sounds more like it came from something digital.*

Near the naupaka growing further up the beach, a woman in a lab coat bustled between machines on rolling carts. The beeping grew more insistent, the woman more frantic, pushing buttons and turning knobs.

Grace recognized her now. "Sofia—"

A wave grabbed her, rolling her under the surf. She hit the reef again, and the air whooshed out of her in a stream in panicked bubbles.

Water surged into her lungs. The salt stung her eyes.

The ocean turned murky, devoid of fish and color. The sunbeams fractured to shards of ice.

The current pummeled her into the rocks again and again. Grace fought for control of the dream—*Rewind. Start over. Or at least put me back on shore*—but another wave caught her and slammed her into a vicious outcropping.

The rock stabbed through her ribcage, through her heart. She sank, blood ribboning out of her chest like smoke.

The beeping of the machines screamed in her ears.

"Stay with me Grace, stay," Sofia pled.

She couldn't tell her friend she was right there, that she could hear her. Her lungs were cement. Her legs spasmed. Her eyes refused to open—*when did they close?* Swollen, everything was swollen, her skin threatening to split like a waterlogged corpse.

*This is my dream. I should be able to fix it.*

*No can fix everything, Grace.* Her grandmother's voice.

Even as Grace was pinned to the ocean floor, a memory swam to the surface. Six years old, she'd found a mongoose, half dead, and fetched her grandmother for help. Tūtū had taken one look at the creature and said the kindest thing they could do was end its pain. Her grandmother released the animal from its life, and Grace cried the rest of the day.

The next day, Grace found the first bruise.

Her family had assumed it was merely a "normal" childhood bump. After that, they'd manifested so often, Grace forgot about the mongoose in relation to the bruises.

James always said it was like she held the whole world's pain in her body. That her compassion let everything in. The rest of the memory played out.

Her grandmother holding her close. *Uku pau, Grace. Let it go. You don't have to carry this.*

And on the bottom of the ocean, in a dream spiraled out of control, she remembered. Her compassion had been there before she had taken on anyone else's pain.

She had made James dig a grave for the creature as she wove a palm leaf into a marker, taking refuge in working with her hands.

She remembered how to use her creativity to filter what she let in. How to let her compassion flow out, but keep the pain from flowing in.

She laid the pain down, embraced the creativity and kicked off the sand.

And then she was on shore, retching and coughing and gasping, and feeling like someone had taken a cheese grater to her lungs, but breathing next to a now-calm sea.

Sofia was still frantic, working on the machines. Grace was free of others' pain, but she knew she needed more—more work, more healing, more time. She couldn't do anymore on her own.

Warmth spread through her shoulder like someone had touched her. She turned, searching, but no one else was on the beach. The heat on her shoulder grew, spread. It caught in her veins, raced to her limbs, stabbed each of her cells like a thousand burning stars. The heat spiraled in her center, burning away the weight in her lungs, easing the pressure on her skin. It flamed into her heart, cauterizing the wound in her chest. The heat consumed her, and she searched her hands, her arms, sure she must be glowing like a supernova.

A hint of wakefulness tickled her mind. She fought it, wanting to see where the heat led, but her conscience prodded her. Something had been happening before she fell asleep. Something important.

*I'd been dying. I'd been dying, and Will and James and Leona went to stop Abaddon. But he kissed me first.*

She knew his shyness. She knew he helped people in spite of it. She knew he had a cat. She knew he loved picture books, and she knew he could punch through walls. She knew he loved Moose Tracks ice cream and hated grape jelly. She knew the pain in his past. She knew who he had grown to become. All of her loved all of him.

Grace let herself wake up. Her eyes opened easily, all the swelling gone. No bruises marred her arms. Her skin was smooth and firm. Nothing hurt.

She pushed to sitting, feeling her compassion beating inside, her creativity keeping it safe.

Sofia was staring at her, mouth open. A clipboard fell from her hands and clattered to the floor. "Grace. How ..."

*How indeed?* Even if her dream experience protected her from future bruises, how would it heal the trauma already there?

The syringe Will had tried to stab into his veins lay on the counter, bent and useless. She touched her lips. There was no way to perform a blood transfusion, but what if blood wasn't the only carrier?

"He kissed me."

Sofia's eyebrows raised. "He kissed you."

Grace threw off the sheets and scrambled out of the bed. All of her loved all of him, and no part of her was going to sit here and wait. "Call Marlena. We're going after them."

# CHAPTER THIRTY-ONE

W ill crashed into the cave wall. Again.

It was the third time the beast had swatted him across the cavern like a bothersome mosquito. He clambered out of the superhero-shaped hole in the wall, brushing rubble off his shoulders, and faced the monster called Abaddon.

Six pairs of legs spiked out of a mountainous, insectile body, the front pair thicker and ending in hooves. A scorpion tail, thick as a tree trunk, curled over a pair of giant wings lying flat against its back. Abaddon's head mimicked the vicious, fanged face on the terrorists' tattoos, but it was the eyes that were getting to Will.

Unlike an insect, there were only two and they had eyelids. They were intelligent—like looking at the eyes of a dog or an octopus. Abaddon knew where it was, and it knew its purpose.

Under that purpose, the cave floor was chaos. Terrorists shrieked and ran in every direction, diving into chambers carved into the wall or behind machinery as Abaddon lurched and crashed around the room.

*Or former terrorists,* Will thought. He suspected any loyalty to their cause or the hulking monster in front of him had evaporated the first time Abaddon had speared one of their own on its stinger, proving it didn't differentiate between humans with tattoos and humans without.

The beast lifted one leg and squashed another of the fleeing terrorists like a roach. Will winced. Terrorist or not, that was a horrifying death.

The lights flickered and a mechanical whirring echoed through the cave.

"Will!" Slingshot's voice came over the transmitter while he waved his arms from the walkway, where Leona was trying to hotwire the control panel for the door blocking the tunnel. He jumped up and down, pointing at the ceiling. The dome was opening.

Abaddon's eyes narrowed and it prepared to spring. It knew its purpose, and it knew where to go.

"No, no, no." Will spun, searching till he spotted the controls. Two men hauled back on levers on the opposite side of the cavern, directed by NineSix. "James!" he called back, gesturing wildly at them. He didn't need to say any more.

Slingshot let fly. Two rocks pinged off the metal control panel. The third took down one of the lever operators. Leona left the door long enough to shoot the second. NineSix jumped out of sight. The dome stopped moving partway open.

Abaddon jumped anyway.

Will dove and grabbed the tail above the stinger. He heaved backwards and spun in a tight circle, using Abaddon's momentum against it. The hooves screeched against the floor like a cymbal in a buzzsaw, scrambling for purchase. Will spun faster, and Abaddon lifted off the ground. Two more circles and he flung the beast through the room, over the pit, and into the back wall. The crash reverberated through the cave. Abaddon slid down the wall, landing on its back with its legs flailing in the air. The wall avalanched, cutting off the quarantine chambers and the stairs.

Will stumbled forward and bent over, hands on knees and chest heaving.

"Brah, you ok?" James asked.

Will gave a wave, still trying to catch his breath.

More rocks flew past, aimed at remaining terrorists. "Was that like a personal best lift or something?"

Will chuckled and straightened, grateful for James' attempt at humor in the face of trying to fight a giant locust-scorpion-horse hybrid. "Yeah, probably. I think my shoulder popped, swinging that thing around."

Abaddon chittered angrily and rocked side to side, trying to regain its footing.

"You know, Grace's never really been into muscly guys." James went for another joke, eyeing the behemoth. "But I think I can talk her into going out with you again if get out of here alive."

Will sobered. "Yeah, and she's gotta be alive when we get back."

James' voice came quieter. "Yeah. And that."

Abaddon found its feet and roared.

Will sighed. "Ok, let's try something else." He ran, stooping to grab a broken metal pole from the debris littered on the floor, and leapt. His stomach flipflopped as he floated half a second at the top of his arc, before plummeting directly over Abaddon's back. The pole speared the beast between the wings, and it shrieked, legs buckling.

Will held on as it thrashed.

It stilled, and he held his breath, his grip loosening on his impromptu spear.

"Are we ... done?" James asked.

The beast's body jerked, shuddered. And gathered itself like Abaddon was holding its breath. It reared, the thorax contracted, and the pole shot out of its body like an arrow, embedding itself in the back wall. The hooves crashed back to earth, and the monster shook itself. The wound closed, sealing as if it had never been there.

"Oh, we're in trouble," Will breathed.

Grinning, Abaddon owled its head around like a horror-show poltergeist, and a sudden surge of sympathy ran through Will for all the criminals who'd ever tried—and failed—to fight him.

Abaddon bucked, tossing him into the air. The scorpion tail smacked him across the room, and he smashed into the wall for the fourth time. Rock collapsed, burying him. Will dug for the top. Air hit his face, and he gasped, coughing out grit and dirt.

The ground rumbled beneath the demon's hooves as it trampled forward. Its stinger rammed into Will's chest with the full weight of the monster's body behind it, pinning him to what remained of the wall, and knocking the wind out of him. Pain lanced through his ribs. He couldn't breathe. For a split second, he wondered if the stinger had actually pierced him—nothing had managed to hit him that hard since he'd gained his powers—but when he looked down, his chest was whole.

Elodie's suit wasn't. The stinger had ripped a gash in the fabric over his ribs.

Will pushed back, struggling to find purchase on the smooth plates of the exoskeleton. Sneering, Abaddon leaned in, pressing harder. The wall crumbled behind Will, drilling him into a crevice, and cutting off any room to maneuver.

A barrage of jagged rocks crashed into Abaddon's eye. It swung its head and backed off, a pair of legs pawing at its face in what Will thought was a good imitation of him when NineSix had pummeled him with locusts.

"Yeah, doesn't feel too nice, does it?" He scrambled out of the rock and waved to Slingshot for the assist.

"Leona's got the door open," the other hero called down.

Marlena and a knot of Seeker Security rushed from the tunnel to position as back up for Slingshot and Leona. Another squad took up places on the opposite walkway.

"Great. We need to close the other one." Will pointed at the dome while he circled Abaddon in a crouch. The beast crept to the side, watching him.

"And then what?" James threw his hands in the air. "Keep it here forever?"

"I don't know! You have any ideas?" Will's foot stepped in a puddle of ooze, and he risked a glance at the broken section of the pit's cement border. Despite the liquid overflowing onto the floor, the level inside the pit hadn't dropped.

Abaddon's gaze followed Will's. A rumble echoed deep in its chest and the edge in its eyes softened a degree.

"What are you thinking?" Will murmured. He crept to the pit wall. Up close, the nauseating colors resolved to a different picture. The contents shimmered, and he realized why the pit had seemed familiar. He'd seen it in his dream in the desert. Here, now, in Abaddon's cave, he saw the same paradise on the other side of the portal he'd seen then.

Green, verdant. Peaceful.

The same longing ached in his chest. The dream, the pull of wherever that place was—they made no sense. Will straightened out of his crouch, mind racing.

Underworld. Hell. Destruction. All of these words had been tossed about like people knew what they were talking about. The portal was a *pit*. Nothing good came out of anything called a pit. Pits never contained beauty.

But this one did.

How furious would its inhabitant be if someone suddenly dumped a scumbag like Hector Strickland on its head? How bent on destruction would it be if it crossed through to find more corrupted beings like the one that had just invaded its perfect home?

Will looked at the pole, invertebrate guts dangling on the end.

*Or if it found someone like me trying to kill it?*

"You want to go home," he murmured. *I don't blame you.* He tore his eyes away from the idyllic picture in the pit, but the intensity of its pull lingered. "Guys?" They couldn't kill this thing, that much was clear. And they couldn't keep it in the cave indefinitely. "What if we send it back?"

"Knock it back in the stew. Got it." Leona braced on one knee and balanced the rocket launcher on her shoulder.

Abaddon wrenched its gaze away from its home and stridulated its wings in a maddened screech. Edge and purpose returned to its eyes, sharp and violent once more, and Will understood. It wouldn't—couldn't—go back until it thought its purpose was fulfilled.

"Wait, Leona, I think—"

A boom echoed off the walls. Abaddon flew backwards, skipped off the surface of the pit like a stone on a lake, and crashed into the remains of the back wall. Dirt and dust and rocks billowed through the cavern, filling Will's mouth and nose and eyes. He ducked behind an abandoned jeep, covering his face with his elbow.

"I was going to say, I don't think us knocking it back in the pit is going to cut it. We have to convince it to go on its own somehow."

Slingshot coughed over the line. "And maybe we don't bring down the ceiling first?"

"Picky, picky," Leona grumbled.

A tremor ran through the ground, setting pebbles dancing. Abaddon was on its feet again. Scrambling for an idea of how to convince a murderous scorpion demon of anything, Will edged around the jeep, still waving away dust. The beast faced away from him, watching something on the walkway opposite Slingshot and Leona. Its tail twitched. Its legs coiled. And it sprung.

The air cleared, and Will saw its target.

The moment contracted to a pinprick. Four thoughts exploded in his brain simultaneously.

Elodie was here, standing on the walkway.

There were no bruises on her skin.

Abaddon was leaping straight at her.

And there was no way for Will to get to her first.

He ran anyway. Everything in him reached for her. His voice—part of him was aware he was screaming. His thoughts—he remembered his words in the medical suite. *I'd give her everything if I could*. And his body. Every cell stretched toward her. But he was too far away, and Elodie was going to die because he'd failed again.

Abaddon's face struck empty air and bounced backwards with a clunk.

The beast staggered back, shaking its head like it had run into a brick wall. Elodie gaped, looking just as confused. Will skidded to a stop, mouth open.

Abaddon lunged again, only to smash its face into nothing again.

The bare bulbs strung along the walkway flickered, and light reflected off a sphere encircling Elodie. It glowed, golden and familiar. Like when he'd kissed her and felt light on his closed eyes.

Abaddon struck a third time and was rebuffed a third time.

Elodie's eyes found Will, awe stretching across her face. She pointed to the barrier, and then to him, mouthing a word.

*Shield.*

He patted his torso like he expected to feel something missing. "*My* ... shield?"

Metal cranked overhead. The dome started to move again, and Abaddon jerked its head up. Will spun to the control panel. NineSix waved, reached for something in his pocket and flickered out of sight. He reappeared right beside Will.

And plunged a knife between his ribs.

Shock froze Will's response long enough for NineSix to stab him twice more, twisting the weapon deep.

Blood wet his torso, his side. He covered the wound with one hand, feeling shreds of skin and muscle tangling with the fabric Abaddon had ripped with its stinger. NineSix leered at him, gloating, and all Will could think was that he was getting blood all over Elodie's beautiful suit.

His pulse whooshed in his ears, obscuring the sounds of the dome cranking open and Elodie's voice, still muffled behind his shield, screaming his name.

His body caught up before his mind did. Some reflex inherent in his gifts kicked in, snapping his shield back to his body. He felt it in his cells, like a wall springing up. The bleeding stopped, the pain vanished, and the knife shot out of his side like it'd been pushed from the inside.

"You're done." Will crushed his heel against NineSix's left foot, then his right. At the same time, a fist sized piece of cave wall rocketed in from the balcony, slamming into his ear, and a shot from Leona shattered his right hip.

He went limp, face in shock. But he didn't jump. Will laid him on the floor and Leona called over the earpiece for a pair of the Seeker Security women to come from outside to deal with him.

"Pretty sure I get the credit for that one," James said. "Middle ear bones!"

Will gave a tired wave. "Good with me."

A mild ding sounded incongruously behind him, and he turned to see Elodie wrestle open the elevator's bent doors. Sofia was with her, a backpack on. He hadn't even noticed the doctor on the walkway. Elodie had been all he could see; all he could think of.

"Will!" She launched herself at him, throwing her arms around his neck. "Are you ok?"

"That's ... interesting." Sofia inspected the stab wound. The mess of flesh was still visible, but it wasn't bleeding. "It *looks* like you should be bleeding out, but it's just kind of frozen there."

The dome ground to a halt, fully open. Abaddon screeched and launched off the ground.

"We'll have to figure it out later." He pulled back to run at the beast again.

"I got it!" Leona let loose with the rocket launcher again. The shot blasted the beast against the wall, sending another avalanche of rock and debris rolling toward them.

Will threw his shield out on purpose this time, stretching it to encompass all three of them. Boulders and broken jeep parts bounced off the shield, the sound muted.

Wetness seeped down his side again. A wave of nausea rolled over him and he swayed.

Elodie swore. "Sof, look."

Will looked too and wished he hadn't. The wound wept like it was making up for every injury he never had.

Sofia whipped bandages out of her backpack and put pressure on the wound. "You have to take your shield back."

Woozily, Will pointed to the enormous monster scrambling to its feet outside their little protected cave.

"Take it back or you're going to bleed out."

Elodie grabbed his face in her hands. "Will, take it back."

He frowned. Images flooded his mind, of a beach, and almost drowning, and then golden warmth. Emotions overran the images—worry, panic—and faintly, barely out of reach, words. *Can't lose him now.*

"Sofia, do hallucinations come with bleeding out?"

But Elodie was frowning too, her eyes unfocused. "You ... fired Hopper?"

"How did you know that?" Will asked. He caught a feeling, a whiff of discovery. Elodie lifted her fingers from his face and the images and feelings cut off. She sucked in a breath and touched his skin again. "Think something. Really loudly."

Outside the shield, Abaddon rampaged through the cave. A few remaining terrorists poked their heads out of hiding and the demon trampled after them.

The edges of Will's vision blurred, and he couldn't see a way out of the situation. He thought the only thing that mattered to him.

*I love you. And I don't care that I was stripped down to nothing and broken, because I found you. And you made me whole. And I don't care if I die here today, because I'll die whole.*

"Oh," Elodie breathed. She kissed the corner of his mouth, his lower lip, softly, like she was afraid to hurt him. "Tell me if you can hear this."

The beach filled his thoughts again. Pain, dying, gold light and bruises disappearing. *That was you. You healed me. I think you sent some of your shield to me when we kissed, just like you're doing now, only on a closer level somehow? I don't know how exactly, but I woke up healed. You made me whole too.*

Sofia's thoughts interrupted them. *This is beautiful, it really is, and I hate to interrupt it.*

Will looked down. Sofia was staring up, apologetically. The tatters of his suit had slipped out of the way and her fingers touched his bare skin.

*And this is a fascinating aspect of casting your shield outside of yourself, and we absolutely need to study it when all of this is done. But that's never going to happen if you die from blood loss. So, as the medical professional here, I have to insist. Take your shield back now, Will.*

He exchanged an amazed glance with Elodie, and she nodded.

"Ok." He let go of her face and called his shield home. It slid into place easily, like a familiar glove. Again, the bleeding stopped, and his head cleared.

Down the other end of the cave, Abaddon snapped at a knot of people cowering in what was left of a carved-out chamber.

Elodie slipped her hand in his. "What do we do about that?"

"Hey, you all okay down there?" James asked over the earbud.

Up on the balcony, Leona threw her hands in the air. "What is Elodie doing here? I still owe you a few more bullets to the face, Will," she ranted. "If anything happens to her, I won't wait till you've got your shield back on you."

Will winced, and Elodie looked at him questioningly. "I don't have an ear bud in, what is she mad about?"

"Uh, Leona wants to make sure you're ok."

James' concern sounded more sincere. "Seriously, are you ok? I couldn't get through on comms while you were in whatever weird bubble you were in, but that looked like a lot of blood. Why were *you* bleeding?"

"We're ok, we're ok. The bubble was ..." Inside the shield, thoughts and ideas and feelings transferred. Whoever was inside his shield could communicate on a different level. Will looked at Abaddon, still stomping around the other side of the cave. "I have an idea. Come on."

"It'll work." *It has to work.* Will held the earbud up while he, Elodie and Sofia leaned in, heads close, to hear Leona and James on the other end.

"Are you crazy?" Leona hissed through the earbud. "You'll bleed out before it works."

"Leona, I didn't know you cared," Will said wryly.

She huffed. "It was just a couple of bullets."

Elodie stared at him, aghast. "We can't do that. Leona's right. It's too dangerous." She touched his side, above the mangled wound.

"When your shield is part of you like it's always been," Sofia said. "Nothing can get through, but obviously, when it's around someone else, you aren't protected. My hypothesis, albeit quickly formed from what we've seen so far, which isn't much—"

On the walkway, Leona waved her hands, gesturing for the doctor to get on with it.

Sofia cleared her throat. "My hypothesis is that an injury you sustain while unprotected ceases bleeding or causing pain once your shield returns to your body. Merely standing inside it doesn't stop it, as we saw. You have to pull it completely back to you. If I had to guess, I would say that you would heal from such an injury over time, provided you keep your shield with you instead of sending it out, but if you ... bleed out while it's outside of you." She spread her hands. "Who knows?"

"There's gotta be another way." Slingshot paced next to Leona, fidgeting a rock in the air.

"James," Will said softly. "In the brief time I've known you, you've been a far better friend that Hopper ever was the whole time I worked with him. But it's like you said, a team is better. And right now, this is my job on the team."

Abaddon turned from the people huddled in the rock chamber and started to claw its way up the mountain of rubble toward the dome.

"Out of time for other options," Leona said, matter-of-factly. "Get on it."

"Your turn, El." Will squeezed her hand before letting go.

Exhaling slowly, Elodie pressed her palms together, then fingers taut, began to pull them apart. Light flared between her hands, and a dark green cord wove itself into existence, stretched between her palms. It lengthened, piling on the ground until she had created a coil long enough to lasso a monster's head. She snapped her fingers, and the cord detached from her skin.

"It's a similar fabric to your suit," she said. "Should be strong enough."

Will scooped it off the ground and kissed her forehead. "You are amazing."

He took her hand and jogged closer to the beast. Sofia hurried back to the elevator to join Slingshot and Leona.

"James, you ready?" Will asked.

"I still don't know if this is the best idea."

"Suck it up, Buttercup," Leona said. "I'm taking the shot."

"Not exactly the words of encouragement I would've chosen," Will muttered.

In answer, Leona sent another rocket into the cave wall above Abaddon. A flurry of boulders burst loose, cascading onto the beast's back. A series of grenades followed, carried by rocks Slingshot sent flying. The wall avalanched, burying Abaddon's back half and pinning it in place.

Still clutching Elodie's hand, Will rushed forward. Abaddon shrieked, throwing its head up in an attempt to scramble out from under the mountain on its back, and Will threw Elodie's cord around its neck, tying it tight against the exoskeleton. The flaps of his ripped suit stuck to his side with dried blood. They'd be wet again as soon as he threw wide his shield.

The last time he'd really bled had been after his final game in high school. Somewhere between the showers and his locker, one of his so-called teammates had slashed him across the back. He hadn't noticed until he'd unwrapped the towel from around his waist and found it soaked in blood.

Fear threaded through his limbs. Once he had his shield outside of himself, they wouldn't have long to convince Abaddon to leave before Will was covered in his own blood again.

*But this isn't high school.*

Elodie squeezed his hand once before letting go and taking her position in front of Abaddon.

*I'm not numb.*

He jumped and caught hold of one of the creature's antennae with one hand, Elodie's rope wrapped around his other.

*This is a real team.*

Muscles straining, jaw clenched, he wrestled Abaddon's head to the ground.

*And this is my choice. This is who I am.*

He flared his shield to include him, Elodie and Abaddon's head. She ran forward and splayed her hands on the beast's face. Abaddon snarled, tried to rear. Will dug his heels into the ground. Wetness seeped across his side. The burn in his ribs sharpened. But he fought to keep the monster in place. Elodie had to be able to reach it.

"Shh," she whispered. "Listen."

Will heard her thoughts through the beast. They made a chain, images and feelings flowing from her to Abaddon to Will through touch.

As soon as her first images reached him, he knew it'd been the right decision to have her speak to Abaddon. He'd spent the last hour trying to kill it, he didn't think it would listen to him. But beyond that, Abaddon's home was a place of beauty. Elodie was an artist. She saw beauty, worked with beauty, moved through beauty.

And she sent beauty.

She started with corals and sand and naupaka. Moved to mangroves, banyan trees, plumeria blossoms. Sent their collective thoughts speeding up near-vertical mountains covered in 'ōhi'a lehua, to burst into a night sky thick with the Milky Way. The images were instantaneous. All at once and yet individual.

Abaddon stilled, caught in the trap of pictures and memories.

Will's left hand went numb. Blood ran down his leg, puddling on the floor. One foot slipped and he scrambled to regain his balance.

Elodie made as if to go to him, but he shook his head.

"No, don't lose it."

She swallowed but continued, adding animals to her message. Multicolored birds, tender crocodile mothers, swift fishes, tight-knit families of wolves.

Vibrations trembled through the antennae Will gripped. Abaddon was humming in approval. And it—she, Will realized—sent a thought back.

*All these will be safe and unharmed. It is what threatens them that I come to make an end to.*

*An end would be premature,* Elodie told it. *There is so much good.* She flooded her thoughts with examples grand and small, far and personal. Countries working on agreements to tackle climate change. One of the keiki at her school hugging a classmate on a bad day. Thousands of people gathering to give disaster relief. Her grandmother singing to her as a child.

Abaddon countered.

Exploitative corporations. Hopper. The thought came accompanied with an impression—his former manager thinking of no one but himself in the moment of death. Fascism, genocide. Abaddon rolled one massive eye in Will's direction. *The scars on your back.*

The hum changed to a growl, the beast straining against Will's hold. A ripping sound came from his side, and he cried out.

Panic shot through Elodie's thoughts.

*Keep going,* he told her.

She spread her hands farther apart, pressing her face against the beast's cheek. *There is still beauty and love in us. There are still people* trying. *This man,* she sent a dozen different images of Will from their time together. *This man is one of them. I was dying, but he gave freely of himself, and he saved my life. He's giving right now. Humans can still give—to each other and to this world.*

Will's right hand went numb. Nausea fluttered in his stomach like a sick bird. *Maybe we are broken,* she admitted. *Maybe we are.*

Abaddon shuddered, and Will adjusted his hold, compensating for the fading sensation in his arms. Another hot wave of blood gushed down his side. His head spun.

Elodie stared at him as she argued for humanity, crying freely. *Sometimes people are so broken that they can't recognize their own brokenness. But people can heal. People can learn wholeness again.* Her memory of kissing him rushed through both beast and hero, filling them. *There is still so much to live for. It is not your time yet.*

The room went dark and light at the same time, Will's vision blurring. He clung to Elodie's memory, willing that to be the last thing he saw. His arms dropped, limp, and his feet slipped in his own blood.

From the floor, he saw rocks being shaken off, and the beast lumbering of her own accord to the portal, but he held the image of the kiss and the depth of Elodie's love above all.

Until he saw nothing.

# CHAPTER THIRTY-TWO

A pair of golden knitting needles gleamed in Will's hands.

At least, he thought they were knitting needles. He'd never actually knit before.

*I'm dreaming again.* The blank fuzz of the start of a lucid dream spread before him. *I guess that means I'm not dead.*

He was lying in a pool of blood, and a sharp ache clawed through his side. His stab wounds pulsed crimson, the pool seeping across the blank landscape.

*Not dead. But so tired.*

The fabric of his shirt scratched and pulled at his tattered skin. He swapped it for the one Elodie had made him. He conjured the bean bag chair from his loft back home, a mug of hot chocolate, and a stack of paperbacks. The pool of blood, he scooted outward, leaving himself a clean patch of ground.

Groaning, he settled into the beanbag and picked his favorite book off the stack. He didn't open *The Black Stallion*, just held it close. The knitting needles he placed in the air over his wounds, picturing the gold of his shield permeating his cells. The needles set to work, mending his torn flesh.

The rest of the dreamscape stayed fuzzy. Will couldn't think of anything to fill it with, anything he wanted in that moment more than rest. And it was his dream, after all.

He shut his eyes and dreamt of sleep.

The knitting needles tapped him awake.

*No, not awake really. Still in my dream.*

He probed his side and found it whole. He also found twenty-seven potholders and three scarves piled around the bean bag.

"Industrious little things, aren't you?"

The needles preened and nestled happily into the chair beside him. Will rose and stretched. The pool of blood was gone, but the dreamscape was still empty. This time, he knew what he wanted.

Elodie was healed. Elodie loved him. And he knew who he was.

Will smiled and woke up.

# CHAPTER THIRTY-THREE

Her face was the first thing he saw. "You're here."

"I'm here." Elodie stroked his face, leaning over the side of his bed. The second thing he saw was her plumeria. "You changed it."

She touched the petals over her left ear and smiled. "Means I'm taken."

They were in a hospital suite much like the one he'd left Elodie in, and he was wearing pajamas that fit him so well and were so soft, he knew she'd made them. He thought about asking where they were, what had happened. But he didn't. That could wait a few minutes.

"Taken." He smiled. "We should get me a flower too, so everybody knows we're both taken."

"Good idea." Elodie crawled under the blanket and laid down next to him, snuggled tight into his side. Tentatively, she slid one hand under his shirt where NineSix had ripped him open. Will moved experimentally, testing his muscles. Everything felt right. He was sore, and weariness still dragged on his bones, but the injury was gone.

Peace settled. Elodie sighed, and they both drifted off.

Images mixed and flashed by as Grace's brain rehashed the events of the last few days. Her hands on Abaddon's face, Will holding the great head, bleeding out.

Will in the bed in the med wing, too still, too pale. The memories resolved into a blurry emptiness, the start of a lucid dream.

She almost woke herself up. She knew she needed the sleep—Will had been out over two days, and she hadn't let herself sleep more than a few hours in case he woke up, or needed her—but he was awake now, he was ok. *Why am I sleeping? I want to be with him.*

But then she saw him there, in the dream with her.

"El?"

She wrapped her arms around his waist. *Not close enough.* With a thought, she banished his shirt and laid her head on his bare chest.

He laughed, like she'd surprised him.

*If I'm controlling the dream, why is dream-Will surprised?* "Wait." She brought her head up to look at him. "Are you part of my dream or are you ... here too?"

His eyebrows came together in confusion. "Aren't you part of my dream?"

She shook her head. "I thought I was having a lucid dream again."

"Me too."

Grace ran through all the accounts of hero lucid dreaming she could remember. None of them ever mentioned encountering another person with powers in a dream. She knew she had never done it. "So, this is something new," she mused.

Her fingers found the spot where NineSix had stabbed him. "It's smooth here. No trace of it."

Will's voice was quiet. "Did it scar in real life?"

"Yes, it did." Grace's words were quiet too, reliving the hell of the last two days, not knowing if Will would heal inside his shield and wake, or if the shield was preventing the medical care that could save him. "We almost lost you. Your shield snapped back to you as soon as you lost consciousness, but you'd lost so much blood." She bit her lip. "The shield cut off the bleeding, of course, but it also meant we couldn't do much for you when we got you back to Fashion Seeker, not even give you an IV to keep you hydrated. Sofia was able to hook up some monitors since those just stick to your skin, so I knew your heart was still beating. But all we could do was wait and hope you'd heal."

He kissed her forehead, as if he could kiss away the stress. "You know you don't have to wait for a dream to get my shirt off, right?"

She laughed, grateful for the distraction, and traced the muscles in his back. "Good to know. You know, Willard never would have said something like."

"You're right. But I'm not Willard anymore."

"No, you're Will." Because this beautiful man holding her wasn't Willard and wasn't Tank. He was who he'd needed to become, who she'd seen inside him all along. "And I love you."

"I love you too."

Will's shirt reappeared. Grace's forehead crinkled. "Did you do that?"

He shook his head. "Wasn't me."

"Brah, you need to keep your clothes on in other people's dreams."

Grace snapped her head toward her brother's voice. "James? What are you doing here?"

He shrugged. "What are you doing here? Usually, I'm in charge of who shows up in my dreams."

Grace exchanged a look with Will. "Three of us in the same dream?"

Something bubbled on the ground. Liquid silver sprouted into a pool, pink iridescence playing across its surface.

"Is that one of you?" Grace asked.

"Not me," James said.

Will shook his head. "Me either."

She turned to face the pool, keeping a hold on Will's hand. "Someone else is in this dream with us."

Will moved in front of her, still her shield. He leaned over the pool, looking straight down, and his eyes grew wide. "Guys, it's alright. Come see."

Grace held onto his arm as an anchor and leaned over the silver, James peering in next to her.

Abaddon gazed back at them with one massive eye.

Grace heard the creature's message as she had inside the shield in the cave. From the looks on their faces, she knew Will and James heard it too.

*I will wait. But you have work to do.*

The beast moved out of sight, and the pool disappeared.

James whistled lowly, and Will blew out a breath. Grace squeezed his hand and reached for her brother.

"Good thing we've got a team."

# EPILOGUE

### One Month Later

Will peeked through the curtain at the room full of reporters. It was the second press conference of the week, and the third event that day.

All of them had centered on the work that Abaddon had warned them needed to be done.

The morning had started with a trauma counseling session. The legal challenge that Slingshot was leading against the AVA proposed quite a few changes, but the one that had spread faster than a gossip column was the idea that the public shouldn't expect heroes to remain unaffected by the things they had to deal with. Social media had picked up the cause, and most cities had voluntarily added mental health benefits for their heroes.

Will and Elodie were attending sessions both individually and together. The individual sessions had comprised the bulk of their time apart in the month since he'd woken up.

That afternoon, he and Elodie had read *A Circle of Cats* to the second graders at Ninth Island Charter School. Will had been nervous. It'd been a while since he'd done a Storytime. But he'd practiced reading it aloud to Lint—who was adjusting to Las Vegas pretty well—the night before. The story of a girl's adventure in cat form, and how she'd been restored to her proper self, whole and safe, had gone over well with both his cat and the keiki.

Elodie joined him at the curtain and threaded her arm through his. After they'd woken from their mutual lucid dream, she'd declared she never wanted to stop touching him. He'd offered no objections. He never wanted to let go of her, either.

Gerard and his mom took their seats in the front row. The boy waved a comic in the air. *We have to talk about the costume choices they made!* he mouthed.

*Absolutely, bud,* Will mouthed back and gave a thumbs up. The mayor and Gerard had arrived the day after he'd woken up. The boy had given his magnanimous approval of Elodie—"She's not too much of a grown-up. You have my permission to date her"—and an offer to Will.

Puffing out his chest, he'd paced at the foot of the bed in Will's med suite. "Since you no longer have Mr. Strickland, I have decided to offer you my managerial skills. You'll find my contacts at the mayor's office to be advantageous. You're welcome."

Mareva had dropped her face in her hand, and Elodie had to turn away to hide her laughter.

"That's a very generous offer," Will had said. "But I'm not going to be using a manager anymore."

Gerard had ceased posturing, his face stricken. "You're quitting being a superhero?"

"Never. But I'm going to be doing some things differently." Will had looked to El. "We have work to do, and we're going to do it on our terms."

Which brought them to the third event. A press conference on the progress of their challenge to the AVA. Mayor Dupont had lent her support to Slingshot's movement and had convinced a number of other mayors around the country to do the same. The online petition had over half a million signatures and counting, and Will had spotted bumper stickers all over town with slogans like *End Superhero Isolation—End the AVA and Bring Back Team-Ups.*

Tonight, Will and Elodie would each speak to their own experiences before Slingshot delivered a rousing speech. They'd all help answer questions at the end.

James clapped him on the shoulder. "Ready, brah?"

Will gave him a fist bump and wrapped an arm around Elodie. He had a team, he had a purpose, he had love. He gave love. He had a new apartment with Elodie, with plenty of well-stocked bookshelves.

And they had work to do.

"I'm ready. Let's talk to some reporters."

## THE END

Sign up for Kelly Fae Wilson's newsletter for news on upcoming books and a free short story!
https://www.kellyfaewilson.com/

# ACKNOWLEDGEMENTS

In this story, Tank had to find his team. Writing a book isn't so different, and I want to say thank you to my own team of superheroes. First and foremost, thank you to my husband, Rus. You were there at every step of the process, from the morning I woke up with the seeds of this story in my head, to the finished product. You read every draft, helped me brainstorm, listened to me babble out loud to fix story problems, and learned so much of the self-publishing process along with me. You knew everything that was going on in the rest of life while I was trying to write and publish, and you pulled me back from despair so many times. Thank you for being my first and biggest fan. I love you.

Many thanks to my kids (who all also write! How lucky is this mamma?). Thank you for reading and cheering me on. Thank you for wanting me to write and believing in your mamma. To my early readers, Lindsay Hiller and Michelle Henrie, your input means the world to me. Thank you for being willing to drop everything to read a blurb for me or to answer questions.

Much love and thanks to Lena Jeong and Tesia Tsai for your mentoring, your friendship, and for talking me off ledges.

Thank you to The Typewriters, and to my indie author group for your support, and to Sally for your editing.

Yenthe, thank you this gorgeous cover, and for fitting me in on such short notice! Working with you was fantastic. I felt like I didn't just have a cover artist—I had a cheerleader.

Mahalo nui loa to Lehua Parker for her expert sensitivity read and generosity in helping me bring Grace and James to life.

And worlds of gratitude to you, Readers. I sound a bit like an airplane flight attendant at the end of the flight, but there are so many books out there that you could have picked up instead of this one. So, thank you for spending your time with Tank and Grace and Slingshot (and Gerard! He'd be mortally offended if I left him out). Thank you for taking a chance on me and on this story. I hope to see you in the next book!

# ABOUT THE AUTHOR

Kelly Fae Wilson writes genre-blending, romantic sci-fi and fantasy. Outside of writing, you can find her teaching dance, playing with faeries, or instigating a food fight at the dinner table. She lives with her husband and kids in Northern Utah. Find her at

kellyfaewilson.com

## Topics for Discussion

1. Throughout the book, Tank deals with how to find and honor his real identity. At different times he hides parts of himself or forces himself to act like someone he isn't. Have you had times when you had to do the same? What made you decide to stop hiding? Recognizing that becoming our true selves is a lifelong process, how has your life changed after deciding to become more of yourself?

2. Similarly, we inevitably find ourselves in situations in life in which we accentuate one part or another of our personality. For example, we may behave differently in a professional setting than in a familiar, personal setting, such as with our families. Does this ever make you feel     inauthentic? Or do you feel it can protect parts of yourself? Both? What has worked for you to balance all the aspects of yourself with different social situations? (Returning to the above example, how do you stay true to yourself while working within the social confines of a more formal work environment?)

3. Elodie faced criticism and opposition from extended family members about her chosen career path. How can we deal with opposition when it comes from those close to us?

4. Tank and Elodie grew as much as they could on their own but then needed each other to go further. Where do you feel the balance lies between doing our own internal growth work and asking others for help? Or is it even possible to grow without any outside help? Many people have a difficult time asking for help. Have you found ways to ask for help when you need it? Who has been a support to you in your own growth? Have there been times when those people offered help or support even though you didn't or couldn't ask? What ways have you found to provide better support for those around you?

5. Elodie points out that the arsonist was correct when he said the fashion industry is high-polluting. Do you believe humans have a duty to care

for the earth? If so, what does that duty look like to you? What are
our individual and collective responsibilities? What are some everyday
actions you take to be a responsible steward of the planet? Some group
actions?

6. At the end of the story, Will and Elodie convince the beast that humanity deserves another chance. How do you feel humans, as a species,
are doing? What do you think humanity would need to change for
Abaddon to be satisfied?

www.ingramcontent.com/pod-product-compliance
Lightning Source LLC
Chambersburg PA
CBHW011916130726
47903CB00016B/3051